light from shadow

The Darkness Within

J. A. FERNIE

UK Book Publishing.com

All characters and events in this publication, other than those clearly in the public domain, are fictitious and any resemblance to real persons, living or dead, is purely coincidental.

Editing, design, typesetting and publishing by UK Book Publishing

www.ukbookpublishing.com

ISBN: 978-1-916572-74-4

light from shadow

The Darkness Within

"Hope can flicker a blinding light, even in the darkest of shadows, in the never ending, ominous corridors of the broken mind. All one needs to do is believe. Believe that there can be hope and the smallest spark can become a raging inferno of light. Just give yourself that chance to believe."

Prologue

The dance of the sunset flames burning across the sky, caused the wild Grandors to roar and rumble, out past the shadowing wall of the City of Randtyph. Wrestling in the distance before the dark of night signalled the commencement of their feeding frenzy. The collisions of their gigantic bodies, covered in diamond flesh and golden fur, causing thunder without lighting, in a starlit sky with no clouds. Along the inside perimeter of the wall, sat marketplaces scattered around the ends of the eight arms of the Outer System. Fabric roofs snapped in the breeze that circled, applauding the primal ritual of the beasts beyond the wall.

This planet, known as Earth until late into the 27th Century, now known as Octdrevion Six, had been blessed and cursed on the same day. The monolith burst through the mantel and high into the sky. An ancient power signalling the coming of a new age. The Turach Vro Aka standing as a talisman for all of Randtyph to see. Centre City, Inner System and Outer System all staring into the same centre. The Outer System masked by the fabric curtain that grows into the sky from the outskirts of the Inner System. Rising from the Diamond Farm, high into the sky and then dipping down to end atop the Great Wall of Randtyph. The wall that separated the Outer System from the Dead Space and the Prison Zone. Separating the living from the damned. From the sky, the city of Randtyph and the eight sections of the Outer System, must have looked like a grand crop circle, left by another race at another time.

The Grandors fed on the Faded in the Dead Zone. The lifeless souls of those who had been tortured and all the light sucked from their lives, whilst held in the Prison Zone. Discarded like soiled water when no darkness or potential could be found within. These lifeless figures, dead behind the eyes, could only slur as they rocked from side to side. Their eyes open, skin whiter than snow, hidden beneath a red cloak, covered in burn marks from the abuse of the prison's guards. The Faded provided the protein and nutrients that the Grandors needed to grow strong enough. Strong enough to drag the enormous sleds, piled high with the stones that fuelled the Empire.

In the Outer System the sound of feet tapping on the mud could be heard, as an excited messenger was trying to shadow run (the name given by the Outer System residents to the art of running down the dark towering aisles of Outer System without being seen. Disappearing in the shadows, then using the next, then the next and the next, until finally reaching their destination) through the aisles and alleyways without being detected. The patting of feet became heavier and more laboured as the messenger pushed through the pain of exhaustion. Stopping at the base of the towering column of shanty huts, pop-up homes for the planet's workforce, he placed his hands on his thighs to try catch his breath, before climbing up to the doorway with candlelight breaking through the sheet door.

"Alenca, it's happening!" Gellon gasped.

Gellon nearly ended up on the floor as he threw the sheet out of the way. His wide but short frame bursting into the home.

In one motion, Alenca spun his massive mountain-like frame round on his stool one hundred and eighty degrees, stood up and caught Gellon. One of his large, paw-like hands nearly filling Gellon's chest, as he grabbed him by the front and scruff of his fabric top.

"Where is she, brother?" Alenca asked eagerly.

The excited question of a man, ready to help his partner give birth to his first child.

"She is at her mother's, with her sister. As soon as the word passed through the Outer System, I knew you'd be here planning." He grabbed Alenca in close and put his arms around him. "Here comes the future. Here comes the light."

Gellon laughed; he was so elated and giddy.

Alenca patted his best friend on the back. "You better believe that the prophecy is real now, brother. Our child, boy or girl, will change Randtyph and the rest of Shadow Empire forever."

Alenca stepped back and stood tall, moving his hair from his face then running his fingers through his dark beard, thick and full like a mane.

"The years of shade. The time of the Hav Guard choking the life and colour from everything we know is ending. It's time to shine." Alenca clapped his hands together and smiled. "Now, brother, I need to get to Jillezi. Take me to her, brother."

The two men jumped out of the second storey doorway, down to the ground below. Even under the curtain, in the grey shadow of night in the Outer System, happiness poured from the men as they darted in and out of the shadows all the way down the long row of pop-up homes. Making sure not to make too much noise and stay as hidden from the Hav Guard's view as possible. Commotion from the birth was allowed by law, but travelling around at night was restricted to only those travelling to work sites. If Gellon or Alenca were seen travelling the streets at night, they would be punished...severely.

As the two crossed over and through the other aisles of endless pop-up homes, the sound of Jillezi screaming through contractions came into ear shot. Alenca gave chase to the sound. The standard dance of the shadows was forgotten. This mountain of a man took off in full stride towards the sound, straight down the middle of the aisles, with no fear for his own personal safety. Alenca just wanted to hold her and take away the pain.

Prologue

"I will be with you soon, Jillezi," Alenca muttered to himself as he tore across the Outer System to get to Jillezi.

Within a few minutes he was throwing the sheet out of the way. Gellon arrived a noticeable amount of time after. Blue in the lips, he was so out of breath. His lungs burning, trying to pull the thick air into his body.

Alenca crouched down next to his partner as she lay cradled on her back. She pulled her legs in by her thighs so aggressively, her sister at her side helping with the strain. As he crouched next to her, he pushed Jillezi's hair back from her wet brow, kissing her forehead so gently, tears flooding his eyes as he then pressed his forehead to hers.

"I'm here, Ezi, I'm here."

Smiling as he squeezed her hand between his and kissed down gently, Alenca's concentration was only broken when he heard the coughing and spluttering of Gellon from behind him.

"Ha ha ha, my brother, do you need me to hold your hand as well, ha ha ha. Need less of that rotten fruit juice and more running through the aisles of the system," Alenca mocked.

The tears streamed down Alenca's cheeks into his beard as he threw his head back in laughter. Drunk with joy and the nerves of being a father.

"Hey you!" Jillezi screached, yanking on the beard of her partner. "Stop messing around and help me push out this Grandor-sized baby of yours!"

Jillezi was a small woman but her voice was so loud and frightening from the birthing pain, it startled everyone.

Gellon tried to jump to attention frantically.

"My Queen, I am here." Alenca kissed her forehead and then squeezed Jillezi's hand as he lifted it to press against his cheek.

"Yvanny, tell me how is she, is it time?" Alenca queried excitedly.

"She is not quite there yet, Alenca, but very soon." Yvanny pressed her hand upon his shoulder and squeezed as she seemed to float by.

Yvanny was a stout lady, covered in layers of robes and throws. Short, powerful and commanding of every room or space she entered. She was dwarfed by Alenca, but he did as she said and if she had asked him to jump, he liked to let her believe he would ask how high. Seeing her daughter was well cared for, Yvanny took a moment to give them their space while she got some fresh air. Her eye line was no higher than Alenca's shoulder as he was crouched down.

"Pull yourself together, man," Yvanny jeered as she slapped Gellon on his back.

Gellon was still trying to catch his breath as Jillezi let out a large scream, causing him to look towards her. The sight of the baby crowning causing him to pass out, slumping to the ground like a wet blanket.

"It's time!" Janya screamed.

Jillezi's sister was straining to hold onto her leg as she pushed. Attempting to dab a cloth to her head and neck at the same time, Janya was sweating nearly as much as Jillezi.

"Get me warm towels and sheets," she shouted to Gellon, shaking her head at him as he dusted his tattered clothing down, trying to pull himself together.

The scratching noise of somebody climbing the ladders caused Alenca's head to tilt towards the doorway. Hav Guard would not climb without announcing themselves first. He quickly eliminated that idea and turned back to his love. Alenca knew it would just be a concerned neighbour or friend. Checking if her screams may be out of fear, signalling that she could be in danger. Everyone remained focussed on Jillezi until the sheet moved to make way for the neighbour's head.

"Jillezi." The floating head of the neighbour and friend, peeked through the doorway sheet, and made eye contact with Jillezi. "Oh my, I apologise."

He quickly realised what was going on. Seeing that she was well cared for he threw the sheet back and scrambled across the buildings back to his own one-room home.

"Solice, it's ok..." Jillezi attempted to shout to her friend, but only managed to begin to utter the words, as she had to stop mid-sentence to clench, feeling another contraction begin to build. As Jillezi let out another scream, the floor, then the whole entire Outer System began to shake. Accompanied by the sound of electricity cracking, like lightning, coming from the direction of Centre City.

"What is going on?" Alenca barked.

He jumped up, still holding Jillezi's hand. As the screaming and pushing stopped while Jillezi paused to try and catch her breath, everything began to settle down apart from an intermittent buzz that could be heard coming from outside.

"Check what that is please, Gellon," Alenca ordered, pointing towards the doorway where the sheet door swayed from the rumbling in the air.

Gellon nodded to Alenca, accepting his mission. With one foot placed inside the home and the other hanging outside, using the wooden doorframe to hold this weight and the sheet thrown behind him, he watched as he thought he was witnessing the impossible. Pale faced, wide eyed with pinned pupils, he turned to face Alenca, revealing that he had begun to sweat profusely.

"The Turach Vro Aka..." He looked to the floor as he felt the vibrations fade.

"Gellon! What is going on?" Alenca's raised voice echoed and bounced from wall to wall for what seemed like minutes but was only really a few seconds.

He looked to Jillezi as she caught her breath before another contraction, then turned back to Gellon.

"Gellon, please, what is going on out there?"

Gellon let out a deep breath, shook his head and ran his hands across his face to clear the sweat. Once composed he regained eye contact with Alenca.

"It's the Turach Vro Aka, it's glowing and there's beams of colour blasting from the top into the sky." The confusion and fear were very apparent on his face.

Yvanny, still moving like she was floating, her long grey hair swishing behind her every movement, was at the doorway in seconds. She peered outside and then looked back to everyone in the room.

"Say hello to our saviour. The unwritten page of a new story has begun," Yvanny yelled in glee, pointing back towards the birthing mother.

Gazing up into the sky in amazement once more, Yvanny found herself caught up in the moment of it all, her body hovering, glowing and lights sparking from her hands. Her emotions were quickly snapped back to reality. Lowering herself back to the ground, she turned round to see the screaming baby, as Janya pulled the blood and afterbirth-covered child from Jillezi.

"Alenca, you have united the Outer System. Your child will unite the Universe."

***

The whole of Centre City reverberated. Marble floors humming like an echo to the swarm-like buzz coming from the Turach Vro Aka. The great halls began to fill with the Hav Guard and the Upper Citizens of Randtyph, rushing to the stage at the foot of their talisman, in an attempt to find out what was causing this earthquake-like event. Were they under attack? Was this the end? The Hav Guard were trying to keep the Upper Citizens calm. Using a distinct change in technique for treatment of citizens compared to that of the

Outer System.

"Can everyone please remain calm. Captain Derza Telema will be here shortly to explain what's going on," the Guard began to plead.

"Please can everybody stop screaming," they ordered as another shudder of the ground sent the Upper Citizens into a screaming frenzy once more.

As each buzz of the Turach Vro Aka intensified, so did the whir of fear exploding from each of the terrified citizens of Randtyph.

There was a loud crack of thunder as Captain Derza Telema stabbed his staff against the marble floor of the stage. By the time he had arrived at the base of the Turach Vro Aka, a frightened few had grown into mass crowd of hysteria.

"Silence! Everyone stay calm." His voice carried right through to the furthest corners of the Great Halls.

Everyone stopped, immediately falling silent, turning to face their Captain, the leader of the Hav Guard. The Royal Guard of the Empire, Derza Telema stood tall like a giant in his black armour. The gold trim of the shoulders and cloak, radiating from the shine of the walls and floors of the Great Hall.

With the crowd beginning to fall into line, the Captain's staff let out another thunderous crack as it was stabbed against the marble once more.

"There is absolutely no need to panic. The Hav Guard can help anybody with questions or needs. You will be safe," he continued to reassure.

A few moments of peace had passed before the next tremor caused a much lesser scream. It was quickly brought under control, knowing the Hav Guard were near. Each hum of the Turach Vro Aka caused it to glow with a beautiful and radiant yellow and white light. Captain Telema looked around the room – confusion and fear was very apparent on the faces of everyone looking on – then looking upwards at the Turach Vro Aka for an answer. His own confusion, only masked by the years of training to hide emotion, behind an unflinching facial expression.

"I need to find the Emperor," he muttered to himself.

Derza quickly scanned for any Hav Guard nearby and looking his way.

"You, guard, here," he barked, motioning him over to his location. "Keep the peace. I'm going to find the Emperor."

Captain Telema dropped down from the stage and made his way through the crowd. Each step he took, made clear by the crowd parting like a Biblical sea.

The echoes from all the commotion, bounced from wall to wall in the Great Halls that sat at the foot of the Turach Vro Aka. The marble stage that stood elevated against it, gave any Captain or Commander the ability to see all, as they demanded any and all attention. The stage lay open to the elements to allow the ability to gaze, in awe, at the great size and presence of the marble stone monolith that grew from the ground. So tall that it seemed to curve into the sky. Shadow never being cast on the stage in daylight.

Sunlight constantly being reflected from the one-way glass, circling the opening to the sky.

On the other side of the glass, the Emperor watched like a God high atop a mountain. Acting as his panoramic viewing gallery. One-way glass, allowing the Shadow Emperor the privacy to stand and stare out over his kingdom, but allowing nothing or nobody the ability to set eyes upon him. With power unmatched, the Emperor wanted to look down on his subjects.

As Captain Telema reached the large, ceiling-high golden doors he paused. Nobody ever went to the Shadow Emperor. He summoned or appeared, like a ghost, when least expected. Rumours and whispers had been heard and travelled from the downtrodden Outer System to the high life of the Centre City. Stories that told of how the Shadow Emperor would just appear in the homes of his enemies, before ending the lives of anybody nearby. It was rumoured that he had the ability to look into your soul and feed off the light and shadow within. Either snuffing out your inner light, or finding that your inner shadow has the dark potential of another Hav Guard.

There were only six who were feared as much as the Shadow Emperor. Six who needed no invitation or summons to enter the Emperor's Quarters. The Havshad Knights. The six pillars of the Shadow Emperor. He fought no battle without them. They won no war without him. They fed off fear and darkness. Experimenting with Shadow Stones had given them eternal life, but they were cursed warriors with unnatural abilities. What once may have been six men of magic, were now six weapons of pure chaos.

Captain Telema placed a gauntlet on each golden handle. Holding each of the gold orbs and squeezing gently, his green eyes reflecting back at him, he took a deep breath in and pulled the doors open, revealing a grand staircase. Like the rest of the Great Halls, it was marble, with golden railings. Mushrooming as they reached another set of golden doors at the top. The last boundary between him and his God. Captain Telema carried his head high, attempting to hide the nervous but fearful excitement he felt.

The doors seemed to sense Captain Telema reaching the final few steps. Inwards they slowly swung open, revealing the Emperor stood half-naked at the wall of glass, staring down on those below. A large visible scar running over the muscular left shoulder of the Emperor, tearing through the Shadow Hammer tattoo covering the rest of his back, inked with oil from the Shadow Stones. Armoured from the waist down, the Emperor stood tall and well-muscled.

"Derza, it is really happening." The Emperor spoke loudly and proudly.

Over his head he threw his chest and back plate, leaving his gigantic arms and lateral back muscles on show. A cloak, dark as night, poured from the shoulders of his minimal armour, the moment it touched his skin. Stopping with a ghostly trim right before it reached the ground.

"You know what's causing this, my Lord?" Captain Telema gasped.

He stopped and bowed his head, banging his right gauntlet against his chest of armour as a sign of respect to his master.

Still with his face to the glass, the Emperor placed his sharp, demonic-faced helmet over his swept back dark hair, covering his scarred and stubbled face, cutting off at the upper lip to allow his mouth to still be seen. Imbued with dark magic, the clouds of black and purple seemed to roll together in a constant battle across the battle attire.

"I have been waiting for this day for over three thousand years," the Shadow Emperor replied as he finished adjusting his helmet. "The prophecy of my demise has commenced. A fraudulent master of life and death is coming to take my throne."

The Captain seemed nervous and reserved as he began to step towards the Emperor.

"I don't understand, my Lord. I thought the prophecy was nothing more than a folk's tale, told by mothers to keep their children from misbehaving?"

The Emperor pulled a set of leather gloves from his waist band and placed them over his hands, almost as though he hadn't heard the question. Pulling down on the gloves and then stretching out his hands, bending and manipulating the armoured knuckles into place. His bones could be heard cracking below. He looked down to his left where the Shadow Hammer rested upside down, against the glass. Too large for a normal man to lift, but for the Emperor, his weapon of choice. Smiling, he placed his hand onto the steel orb at the bottom of the handle, with one finger on the spike.

The Shadow Hammer had been forged in the dark mines of Vexora by the Mages of El Radith. Made from Vexorian Steel, blended with Shadow Stones and sealed with the hatred and evil that burned inside the makers of this malevolent weapon.

Captain Telema looked around the room, at the massive golden-framed bed where three beautiful naked women and a slender naked male huddled together in fear. Whimpering in their home planet's tongue and shrieking with every vibration of the city. Trails of crushed Quaba (a crystal-like substance made from a synthetic form of the Shadow Stones. Found during trials to use Shadow Stones to enhance the Shadow Emperor's power. It gave a huge rush of energy and sense of euphoria, but was outlawed for use on any planet not currently occupied by the Emperor) sat on the golden table that sat aside the bed.

Sniffing and smoking Quaba had become a way of life for the Shadow Emperor. Giving him the rush that he craved but no longer got from life since he had settled on Octdrevion Six after the annihilation of nearly the entire population, wildlife and all its natural resources. The sight of their bodies caused him to snap his face forward nervously, making his fear and confusion about the whole situation multiply.

"My Lord, what do you want me to tell the Hav Guard and the citizens of Randtyph?" Derza asked.

The Emperor lowered his head and clapped his hands together, releasing a cloud of Quaba into the air, holding them against his lips as though to pray. But really, inhaling the fumes that were given off. Grabbing the handle, he swung the gigantic hammer over, rested it on his shoulder and then turned to face the Captain. This mountain of a man stood tall and wide. The darkened steel-face covering most of his. Still, the smile lingered on his face. Chiselled abdominal muscles showing below the chest plate. Behind him, the Turach Vro Aka shone a brilliant white, now all the vibrating and humming had died out. With the snap of his gloved fingers, the hammer, helmet, his eyes and the trim of his cloak were engulfed in purple flames.

The Emperor's smile turned into a snarling smirk.

"A light has been born. It's time to snuff it out."

Chapter One

"Oshi…"

Feroshi heard a rumbling murmur in his dream. Like a higher power calling his name to wake him from the nightmare.

"Feroshi, wake up. You're dreaming of him again, aren't you?" Simeskey's voice broke through the fog of the nightmare.

She dabbed a rag to his head as he awoke in a cold sweat. The rushing sounds of the troop transporter above, heading for the Prison Zone from the barracks in the Inner System, caused the supports of their little home to vibrate. Feroshi looked at her, then to his calloused hands.

"Yes, and they are getting worse," Feroshi said while rubbing his hands together trying to stop the tingling in his fingertips.

He gently took the rag from Simeskey and wiped the cold sweat from his neck.

"Talk to me...what's going on in that little head of yours?" Simeskey asked.

There was so much love in her words. Nothing but worry and concern for her partner in this life.

Feroshi gazed around their home. Nothing but a bed, a stove, a wooden table and utensils, bucket of water, three stools and the love of his life. It was their reality in this ominous and perilous world they lived in. Everything in the centre of the city was so marvellous and new. The centre of the City of Randtyph had forgotten about the world and Outer Systems under the sheet.

"It's like, with every nightmare the feeling in my hands and the tingles in my hands are getting more intense. I've even started to feel a burning in my chest," he replied.

Feroshi stretched as he stood up and made his way over to the sheet that hung as a doorway.

"It's like something...or someone is pushing, pulling, trying to break something free from inside."

He cast the sheet aside to gaze out, along the rows of little huts and pop-up houses that were stacked high and far. People living with nothing to supply those who have everything. Everyone awaking to the day ahead. The first transporter to the Prison Zone of the day acting as a muster call to all those below. Feroshi took a moment to take it in: the smiles of children; the tired looks on the faces of parents. He gazed back at Simeskey and noticed the smile she had was radiating. It was as though she gave off heat and light that called for him.

Simeskey caught his smile and blushed.

"What are you looking at?" She giggled.

She smiled and covered her face with her shoulder, bashful like a younger girl would have been.

"You are just a whole lot of beauty in a very ugly world."

He walked over, all smiles as he kissed her on the top of her head.

There was a clattering of pans and stacked piles of wood outside, as children ran down the dirt path that divided the two separate sectors of houses. No electricity, no power, just eight aisles separating eight densely populated sections of one-room homes. Made of nothing but wood and corrugated metal found lying around. The entirety of the Outer System knew nothing other than the life in the shadow that was cast by the Empire. No happiness was to be shown...only conformity to the City of Randtyph's Shadow System. Only the "exceptional few" were ever selected, or in better words taken, at the Joining Ceremony because of the darkness within. Taken to the Hav Guard, to become and serve. Never seen by their families again.

The Turach Vro Aka stood as a monumental stone spear that radiated light and stood, what seemed like, miles and miles into the air. A reminder to the Outer System's residents that there was always a higher power watching and controlling everything. All aspects of life past, present and future; and if anybody forgot, the Hav Guard would be there to remind them.

The Outer System had no connection to their past due to all records being concealed within the Havshad Archive. All history to them was word of mouth. Parents using the dirt below and a finger as their canvas and tools. No one was to speak of a time more than one generation above or below, forbidden and enforced by the Hav Guard, happily using this as an excuse to physically and verbally attack anyone they please. Anyone with a little too much joy in their eyes. A boot to the face of a child smiling at their parent, unaware of their mistake. A shove to the back of an elderly cripple, too broken to move out of the way as the Hav Guard approached. These bullies of the Outer System were like robots, programmed to bring an extra level of shadow to the already darkened life in the outer rims of Randtyph. Never a face...just a cloaked suit of armour, with ghostly white masks.

Feroshi moved towards the doorway, throwing his fabric fashioned top over his head, to see what the commotion was outside.

"That better not be the Hav Guard again, Keskey. I honestly can't stand the way they treat us...and everybody just takes it!" Feroshi grabbed onto the wooden door frame after throwing the sheet aside. "Why do we just take it?"

"Oshi, please just ignore it. They will just be looking for trouble and if you say anything they will beat you, if not kill you."

Simeskey walked up behind him and put her hand on his shoulder. She noticed that Feroshi's knuckles were going white from grabbing onto the support with so much force. It almost seemed like his hand was sinking into the wood. Leaving an engraved handprint.

"Oshi, what's going on with your hand?" she pleaded.

Chapter One

He was in a daze. His body was there but his mind was gone. His thoughts were running away from him, causing an uncontrollable rage to begin to burn inside.

"Feroshi..." Simeskey squeezed his shoulder.

His grip on the doorway loosened, revealing a recessed handprint in the wood. He looked panicked as his hand shook and beads of sweat ran down his face.

"Keskey, I don't know what's happening. What just happened? My hands feel like they're full of broken glass trying to rip its way out."

This panic and worry was not one that Feroshi was used to. He was fearless. Always had been. Simeskey pushed the hair out of his face and put her hands round his.

"It's ok, just lie back down," Simeskey said soothingly.

Feroshi immediately began to fill with calm. His thoughts coming back under control. Simeskey ushered him towards the sheet and pillow on the floor, helping him down onto the ground.

"I've only just got that pillow dry after you soaking it with your nightmares," she joked, trying to help him forget. "You're going to be..."

"What's wrong with this piece of trash then? Worthless Outer System skaff. You waste of space struggling to function?" a voice yelled from outside their home.

Feroshi and Simeskey turned to see two members of the Hav Guard stood inside their doorway, unaware that their sheet had got caught, leaving the door frame open like a glassless window. Accidents like this on the groung floor homes were easy targets for the Hav Guard.

"I'm fine, just wanted a bit of a lie down to think about how good life is as a, what was it again...worthless Outer System skaff," Feroshi barked in reply.

Any weakness that had been seen was now gone. Feroshi was stood tall, reinvigorated and ready to go as he moved in front of Simeskey. Blood coursed through his veins as they protruded from his tensed arms.

"Now what does the Hav Guard want with us worthless lot anyway?" Feroshi jeered.

"What the fu...."

The Hav Guard was interrupted as a white glowing staff pressed against his chest and a Hav Guard Captain moved forward. The gold trim on his black mask and armour radiating, even in the dark and damp home.

"It's ok, Hav Guard, there's no need to beat this one today," the Captain said as he moved through the room.

The Hav Guard Captain rested his staff against the wall, removed his helmet, revealing well-kept blond hair and a complexion that showed he had never lived a day in the dirt, in his life. Perfect skin, shaved down the bone so his finger ran smooth against it.

Simeskey began to feel panic, knowing that anyone who spoke back and spoke up against the Guard were brutally punished.

"Captain, what brings you to this sector of the Outer System?" she asked softly, trying to defuse the tension.

"There has been a lot of chatter back at Hav Guard barracks. Chatter that tells me there is something in the Outer System that is calling to the Turach Vro Aka."

The Captain placed his helmet on the table and sat himself down on a stool. With a single hand gesture, he ordered the Hav Guard outside.

"Now tell me, why would there be something in the Outer System calling to the Turach Vro Aka? There is nothing here but damp and disease."

He wiped his finger across the table with a smug disgusted look on his face; he rubbed his thumb against his two fingers and then shook the dust off his fingertips.

"If you have any information, it is your duty to divulge said information," the Captain finished with a menacing smile creeping across his face.

Feroshi began, but was immediately interrupted by Simeskey. She was determined to calm things down before they got out of control.

"We know nothing of the Turach Vro Aka apart from what we can see. It is our talisman at the centre of Randtyph," Simeskey pleaded.

"Yes, hmmm. What's your thoughts on this?" the Captain enquired.

With his elbow resting on the table and keeping eye contact with Simeskey, he pointed his gloved finger towards Feroshi and then his eyes followed.

Feroshi looked towards Simeskey and could see the nervous look on her face. He exhaled, not wanting to cause any more problems, knowing that if he pressed any longer, there was every chance he would be taken away. It was time for him to admit defeat.

"Exactly what my partner said, we know nothing about anything calling. It's quiet here, always quiet," Feroshi answered.

The Captain looked from Feroshi to Simeskey, and then smiled as he exhaled and stood up from his stool, pushing up with both hands on his thighs.

"Well if you hear anything or see anything, you make sure to let one of my guards know." He placed the helmet back on his head. "I think you'll be seeing a lot more of me until we get to the bottom of this."

Simeskey breathed a sigh of relief, but Feroshi still had eyes locked on the Captain. There was a pause where both men seemed to be in a standoff. The Captain broke it to face Simeskey.

"Is there anything else we can do for you?" Simeskey blurted, panicked and just wanting for the Captain to leave.

"No that will be all...for now."

The Captain stroked Simeskey's face with the finger of his gauntlet and then nodded towards Feroshi, before he turned, grabbed his staff and started to make his leave. As he took a step towards the doorway he stopped.

"Now what is this?"

"What now?" Feroshi exclaimed.

The Captain threw the staff into the opposite hand and placed the tip against the handprint.

"What is this and how did it happen?" He removed his right glove and ran his fingers across the handprint. Then placed his hand as though he was reliving the moment. Feeling the power that caused it. "I can feel it."

"Yes, it's wood and it feels like wood."

Feroshi tried to use humour to get the Captain's attention away from the embedded handprint and whatever strange connection he was having with it.

The Captain broke from his connection to the imprint and faced Feroshi.

"You know what I'm talking ab..."

A member of the Hav Guard crashed into the Captain, knocking him down.

"What in the name of the Turach Vro Aka do you think you are doing, Guard!" he shouted before realising the body was limp and his mask had been shattered, showing a face broken and covered in blood. "What is going on out there?"

He pushed the limp body of the guard off him and moved outside. A makeshift ladder had fallen from a few storeys up and swung down and hit a few members of the Hav Guard. The one lying limp on the floor had taken a direct hit to the face.

"It's the Outer System, Sir. It's all shit and falling apart," another member of the Hav Guard began to explain as he stood to attention in front of the Captain.

"Get him up and let's get back to the barracks, we have made some interesting discoveries today." The Captain pointed to the Guard on the floor.

He turned and walked back towards the centre of the room.

“Let me introduce myself properly, I am Captain Theron Magda of the Hav Guard. You should probably introduce yourself to me, because I have a funny feeling that we will be seeing a hell of a lot more of each other,” he said in his most condescending tone while resting his hand on Feroshi’s shoulder.

Feroshi showed no emotion or pain as the Captain began to apply pressure.

“I am Feroshi Enlit of the Outer System. Orphaned by the Hav Guard when I was just a child, in the War for Randtyph,” he said through gritted teeth.

At the sound of Feroshi’s name the Captain’s head picked up.

“Enlit, you say. I have definitely heard that name before. That is something I shall need to discuss with the Higher Powers back at Centre City.” He turned towards Simeskey. “And your first name please, Lady Enlit.”

“Her name is...” Feroshi started, but was interrupted by the Captain’s staff being placed onto his lips. He scrunched his face up in a show of disapproval.

“Now don’t be rude, Feroshi. We have had plenty of time to get to know each other, it’s her turn. So then, what is your name, my lady?” Captain Theron Magda removed the staff from Feroshi’s lips, stabbed it against the dirt floor and turned to face Simeskey again.

Simeskey gave Feroshi a reassuring squeeze on his arm.

"Captain, I am Simeskey, or Keskey to my friends. Originally Simeskey Fawn but when it was time for my pairing I became Simeskey Enlit." She exhaled and held onto Feroshi, still trying to keep him calm.

The Captain looked from Simeskey, then to Feroshi and scoffed with a smile.

"Well like I said, I'm done here for now, but I know we'll be seeing each other again, Feroshi."

The Captain replaced his helmet and stood square in front of Feroshi. Feroshi braced up, refusing to back down. Feroshi was broad, and even though his tattered top was loose, the definition of his wide chest and enlarged arms could be seen. But Captain Theron Magda was wearing his suit of armour and would not back down to a citizen of Randtyph, let alone a citizen of its Outer System.

Simeskey pulled on Feroshi's hand and through her teeth pleaded with her partner. "Oshi, please," she begged.

"Listen to your partner, Feroshi."

The Captain leaned in so as to have his mask millimetres from Feroshi's ear, so close Feroshi could feel the cold of the metallic helmet on his cheek.

"I really wouldn't want to have to make an example of you in front of the rest of the Outer System," Theron hissed into Feroshi's ear.

He then stepped back, turned to face Simeskey and slightly bowed.

Feroshi stayed tense and rigid as he watched Theron Magda step outside and his men came to attention, then followed in file as he headed out of sight. Simeskey watched in the doorway to make sure all of the Hav Guard had left and then unhooked the doorway sheet so that it fell. She stood as if to listen to someone speaking on the other side.

"I don't know whether to love you or kill you. Nobody else fights apart from you and Rue and I hate that you pair won't fall in line." She turned and charged past Feroshi. She paused and brushed herself down. "But I love that you want things to change."

The aggression left her voice and was filled with love again as she turned and hugged onto Feroshi. Simeskey was swallowed up as he wrapped his arms around her.

"I don't know what it is. Every time they start throwing their weight around, it's like my hands are on fire and then I lose control."

He kissed her on the top of the head, before stepping back and picking up a wooden beaker. He then filled it with water from the bucket Simeskey had fetched, prior to waking him earlier that morning.

The world had grown darker with every year that passed. The world that Feroshi had come to know, was that of darkness and quiet. Peace found in darkness and shadow cast by the Higher Powers, was the way of life that the Outer System of Randtyph had come to know.

As Feroshi stood in his doorway, gazing up and down his aisle that separated his row of homes from the other sectors, he wondered how there could be this peace, when all he could remember was fire and pain, the battles for Randtyph.

Is that all these flashing memories were? The tingling in the hands, the inner rage...was Feroshi the problem, or was he the only one that could not remember clearly? Blaster holes and entire homes turned to rubble, were signs that the past was more than a memory. The reminder of the power of the Shadow over the Light.

Even when the talk of how the sectors used to rage bloody battles in the streets against each other. Poverty fighting poverty for just a little bit extra for the families in their section. A sick game, that began the day the Emperor filled the original homes with different races from different planets. Buying land with blood as the currency. The more that was spilt, the greater a hold on that section they would have.

The battles of the gangs of the eight sectors used to be of great amusement to any onlooking Hav Guard. Now out of fear, with the Outer System united for over two decades, the residents allowed themselves to be held as prisoners of misery. Feroshi still could not get on the same level of fear as his neighbours and friends. He was not afraid to die protecting others. He was afraid to die for the amusement of others.

"Do you want to talk about the nightmares? You know I'm here for you no matter what," Simeskey asked reassuringly.

"I don't want you to worry, Keskey. The dark figure with burning purple eyes keeps haunting me. From the moment he enters my dreams they all go the same way; flashes of the Outer System burned to the ground. The dark figure standing over all the dead bodies. Yours and Rue's were at the top, under his boots. Then it ends with everything going dark as he rushes towards me. What if I'm the dark figure? What if I'm the death of you?" Feroshi hung his head, almost ashamed to be fearful of a dream and what it might mean.

Simeskey approached Feroshi from behind and wrapped arms around him. She placed her hand under his tattered top and began to soothingly tickle his stomach. Running her fingers over the ridges from scars on his abdominal muscles.

"Scars remind us where we've been, but your dreams... your dreams only show you a path you might take. I know that dark figure isn't you, and more importantly, you show me every day how much you love me. The only way you'll be the death of me, is if you roll on top of me."

Feroshi turned to face Simeskey with a new smile on his face.

"You really do shine bright, even under all this shade. If only I could keep my mouth shut." He innocently chuckled as his reply came to an end.

"Well I love you and your big mouth." She kissed Feroshi on his lips. "Do you remember what the old crazy lady used to say when she worked at the market? The most scarred of us are the ones with the biggest stories to tell."

Chapter Two

Eight members of the Hav Guard accompanied Captain Theron Magda on the troop transporter back to Hav Guard barracks, to debrief with the council. The Hav Guard onboard made conversation and laughed among themselves whilst the Captain stood at the front of the transport, deep in thought about earlier that day; the handprint embedded into the door frame, the insolent insect that he suspected was the owner of the handprint, Feroshi's partner and how he craved the feeling of her hair in his hand, her perfumed aroma that lingered in his nose still and to touch her skin, instead of her being with him. He knew that there was something else he was supposed to have on his mind from today. Prodding at his cuff he brought up a rotating hologram of Feroshi. A voice relayed incident after incident, date after date, of his incursions and skirmishes with the Hav Guard. He exhaled and gave a little shake of his head to himself.

"Pft, I'll deal with that later," Theron muttered to himself, in an attempt to shake the nagging feeling that he was forgetting something... "ENLIT!"

A few seconds later, his time of thought was being brought to an abrupt end as the transporter's tannoy announcement began.

"You will be arriving at your destination in a few moments. Be ready to depart shortly. Have a lovely day."

The cheer in the female voice was drowned out by the clatter of armour once Captain Theron Magda called the troop transport to attention.

"Men, go back to your quarters. I need to speak to the Higher Powers," he ordered.

The Hav Guard shifted forty-five degrees to their right on their heels and all marched two steps forward to fall out of line, clattering their left gauntlet to their chest plates with each step. They all turned to make their way off the transport, single file, one by one they exited.

As the final Hav Guard disembarked the transport, Theron Magda turned to lean into the railing that ran waist-height along the walls of energy that made up the transporter. Searching his mind for the answers. All through his training as Hav Guard, then his rise through Hav Guard Command Selection he had been taught the same message: "From Light came the Shadow. From Shadow came peace and conformity. Snuff out the Light and the Shadow shall rule." The stories of the Outer System's Uprising were taught as lessons on why the skaffs, at all costs, must remain in shade, their purpose...to serve. The Shadow Emperor had vanished at the end of the war. Nobody knew where he had gone after the final battle with the Outer System rebellion.

Chapter Two

Captain Theron Magda knew he had heard that name before. He was sure that the name Enlit was one of those that belonged to one of the leaders of the rebellion. He gripped the handle and then threw his weight toward the doors as the energy wall parted, creating a doorway for him to walk through, grabbing his staff from its holder on his way. He stepped off the transporter onto the marble floors of Centre City. Walking through the halls, past the stage and the Shadow Hammer.

"Captain!" he heard from behind him.

Theron Magda turned to see the six Higher Powers stood only a few paces away from him. There had been no footsteps. No noise. Nothing to signal the approaching of the phantom stewards to the Emperor's throne. He took a step backwards and bent down on one knee in respect.

"My Lords, I did not expect..." he began.

"We move with the shadows, Captain." Marra El, the head of the Higher Powers, stepped forward. "Remove your helmet and tell us what you know, Captain."

The dark figure stood cloaked, with a dark silver mask just seen in the shadow beneath, sinisterly towering over the Captain knelt below.

Theron Magda stood up quickly and nervously, leaving his staff on the ground, he removed his helmet and placed it under his right arm and adjusting his blond hair that had fallen in front of his face, before addressing his masters.

"My Lords, I know nothing yet. I have a lot of investigating to do before presenting any findings to the council," Theron answered nervously.

Marra El raised a dark armoured arm from beneath the haunting cloak. He raised the gauntlet and pointed towards the Shadow Hammer that hung above the stage.

"The Shadow Emperor will return to us soon, we can feel it."

He returned his arm to be hidden in the cloak and moved back into line with the other Higher Powers.

"Do not fail us, Captain. Find the light. Destroy the light. That is our way."

"Find the Light. Destroy the light," the five other members of the Higher Power returned loudly in a demonic echo, before all six flickered, merged and vanished with the wind and shadows.

The Captain remained still for a moment, feeling a bead of sweat drip down his face, he tried to rid himself of the nerves. He expelled a large lungful of air and then replaced his helmet, covering his head and face once again. He took a look towards the Shadow Hammer that hung above the six thrones of the Higher Powers. A sudden feeling of fear filled him. What would the return of the Emperor mean? Was this the beginning of a new chapter in the Empire's history? Would expansion begin again? The Captain had spent his whole life on Octdrevion Six, but had heard and read stories of the Shadow Empire's armada conquering Galaxy after Galaxy. Cutting through any defence system like a hot knife through flesh.

Chapter Two

"I need to go to the Havshad Archive. Why did he settle here? Where did he go?" he muttered to himself, questioning anything and everything that popped into his mind.

A Hav Guard Lieutenant approached the Captain from across the marble hall. The bronze lining and trim had caught the Captain's eye.

"Captain, what are our orders?" he shouted on approach prior to stopping a few paces from Theron Magda.

"What...emm..."

Theron had been caught deep in thought by the Lieutenant, so needed a moment to compose himself. He coughed and spluttered the haze away to bring his thoughts into focus.

"No orders, Lieutenant. I will call if needed. I'm going to the Havshad Archive to study. I do not want to be interrupted, understand?"

"Yes, Sir. No disruptions," the Lieutenant replied before turning to face the opposite direction and marching off.

The Havshad Archive was located on the opposite side of the Turach Vro Aka from the stage and thrones of the Higher Powers. Theron Magda marched round with speed in his step. His thoughts were bouncing between the return of the Shadow Emperor and the name Enlit. He had so many questions that only the archive could begin to answer. There was a new excitement bubbling beneath the nerves and the Captain began to embrace it on the journey.

The marble halls were filled with the intellects and Upper Citizens of Randtyph, discussing past conquests, planets, the solar systems and future plans. Science and technology filled their minds and mouths. Their chatter filled the halls. Excitement began to overtake fear, so much excitement the Captain had not noticed that groups of intellects were having to part to avoid collision. They scoffed and shook their heads in disgust, believing the pen is always mightier than the sword. Their disapproval was kept quiet enough to not be heard, as they did not want to test that theory with the Octdrevion Six Captain of the Hav Guard.

Before too much time had passed, the Captain had made his way around the base of the Turach Vro Aka to the archives. The golden doors, while closed, showed six golden figures, one to symbolise each of the Higher Powers before the disappearance of the Shadow Emperor, back in their time as the Havshad Knights.

Marra El, Zenta El, Warla El, Akorth El, Delna El and Karantha El were said to have been Dark Mages, beginning as men that craved power and immortality over anything else. Through lies, deceit and manipulation they took everything they had been longing for. From the moment they arrived on Vexora, the birthplace of their leader in the Octdrevya Galaxy, they felt the pull of the Shadow Stone and knew with that strength they could consume all.

As the Captain pushed open the massive golden doors, he felt like he was fully aware of his surroundings for the first time in what felt like a long time. He paused for a moment, and looked back, just now realising that he was about to enter the archives. How had he got here? He had been so deep in thought that he had taken no notice of his journey to the archive or the people around. The pause was only for a moment. His field of view was brought back forward as he pushed through the golden doors, revealing towering tall golden bookcases filled from floor to ceiling with scrolls and books filled with writings from planets and records of conquest spanning over thousands of years.

The archive attendants, known as the Keepers, were elderly members of the Empire. Gowned in silk with golden trims and a golden Shadow Hammer stitched with gold into the left breast of the silk, they spent their days absorbing as much knowledge as they could from all the documents and transcripts that filled the archives from wall to wall. Studying the Shadow Stones and what dark power and secrets lie within. Their nights spent satisfying their urges on the Faded as a Keeper had to take a vow of celibacy.

In the Outer System, the power of the Shadow Stone was only whispered about in the smallest of circles, hidden away in the dark. Before the taking of Earth, and the creation of Octdrevion Six, there had been relatively few opportunities for large amounts of study as the Shadow Emperor was continually moving, growing his armada, taking, conquering and destroying planets. Even the total annihilation of galaxies in his quest for more. More soldiers. More power. More shadow. Never seeming to have his thirst for battle and blood quenched. Until Earth. Until the Turach Vro Aka called to him. Called for him.

The Keepers of the archive searched to answer the questions that had been asked for many years. Why, on what was only seen as a primitive planet by them before, had the Shadow Emperor stopped here? Why had the Turach Vro Aka been found so many galaxies away from the Octdrevya Galaxy? The Turach Vro Aka had been a thing of prophecy and legend in the temples on Vexora, built upon the ruins of the original. Before the time of the Shadow Emperor, turning what was a peaceful planet, into the home of a demonic and cursed army, home of the Shadow Stone and the Dark Mages of the House of El. No light. No happiness. Just his armies marching the scorched planet, waiting for his return.

Two of the Keepers greeted the Captain as he entered. Both with matching swept back white hair, peering over their golden rimmed glasses. The lead Keeper, Keeper Thon, clearly identifiable by the scar running across his face.

"Good day to you, Captain. Praise be to the Higher Powers and may the return of the Shadow Emperor be nigh," they greeted in unison.

Both voices filled with joy at the sight of a visit from the Captain. They bowed their heads to finish their welcome.

"Good day to you, sirs. Praise be to the Higher Powers." He bowed in reply.

After adjusting his head back upright, the Captain, removed his helmet, placed it onto a table along with his staff just beside them, then his gauntlets, before finally adjusting his hair. Always making sure his appearance was perfect, especially in front of the highly educated eyes of the Keepers.

"How can we help you today, Captain? What questions do you need to ask? We Keepers can answer what we know, and what we know can be only answered by us."

The two Keepers began to riddle to the Captain, smiling and chuckling at the end of every sentence.

Theron Magda scoffed and rolled his eyes at the joy the pair were getting from the sound of their own voices.

"I am looking for answers relating to the disappearance of the Shadow Emperor," Theron barked.

Every Keeper in the archive gasped at the sound of the question. The slap and clatter of books and tablets being dropped filled the deafening silence that had consumed the room. Any questions or statements painting any weakness of the Shadow Empire was seen as blasphemy.

Keeper Thon placed his hand on the shoulder of his startled companion, the Keeper looking at the Captain with utter disgust.

"There now, the Captain means no harm or disrespect. He only looks for clarity of mind." He patted him on the back and then outstretched his arm to greet the Captain. "I am Keeper Thon, the head of the Archive Council here on Octdrevion Six. You may speak plainly, Captain."

Captain Theron Magda placed his hand around the Keeper's forearm, his hand reaching right around Keeper Thon's arm, his middle finger and thumb nearly meeting. Whilst the old frail hand sat like a design on the forearm plate of the Captain's armourer.

"I know who you are, Thon," Theron snarled as he pulled Keeper Thon in close. "I am looking for any clear information or details of what happened. We are told the Shadow Emperor defeated the Outer System rebellion before disappearing. What happened, and does the name Enlit mean anything to you?"

Keeper Thon hurried to guide the Captain to sit down at the table to discuss further with a bit more privacy.

"What do you know?" Theron continued to press for answers.

Keeper Thon took a seat at the table across from the Captain. Thon's fellow Keeper shook his head as he made his way back to the shelves full of books, tablets, paper and parchment to try and find peace in knowledge. The solid marble table was cold to touch and caused the conversation to echo slightly.

"Very strange, but strong questions you ask. Let me think on this for a moment," Keeper Thon mocked.

He rested his elbow on the top of the marble table, placing his chin into his hand and looked away as if to imitate falling deep into thought.

The Keeper's moment of thought turned into an awkward moment of silence, with Captain Theron Magda left looking from side to side for an answer. Was he to speak? He waited a moment, more to see if the Keeper would make eye contact again, or remain staring towards the ceiling, acting as though he had forgotten about the Captain.

Chapter Two

"Keeper Thon, if I show you and the rest of your Keepers the respect of ignoring your depraved, sexually sadistic, extracurricular activities with the Faded, then I would strongly advise you show me the courtesy of not acting as though I, Captain of the Hav Guard, do not exist. So once again, what do you know?" Theron said sternly while slamming his hand against the marble top.

"Well nobody knows, not even the Higher Powers. It happened after the battle for Randtyph–" Keeper Thon began.

"Please don't give me the usual Keeper nonsense. I know that nothing has happened through time and space without you lot studying it." Theron looked around him before leaning in, closing the gap between himself and Thon. "I know you fought in the battle for Randtyph. That scar that runs down your face–"

There was a swoosh, a flicker of light and then a loud slam behind as the doors crashed shut. The Captain and Keeper Thon jumped and turned to see what had happened. In front of the closed golden doors stood Karantha El. The Captain jumped up from the marble bench and turned to face the Higher Power.

"My Lord, how can I help?" Theron asked nervously.

Keeper Thon had graciously dismounted his marble stool and made his way round the table to stand side by side with the Captain.

"My Lord." Thon bowed. "Praise be to the Higher Powers and may the return of the Shadow Emperor be nigh."

Theron Magda took a second look at the Keeper before bowing his head.

Karantha El stood and exhaled large rasps of his cursed breath. The archive lay silent and still since all the Keepers had stopped what they were doing, startled by the crash of the doors slamming shut. Even more so by the sight of Karantha El, infamous for being the most bloodthirsty, savage, cruel and merciless of all the Higher Powers.

Karantha El stood there silent, his haunting cloak covering the tall frame, the darkened mask breaking through the overcast hood. His head turned to face Keeper Thon, still bowed, and then to the Captain who was stood up straight, waiting to be addressed.

"Captain, the time for study has passed. We must prepare for the Emperor's return. The Turach Vro Aka has spoken and it is once again time for the Outer System's Joining Ceremony. Our numbers must grow," Karantha El's demonic voice spoke.

"The Emperor is returning?" Keeper Thon asked in shock.

He momentarily raised his head before bowing once again. The fear that the Higher Powers instilled by simply being in the room, was highly apparent in the Havshad Archive at that very moment. Elation, adulation and salutations seemed to have never graced these walls. Their place and memory replaced by that of the bitter, crisp frost of unease and worry. Once again, the silence was deafening as the archive waited for the Higher Power to speak.

The pause continued until the Captain refused to wait any longer. He picked up his helmet and replaced it over his head. Grabbed at his gauntlets and ripped them over his hands quickly, in a hurry to escape the awkward situation he was now in, growing more and more tense by the second.

"I'll see to it right away, my Lord. I will have the preparations started, immediately," Theron voiced in a hurry.

He bowed to excuse himself before there was an opportunity for any reply, joining the still hunched over Keeper Thon, too afraid to look upon his master.

Whilst both the heads were bowed, there was another swoosh and flicker of light. Both men looked up to find the space in front of them empty.

Keeper Thon turned to face the Captain and chuckled unbelievably.

"We often wonder if the time shall come when we are the targets. We are spread far across the Cosmic Web. Give anybody a big enough target and they will eventually point a finger at you. There is a lot of strength in the shadow. We should not be trading Quaba for loyalty. Only in becoming a master of death can one seize and wield true power. I ramble. Good day, Captain Magda."

He smiled as he made his way over to the shelves, removing pieces of parchment as he searched for new information to absorb, ending the conversation very abruptly, in fear of Karantha El or another member of the Higher Powers returning.

The Captain stood patiently for a minute, in shock from how quickly things had turned. After a few moments of staring at the empty space in front of him and the Keepers going back to their routine, the Captain turned and made his way towards the doors to exit the archive, completely forgetting about his staff. It was something he had never managed to get used to. Vulnerabilities exposed the minute one of the Higher Powers appeared in a room. Any Hav Guard that did not fear them, usually found themselves moving up through the ranks quickly. The Higher Powers were always looking for their own personal spies and assassins.

Chapter Three

Feroshi washed away the stress of the morning's troubles with a bucket of water and a rag, while Simeskey made their bed. So precise with every fold. Gently running her hand over every intentional crease, smiling and humming with every motion. With one final pat of her hand on the top of the bed, she stood up and turned to face the back of Feroshi. She reached out her hand and grabbed his shoulder.

"You'll need to be getting yourself off to work soon. After you giving away the last of our rations to those kids, we need something to put in that belly of yours. Oh, please no more trouble," Simeskey joked.

She smiled, revealing her beautiful white teeth. Feroshi turned and smiled back as he pulled her close in to kiss her.

"You love trouble. We all need a bit of trouble in this hell, otherwise we'll all end up like old crazy Yvanny, screeching at the moon." Feroshi laughed.

Thud! There was a loud sound of a huge physique landing firm against the dirt deck outside.

"You know I'm coming in there, Mumma. I'll take a mug of water while I wait." The voice boomed through the doorway sheet.

Simeskey flinched and tightened her grip on Feroshi, startled by the loud unexpected noise that had just rung out from right outside their home.

"Now here is the real trouble." Feroshi swept his hair behind his ear as he rushed to greet his friend. "Ruevanlynn, my brother. You're back."

Ruevanlynn's dark skin caused his huge frame to move like a stunning silhouette through the doorway. But not even a shadow could stop reflections of light outlining his muscular torso. His head shaved smooth and close to the bone. Charcoal make-up used to highlight and make the whites of the eyes pop around the dark brown. Finished with his famous cheeky smiling pout.

Feroshi grabbed Ruevanlynn's arms. Not even his large working hands could engulf the large muscular arm of Ruevanlynn. They pulled each other in close, patting each other on the back, laughing and giddy to see each other.

"Bitch, I've been here all morning. You think I'm jumping two storeys because I love falling. You think my ladder just fell from the sky this mornin'." Ruevanlynn laughed.

He backed into the stool and sat down, taking his sheet tied round his wrist and applying it to his head and tying at the back.

"I'm the motherfucking black magic baby. I got back just before the Hav Guard came knocking. I thought Theron

Magda needed a little help leaving this humblest of *abodes*." He circled his finger to map out the walls. "Now even Mumma Rue must admit, it worked a lot better than I hoped. Pretty sure I killed that bitch."

Feroshi and Ruevanlynn laughed and joked, while Simeskey grimaced awkwardly as she filled a beaker with water. She tried her hardest to love everybody and everything. There had been no joy taken on her behalf at the sight of the mangled Hav Guard.

"Oshi, we really gotta get moving, baby," Ruevanlynn stated.

He jumped to his feet, patting down his fabric shorts and sheet shirt, before pointing to the doorway and gently taking the mug of water from Simeskey, as she handed it to him.

"What are you like?" Simeskey smiled and leaned into kiss Feroshi goodbye. "Now you pair behave yourselves."

Taking the mug back from Ruevanlynn in one hand, she placed her other hand on Feroshi's back and let it fall down his spine as he moved towards the doorway.

"Rue, you will need to come by this evening and tell me how your man is getting on in the Prison Zone," Simeskey called out.

She placed two fingers, her index and middle of her right hand, to her lips and motioned towards the doorway as the men moved through.

Ruevanlynn stopped in the doorway, only just now noticing the handprint upon his exit.

"So Mumma Rue did miss a party this morning."

He winked, ran his finger over the handprint, smiled and made his way outside.

Feroshi returned the motion to Simeskey, then turned and made his way outside. He placed his massive paw like hand on Ruevanlynn's shoulder. Both these men stood like mountains in the street. Massive with muscle from the work at the Octdrevion Six Diamond Farm – the Light Stones caused the men working with them to mutate into massive muscle bound warrior-like men, allowing them to break down the massive diamonds, releasing the stones inside.

"How is Zed getting on?" Feroshi asked.

Ruevanlynn rubbed his face with his hand and then removed his rag bandana from his head.

"Brother, he's not doing well, I'll tell you that. Looks pale and thin. Don't get me wrong, my boo was never big like us but still. They barely feed them and do all sorts of tests. I think he'll just be another one of the Faded soon. Grandor chow in the Dead Zone. What you gonna do?" he replied.

A teardrop began to form as he shrugged his shoulders, trying to compose himself, wiping all sentiment away with his finger under the tip of his nose, masking the splutter and cough of emotional pain with the rest of his hand.

"The Guard stopped him before he could let on too much. I don't think he's going to last, but nothing Mumma Rue can do."

He just swung his hands out in front, motioning forward.

Chapter Three

The street between the two towering aisles of homes, seemed endless. The chattering of children playing, as they made sure to keep an eye out for the Hav Guard, chased after the two men.

"Feroshi, where are you going?" they yelled out.

"Ruevanlynn, look at this," they continued.

The children acted as cheerleaders. The two men were like talismans of hope to the Outer System of Randtyph, standing so tall and muscular. The bravery these two had shown over time, defending the lesser from the Guard and taking the beatings and punishment themselves. Instead of allowing the young or old and weary to suffer, had given them status in the forgotten. Even before the Light Stones had started to take effect on the size of these two friends, they were fighting back to help anybody they could.

Ruevanlynn and Feroshi smiled and waved to the children.

"Off to work we go. You make sure you keep an eye out and go home quickly if you see the Hav Guard coming. Promise? Listen for the pots and pans." they replied.

The joy the children were experiencing seemed to resonate through the two. Even though Feroshi knew the rule was conformity over joy, he thought to himself, "... but the children shouldn't suffer for what they couldn't understand, and they couldn't understand the Hav Guard without taking a beating first."

As the Curtain began to lower to signal the entrance to the Inner System, Feroshi placed his hand across

Ruevanlyn's chest, stopping him where they stood.

"There's something I need to tell you. You're my brother and I need your advice." He ushered Ruevanlynn over to the side, to avoid the fuss of people trying to pass them. "Do you know what that was about this morning?"

Sweeping his hair out his face nervously, to try and almost hide the words.

"Oshi, you ain't got to go explaining your pretty little self to me. I'll have your back no matter what," Ruevanlynn reassured.

He gently punched at Feroshi's shoulder and then used his hand to scoop his drooping head. The fear was well hidden, but Ruevanlynn knew his best friend was troubled.

"Baby boy, what's got you twisted? Talk to me then. Pour your big bear heart out into my darkened cushions, baby." He taunted Feroshi as he pulled his head into his chest, patting him gently on the back of his head.

Feroshi laughed and slapped his hands against Ruevanlynn's waist.

"You know me too well, Rue." He stepped back, took a deep breath, swept both his hands through his dark hair, preparing himself.

"That handprint..." He looked at his right hand. "These tingles are getting worse. I don't know what's happening to me."

The sweat had begun to fall from Feroshi's brow.

"Think of all the trouble we've been in. All the fights with the Hav Guard. You don't think they've changed me, do you? Or maybe there's something wrong with me."

Ruevanlynn burst out laughing with so much force, so unexpectedly that his head was thrown back before he was able to try and stop it. Covering his mouth left him blowing bubbles through his fingers.

"Baby, baby, baby...if the Higher Powers and the Hav Guard were going to change anybody, I can guarantee you, my beautiful ass would be sat on that stage shouting up at the Turach Vro Aka. Damn, I might even get me one of those floating cloaks they wear." He patted Feroshi on the arm while cupping his face with the other. "Your heart is good. Just never end up in that Prison Zone, there's some weird shit going on there. The transport gets strange after you leave the walls of Randtyph. The energy walls of the transport black out so you can't see outside. Not until you get inside to the visiting room. Don't know what they're hiding, but it ain't good."

Feroshi could feel doubt becoming just more confusion as Ruevanlynn spoke.

"Oi, you two...keep moving!" a voice yelled.

A member of the Hav Guard had spotted the two speaking instead of heading to work. He pointed his baton towards where the curtain of shade met the ground. The direction everybody else was travelling in that was bound for work at the farm.

"Diamonds won't harvest themselves, will they...Outer System skaff," they snarled.

Another few members of the Guard had noticed the commotion and began to join in with the heckling.

"Pft, let's get moving, brother. Don't need to be stamping the shadow out of these fools today, do we?" Ruevanlynn scoffed. "I'm only joking, don't rise to it, baby."

He nodded towards the Hav Guard in acknowledgment and then raised his hand to apologise with it.

Feroshi and Ruevanlynn turned and made their way towards the entrance of the Diamond Farm. As they approached the base of the curtain, it raised to form a doorway as each worker and Hav Guard approached. The Octdrevion Diamond Farm formed a border between the Outer System under the shade of the curtain, and the Inner System out in the light.

The Inner System housed the rich and powerful of the Octdrevion Six extension of the Shadow Empire. The Diamond Farmers, the Hav Guard, Captain Theron Magda, Troop Commanders and his Lieutenants were among its residents, along with the Upper Citizens and Higher Intellects of Randtyph. Only the Higher Powers and the Shadow Emperor, upon his return, stayed in the Centre City of Randtyph. Only they had the honour of the brilliant marble halls with great ceiling-high gold doors.

Under the Inner System and deep below Centre City lay the Mines. Dark, damp and dangerous. The Light Stones powered everything in the Shadow Empire, from weapons to accommodation, lights to Space Jumps. Whereas the Shadow Stones fuelled the dark powers of the most malevolent of weapons and testing. They only grew deep beneath the surface near the base of the Turach Vro Aka's roots, where the crystals feed on its power. In recent years the Higher Intellects had managed to infuse Light Stone technology with the Shadow Stones, bringing about the new era of Shadow Tech.

Feroshi and Ruevanlynn walked into the entrance of the Farm, collecting their leather cuffs and pickaxe as they made their way through. The cuffs tracked their work rate and location, allowing the Hav Guard to know if anybody needed an incentive to work harder.

"Time to earn some food and water," Feroshi called out.

He threw his axe over his shoulder and made his way into the fields of light. Having to pause as radiated out, to allow his eyes to adjust. He held his axe, pointing towards the sky.

"Lord of light–"

"I think not." Ruevanlynn placed his axe against Feroshi's handle and pulled the axe to the ground. "You've caused enough bother today, Mr Handprint. Look at the colour of the sun...purple...ain't no Lord of Light here, baby boy. If you need cheering up, we got ourselves a couple greenies over there."

Feroshi turned to see two very slight men. Not a callus to be found on either of their pairs of hands. Chewed up, turned red raw and blistered from clenching onto the handle for dear life. The sun blinding to them as they swung their tools. Out of breath and exhausted, needing to break for air, every couple of swings. Each collision with the giant diamonds left nothing more than a graze on the outer skin.

"I still remember when that was us, brother. Well I don't think either of us had that little muscle, did we? Anyway, won't be long until they get strong enough to break into the stones. Then after that they'll be bigger than you in no time," Feroshi joked.

"Damn, bitch, that's cold."

The men began to laugh as they hacked away at the enormous white diamonds that burst out of the ground like miniature Light Shadows. They then collected the rubble in piles on the floor for the Farmers to come and gather on the back of their Grandors, using their scoop-like shovels to direct the piles of Light Stones into the cart being dragged behind.

"Let's just keep an eye, if you see the Farmer coming let me know and we'll hustle some of our pile over to the newbies," Feroshi stated.

Anything to protect the citizens of the Outer System.

***

As the Sun began to fall, the crystals slightly retracted, signalling the end of work. At the end of the shift, workers were allowed to shower, collect meal rations for the evening and tomorrow morning after returning their axe and cuffs.

Feroshi and Ruevanlynn headed through into the shower rooms to wash away the day's labour.

Chapter Three

"We tore it up today!" Feroshi exclaimed as the water began to pour over him from the ceiling above.

Ruevanlynn noticed a farmer heading their way with parchment in hand whilst stepping into the shower room.

"Heads up, brother. Mumma Rue's got eye on trouble heading this way."

The farmer, an elderly man with a dark black tunic and cloak, the white hair sat long but neatly on his head, brushed back with no tangles or loose hair, purposefully made his way to a little mound outside the shower room. The fogged glass sat chest high and above, so as to allow the workers to have eyes on the farmer during the address.

"The Higher Powers would like to invite you all to attend the Joining Ceremony of the Outer System for all males and females that are of age and ready to serve the Shadow Emperor and his Higher Powers. Please be ready, in your sector's arm, to board the transporters leaving the Outer System at the break of morning. All persons that are of age are to make their way into the Akaveash Colosseum. Drop their blood sample into the burning rocks. Go to the waiting room and from there, walk into the Havshad Curtain of Calling."

"That will be all."

The moment he finished reading, he folded his parchment, turned, dismounted the mound and headed towards the Inner System's entrance. Each farmer giving their section the same address.

Ruevanlynn washed away the soap from his face and turned to pick up his towel hanging next to him.

"Do you remember when we had our Joining Ceremony?" He chuckled. "Man, I remember when I first saw you and Simeskey together after you reappeared. Mmmmm, you were glowing. Baby, you are a lucky man."

Feroshi threw his head back with laughter as he dried his body.

"Brother, I thought you had hidden the Shadow Hammer down your shorts when you introduced me to Zed."

Ruevanlynn grabbed at his crotch.

"I've still got it, brother."

He released his grip on himself and lifted his hand to his face before blowing a kiss to Feroshi. He picked up his garments that had been laid out for him to wear while they washed.

"Gorgeous as ever. The grey really makes my eyes pop." Ruevanlynn removed a bit of charcoal he had hidden in the rag bandana. "That's why I got to make them dance when they pop."

He applied his charcoal eye liner, making sure to overextend the line like a black wing coming from the sides of his eyes.

Feroshi didn't give a second look to the sheet top he had thrown over his head or the fabric short bottoms he'd pulled on.

"I didn't even think." Feroshi stopped dead in his tracks. "Theron Magda will be there tomorrow. Bet you your eye-liner that they find a reason to pick me out tomorrow?"

"Don't you be getting yourself all worked up, baby. He'll be good as gold in front of the Higher Powers." Ruevanlynn tried to comfort the panic away. "Let's just grab our ration packs and get back home to the beautiful shade under the curtain."

Both men paused for a moment, looked each other seriously in the eye and then burst out laughing.

"Oi...enough of that laughing and joking, skaffs!" The Hav Guard had become impatient waiting for everyone to get showered and get off the farm. "Get off the farm and back to your shithole of a home."

He was throwing his baton in the air side to side, as if to motion for more speed.

The two men just shook their heads and left their gaze at the ground as they headed for the ration packs at the curtain and then to the Outer System entrance where the curtain lifted, avoiding any extra commotion.

"Ok, ok, I really mean it now...what a day." Feroshi chuckled.

The two men made their way home, walking with the group of workers that had been heading to their section of the Outer System. As they got further down the aisle and the group began to thin, the wild wailing of Yvanny could be heard shouting in tongues at the moon. For as long as the two could remember, this went on for a few minutes every night. Nobody knew why this old hermit sat atop the building, carrying out this ritual every night. All anybody knew is that it was more important to avoid her crazed rants, than to find out why.

Chapter Four

There was a buzz in the air of Randtyph that hadn't been felt in a long time. Cruisers and transporters coming in from all different planets, from all across the Shadow Empire's stretch through space. The electricity in the air, the noise of cheering and conversation could be heard and felt from Centre City all the way through the Inner System and into the slums of the Outer System. The Joining Ceremony of the Outer System was rarely attended by any members from the Inner System and Centre City of Randtyph, let alone anyone from off planet. The children who were of age, known as younglings, had already arrived and began to go through the pairing process.

The transporters for the Outer System were beginning to fill the eight aisles of the housing set up, collecting the participants one section at a time. Like large fogged pyramids they landed to the silent residents waiting below, on the dirt outside their high rise pop-up homes. Even from above, the faces of the Outer System residents were beacons of fear and confusion, at the sounds of excitement and commotion that could be heard from so far away.

Chapter Four

Noise, excitement or any form of commotion, excluding the birth of a child, was so highly frowned upon that nobody knew what was different about this Joining Ceremony. Usually only manned by a few members of the Hav Guard and the Captain, meaning the sight of enormous battle cruisers coming from the sky, filled anyone old enough to remember with fear. Old enough to remember that noise like this hadn't been heard, since the time of the Shadow Emperor. Vexorian battle cruisers began to appear. Jet black in colour. Enormous in size. Each carrying over a thousand Vexorian and Eissolian soldiers.

The beasts of Eissol were more than man. They were abominations of nature. Birthed by the Tempest Witches from the planet Manviewa, using the power of the Shadow Stones to splice themselves with the demonic creatures that control Buie Craiga. A dead planet. No light or life. Only the vile survive. These soldiers placed fear even into the bravest of the Hav Guard. These cruisers and soldiers had not been seen since the Shadow Emperor had vanished. Their snarls and putrid breath steaming out, were followed by the toxic odour, seeping from their leathery scaled skin. Eyes glowing like fire in water.

"Why are they here?" could be heard in the crowds of the hundreds of higher intellects and Hav Guard, that were gathering in the Great Hall.

From below, in the aisles of the Outer System, Feroshi, Simeskey and Ruevanlynn stared with fear, as did the rest of the Outer System residents. Looking backwards and forwards at each other's faces. Simeskey's face was filled with dread so Feroshi, standing by her side, took her hand in his and kissed her cheek.

"Don't be afraid, beautiful, I've got you," Feroshi whispered to her.

He kissed her once more on the cheek and looked toward the transporter landing to the left of them. Ruevanlynn put his bulging arm around Simeskey as extra added support.

"You know that while you got these two Grandors either side of you, there ain't shit going to happen to you, Mumma."

They smiled back at each other and Ruevanlynn pulled her in with his arm to comfort her more with his embrace.

"Something's wrong, this doesn't feel right," Feroshi muttered.

Ruevanlynn and Simeskey's moment of peace was broken by the tone in Feroshi's voice. People had begun to be thrown from the transporters to the ground below. Only the younglings participating in the ceremony were being left onboard and taken away on the transporters.

Once all the younglings had been taken away, the rest of the Outer System residents, old and young, were being forced back into their homes. Barged back into doorways that weren't even their own by the Hav Guard with their batons drawn.

"Everyone is to return to their homes immediately, apart from Feroshi Enlit. Feroshi Enlit, make yourself known to the Hav Guard immediately!" The tannoy from the transporters echoed and repeated, until the message had been passed through the entire section of the Outer System.

"What? No. 'Oshi, why do they want you?" Simeskey screamed.

Tears began to stream from her eyes and down her face the moment she heard his name. She broke free from her two protectors and grabbed Feroshi. Simeskey hugged him like she was trying to squeeze all her love into him as a blanket of protection. Feroshi wrapped his arms around Simeskey and looked straight into Ruevalynn's eyes.

"Take her and hide her, brother, please. I don't know what they want with me, but whatever it is, you can't let them find or hurt her. Promise me, brother, please!" Feroshi begged.

Ruevanlynn took a step towards Feroshi and Simeskey. He placed one of his hands on her shoulder gently, the other he placed on Feroshi's and gripped assuringly.

"We chose this family the minute they killed ours. Nobody is coming near our family. They took Zed from me, these bitches got another thing coming, if they think they're taking the only other two people, on this fucked up planet, that I love." He placed his forehead against Feroshi's. "I'll get her safe. Then I'm coming to save your ass."

He grasped the back of Feroshi's head, looking into his eyes before Feroshi turned to face Simeskey as she grabbed him away from Ruevanlynn.

Feroshi moved back and gently removed her arms from around his waist.

"No, Rue, not this time, brother. Get her safe and stay there with her."

He kissed Simeskey with so much passion, picking her up with one arm around her waist and held her face with the other. After a moment he placed her down and kissed her on the forehead, before turning to face Ruevanlynn again.

"If that fool Theron Magda wants to play games..." Ruevanlynn started.

He clapped his hands and then rubbed them together. At the same time there was a truly joyful smile beginning to form on his face accompanied by his soft brown eyes.

"I will play his games to keep you two safe."

Feroshi grabbed them both in one final embrace, kissed both their foreheads and turned to walk away. He knew what this meant. Once a name had been called by the Hav Guard, nobody ever saw them again. He was determined to show no fear or weakness while Simeskey could still see him.

"No, you can't!" Simeskey screamed.

She went to grab the back of his top, but was stopped by Ruevanlynn pulling her in as she cried and attempted to reach out for him.

Ruevanlynn held her back, but even though she was so much smaller than him, her emotion and rage was making her strength almost too much for him.

"What the hell?" he yelped, finally managing to get both arms around her and lift her off so her feet were off the ground. "Simeskey, look at me."

Simeskey was becoming feral like a wild animal, backed into a corner and fearing for its life. She was ferocious. This beautiful woman and her smile, ever since a baby, had been a bright shining light, in everybody-she-met's life. Her bright blue eyes remained like glass, even under the cover of the curtain. Long golden blonde hair always sat in a neat pleat running down her back, but not now.

There was no smile. Her pleat was not sat neatly. Sweat and tears had caused her hair to break free. Those hairs looking unkept and straggled as they pointed off in different directions, with different angled kinks all through each strand.

"Fero..." she started to scream.

Reacting as quickly as he could, Ruevanlynn covered her mouth with one hand as he placed her down and turned her to face him. Panicking that if he did not silence her immediately, she would catch the attention of the Hav Guard that were honing in on Feroshi.

He held her tight with his other arm, so tight that the veins from his bicep, forearm and hand were swelling as he used all his might to restrain her in her current state.

"Bitch, you better calm that shit the fuck down before I slap you in that pretty little face, or one of the Hav Guards will beat the shit out of you...or worse. Please, baby."

He pouted with his lips as his eyes tried to find a way to look through the torture in her eyes and find the real her. The bright blue-eyed girl whom he loved like a sister and the love of his best friend's life.

"There you are," Ruevanlynn spoke softly.

As he removed his hand from around her mouth, his expression began to soften and tears began to fall from his eyes. He pulled her in close and kissed the top of her head. Squeezing on to Ruevanlynn, she began to come back from the depths of the pain and desperation that had just overcome her.

"Rue, what just happened?" She seemed startled and confused as though the last few minutes had been nothing more than a bad dream.

Ruevanlynn moved back but held onto her hands, so she knew he wasn't going anywhere.

"Baby girl, I have no idea. All I know is that we got to get out of here before the Hav Guard stop paying attention to Feroshi and start looking at you, little Miss Temper Tantrum."

They chuckled for a moment, before the reality set back in and her face drooped as she attempted to see what was going on with Feroshi.

"If we know one thing, Keskey, it's that he is our beautiful bear, and if he tells me to get you somewhere safe and then stay wit' you..." He scooped her legs with one arm and supported her upper half with his other, and she snuggled into his chest, using it like a pillow. "Then, baby, we about to be room mates for a while until Mumma Rue shakes a few trees and sees what the next move is."

Hesitantly and reluctantly, Ruevanlynn carried Simeskey in the opposite direction from where Feroshi was being slammed to the ground, for resisting arrest by the Hav Guard.

Chapter Four

Feroshi had walked towards the Hav Guard troop beside the transporter with his hands raised as a sign of his passive intentions. It did not matter as the Hav Guard were laughing and shouting slurs at Feroshi well before physical abuse had started. Electrocuting and beating him with their batons, but he made no noise. He lay there on his side allowing this to happen. No fighting back. Just lying there with his eyes on Ruevanlynn carrying Simeskey away. Thud! Crack! Thud! Another barrage rained down as he kept his vision focussed. His family, brother and love, would be safe while he played along with whatever the Captain had planned for him.

Smash! Finally, a toe punt from one of the Hav Guards caught Feroshi in his solar plexus, causing his head to be thrown back in an attempt to breathe. His mouth filled with blood and the metallic taste along with it. His vision blurred and ears pulsing. He brought his head back forward and his vision came back into focus. Feroshi checked to see if Ruevanlynn and Simeskey were out of sight. They were gone; not even he could know where, neither could the Captain. There were no witnesses because all the transporters from the Outer System, that had emptied their occupants back into their homes, had taken their Hav Guard back to Centre City. The Hav Guard from this section were all too focussed on trying to beat down the hero of the Outer System, Feroshi Enlit, to have noticed where anybody had gone. Simeskey was safe while nobody knew where she was.

Now that nobody had seen where Simeskey and Ruevanlynn had gone; Feroshi's plan had worked as he had been hoping. All that was left to do is to see what would happen after the abuse. He began to laugh and got up to his knees, facing the member of the Hav Guard who had, not long before, toe punted him in his solar plexus, causing him a great deal of pain and discomfort. Feroshi whipped his hair back to remove it from his face. Soaked in blood, dirt and sweat it draped down behind his head and neck. His vision now clear, allowing him to stare deep into the white mask of his abuser.

"I promise that I will hand myself into the Captain peacefully," Feroshi offered himself.

He turned to stare at as many of the Hav Guard troop as possible. Then looked the toe punting bully from boot to mask.

"But first..."

Feroshi spat blood onto the bully's toes, keeping eye contact with the white face of his mask the whole time. Predicting the disgust of this action to cause him to try and knee his face, Feroshi blocked the knee. Thump! Both forearms landing like logs against the Hav Guard's thigh. Still staring at the Hav Guard and smiling. The block sent the Guard's leg into a limp and lame state, unable to hold his weight, causing him to drop in pain to his knees. Feroshi jumped to his feet, grabbed the Hav Guard by the back of his neck and quickly stood behind the Guard. A human shield? Or to show that even though the Hav Guard may be part of this Shadow Empire, they could still be made to look weak and vulnerable if the forgotten many decided to rise up.

Chapter Four

Holding one hand firmly against the back of the bully's head, forcing him to face the dirt whilst on his knees, the other hand held up in peace, to the other members of the Hav Guard that had formed a semi-circle around him. Batons drawn but not moving closer. Feroshi remained with his hand up and his head bowed. He took a deep breath in and then sighed.

"As I said, I will come peacefully. I have no quarrel with any you. The Outer System are here to serve as we must, but I do have a problem with this one."

Ripping his helmet and mask off and throwing it to the ground, revealed a middle age man with not a single scar on his face. Well kept eyebrows and other facial hair with a thick mane of dark hair atop his head. Feroshi was taken aback when he recognised this man. He had not always been Hav Guard. He was once Outer System living not far from him as a boy. Struggling every day like everybody else, but this Guard was already a man then? Solice...Solice Roid, that was his name. How could he still look the exact same; in fact, better and pampered? How had he become Hav Guard?

"Solice..." Feroshi muttered as he stared straight into his soul through his eyes.

Solice began to smile at Feroshi and opened his mouth as if to speak.

Crack! Snap! A sound much like wood breaking, rang out for a second. Followed by a dull thud. The echo bounced down the corridor of houses as Feroshi, with one hand on Solice's shoulder and the other holding his face to keep eye contact, with one twist of the wrist, Feroshi snapped his neck. Letting Solice's body fall to the floor by gently throwing his face away, which now faced the opposite direction from the rest of his body.

Feroshi remained still, breathing heavily for a moment while a tear ran down his cheek, but his face was a picture of confusion and anger. He had never killed a man before. His last attachment to innocence, fading away with the blooding. Still staring at where Solice's eyeline had been moments before, he then dropped to his knees and placed his hands behind the back of his head, to show he surrendered and meant no harm to any other member of the Hav Guard troop. This meant nothing to the Hav Guard; they paused for a moment in disbelief at what had just happened, then began to slowly move forward, staying with one foot forward and energy batons raised high.

"No, leave him alone!"

The children of the Outer System ran out of where they had been hiding and began to scream at the Hav Guards below. Still far too young for the Joining Ceremony, but with so much bravery to protect their protector. Grabbing and pulling at their arms and legs.

"Please don't hurt him," they continued.

The Troop Commander stood front and centre of the Guard troop. His purple flashes dancing in the wind. He grabbed one of the children by the hair that ran to Feroshi's aid and threw him violently to the side. As he did this, he noticed that all the members of this section of the housing corridor had begun to leave their homes armed with pans, stools and any other item that could be used as a weapon. It had been over two decades since the end of the uprising, but this section of the Outer System seemed ready to relight the fire of rebellion.

"Stop, or we will kill every last one of you," he scoffed towards the armed mob in disgust.

Feroshi stood up, hands still behind his head.

"Leave them, it's me the Captain wants so let's get on with it," Feroshi called out getting back to his feet.

He dropped his hands behind his back so he could be cuffed and then turned to the other members of the Outer System.

"Please, everybody go home. Stay safe and look after each other," he pleaded with them.

Feroshi would never want any of the fellow members of the Outer System to suffer because of him. Ruevanlynn and Feroshi, from a young age, had thrown themselves into minor skirmishes with any Hav Guard that tried to bully the weak and helpless. Always ending the same way. Ruevanlynn and Feroshi swarmed by supporting Hav Guard. Both of them battered and bruised on the floor. Then when conscious, carrying each other home, laughing and wincing with every chuckle. As they grew older, enhanced by the power of the Light Stones, stronger, faster and smarter, they would attack quickly with knockout power and escape, before any of the other Guard were able to react.

The Troop Commander walked behind Feroshi. The top of his helmet barely reaching the top of Feroshi's shoulders. Thud! He used his baton to take Feroshi's left leg down on to his knee. Low enough and in a position where the Hav Guard felt like he had total power over this enormous specimen. As he applied the energy cuffs to Feroshi's wrists, the Troop Commander leaned forward next to Feroshi's ear.

"Fuck the Captain. I'm going to break you, you worthless skaff scum," he hissed.

Smash! The Troop Commander struck Feroshi across the back of his head with his baton. Knocking Feroshi to the floor. He stepped forward and placed his foot on the back of Feroshi's throat. Applying just enough pressure to dig his face into the dirt.

"This is your hero?" he yelled out with the baton pointing down at Feroshi. "You Outer System skaffs live because I allow it. Me! Troop Commander Drathon Telema."

He removed his boot from the back of Feroshi's neck. Feroshi tried to get the dirt out of his mouth and spat the dirt onto the ground next to his face. Forcing his head so he was able to look up at The Troop Commander and then laughed.

"Drathon Telema. Theron Magda. Hav Guard. You are all the same, just cowards in armour," Feroshi jeered.

With another mouth full of dirt and blood, he spat to the side and placed his chin on the ground with his head facing straight ahead.

"How dare you!" Drathon screamed.

Chapter Four

Commander Telema began to beat the back of Feroshi. Thud! Thump! Thud! But not a noise was made from Feroshi. Not even a grunt while the thumping and thudding of the baton against his back continued. Muffled cries of hidden friends and other members of the Outer System could be heard with every strike. Everyone trusted in Feroshi's statement. Everyone believed in Feroshi, so nobody screamed out.

Trying to not look weak, Drathon ended his assault, stepped back and turned towards his men.

"Drag this scum into a transporter and take him to Karantha El." He barked his orders.

Drathon turned to face Feroshi and noticed that the smile wasn't there anymore. He lifted his helmet, just enough to show Feroshi the smile his mask was hiding.

"Karantha El. Should be fun, let's do it," Feroshi taunted.

Feroshi placed himself face down and waited for the Hav Guard to carry him away. Four members of the Hav Guard stepped up to carry Feroshi, grabbing onto his muscular arms and lifting. Feroshi hung his head as his feet dragged along the floor.

"Wait!" Drathon ordered.

Walking over to the lifting party, he walked slowly, shaking his head as he stared at Feroshi. Drathon stopped in front of him and waited for a moment, but Feroshi refused to look up.

"Look at me!" Drathon screamed furiously.

He didn't give Feroshi a chance as snatched at his long, dirt- and blood-filled hair and pulled his face up to be eye to eye with him. Drathon removed his helmet to reveal a head full of thick silver hair and piercing green eyes, a face stubbled with hair that matched the colour on his head. Only his eyebrows and eyelashes were dark in colour.

"You realise you're nothing, don't you?" he said rhetorically while smiling, revealing a set of perfect teeth.

Feroshi coughed, spluttered, looked to the ground and then spat a mouthful of blood onto the floor in front of Drathon's armoured boots in a final act of defiance.

"Nothing," he spluttered

His face, blood and dirt covered. Any hair not held in the grip of Drathon had fallen forward slightly covering Feroshi's face. Feroshi, through swollen eyes, looked Drathon dead in his, and mustered a smile.

"Screw the Shadow and fuck you." Feroshi continued to splutter and giggle.

Rage filled Drathon as he watched Feroshi break eye contact. His laugh was the final straw. Smash! Drathon smashed his helmet against Feroshi's head and face, causing him to fall limp and unconscious. The Troop Commander was deep breathing through relief. Glad to have finally ended the exchange. He threw his head back and used his free hand to push his hair back over his head, as if to gain composure. He then looked back at the lame Feroshi and a menacing smile began to creep across his face. Watching the blood pour from Feroshi's head, then to his face and dripping onto the floor was causing arousal from the rush of adrenaline.

Drathon replaced his helmet. Blood splattered across the white mask. He took a few steps backwards before pointing his gauntlet towards the transporter.

"Get that filth on to the transporter," Drathon shouted sadistically.

Limp and blood soaked, Feroshi was dragged onto the transporter. As it took off, the Outer System section that had just watched the onslaught, filled the corridor. Each one in sync, kissing the index and middle finger on their right hand and then pointing them up to the transporter. As if to say goodbye to their protector. For so many years giving the Outer System a reason to smile as he would walk the corridors of the Outer System. Like a talisman of light to and for the people, that were to live their life in the shade of the Shadow Emperor before and now, the Higher Powers and their Hav Guard.

From the back a thud was heard, breaking the concentration of everyone stood there staring up to the troop transporter as it rose into the sky, causing a parting in the curtain to allow the troop carrier to rise high, before heading in the direction of the Turach Vro Aka.

Apart from Feroshi, there was only one other member of this section of the Outer System that would make a thud like that dropping from a couple of floors up.

"People...don't let those bitches win," Ruevanlynn said with encouragement. Standing tall as another hope in this defeated population's eyes. "Now I know you don't think that this is the last time we're going to be seeing that man. That's motherfuckin' Feroshi Enlit."

Ruevanlynn moved closer, beating his chest and raising his voice, trying to raise morale. He stopped where Feroshi's blood still lay drying on top of the dirt and pointed.

"He bleeds for all y'all. For all eight sections of the Outer System, baby. He bleeds and breathes for every one of us."

A young girl from the crowd ran over to Ruevanlynn and wrapped her arms around one of his tree truck thighs and squeezed tight.

"Please save him, Rue," she asked with her sweet innocent voice.

Ruevanlynn knelt down and placed his left hand on her shoulder.

"Baby girl, I promise you this...he will bring himself back. Someway. Somehow. We just have to believe." He then stood, picking up the girl and placing her on his shoulder. "Right now I need every one of y'all to stay safe, because this right here, is the beginning of some dark times. It will get darker before the light can shine again. We are going to tear it all down...and it will burn. They say they give us peace. Well maybe it's time for a bit of chaos up in this bitch."

He placed the little girl down and watched as the crowd dispersed.

"Yo, Rue." He heard from behind him over the slapping of feet closing in on his position.

Chapter Four

"Ranoa, baby boy, what you up to? We ain't seen you around in a minute." Ruevanlynn asked, hugging his friend as he approached.

"I have been sent by "The Pit", to tell you and Simeskey to come to over to mine and Shajo's place tonight. You want to save Feroshi and the others want her off planet? Trust me, brother," Ranoa explained before rushing off.

For a moment Ruevanlynn stood confused, contemplating his options. He had known Ranoa and his partner Shajo since they were all boys. Including Feroshi, the four of them went way back. This was just such a random and unexpected turn of events. The Pit and the others? There wasn't much of a choice here for Ruevanlynn, though. He had to get his brother back.

Chapter 5

The Centre City of Randtyph was buzzing with thousands of members of the Shadow Empire. Usually the Akaveash Colosseum of Centre City was filled with members of the Outer System, and a few Hav Guard, watching on as the males and females were joined with their "life partner", in the eyes of the Shadow Empire. Each male and female of age, roughly when puberty would set in, would drop blood from their hand into the burning rocks, climb the steps behind the Havshad Curtain of Calling and disappear. The Veils hung as though held by nothing. Flowing without wind. Casting a shadow as dark as the night's sky until a pairing was made and they passed through. The shadow would then begin to glow bright and blind with light, only for a moment.

This seated colosseum was nearly blinding to the participants, as the reflection of light on marble caused them to shelter their eyes as they entered. The brightest thing these younglings had ever seen before this, was through the curtain above the Outer System.

Chapter 5

Two at a time, male and female, female and female, or male and male, the new couples would appear from the blinding light beneath the Curtain of Calling. As each pair of the Outer System's younglings would exit the veil, they would turn inward to face their partner for life. It was said from the droplet of blood on the rocks, the power of the Shadow could see into the deepest fibres of your soul. Knowing whether a male walked out with a male. A female with a female. A female with a male. The Shadow could see if you were worthy to serve. The Curtain searched for the Light as well. Many children had walked through the floating veil but had never reappeared on the other side. To where, nobody in the Outer System knew. All they knew, is that if you did not reappear by the end of the ceremony...a light flickered far too bright inside for the Shadow to allow them to be, or their inner darkness was of such potential that the Shadow Empire could use them.

Members of the Shadow Empire rarely appeared in such vast numbers to such an event though. To them, a planet's Joining Ceremony was merely a formality. Each planet needed farming. The Outer System residence of all the Shadow Emperor's planets served a single purpose: to do whatever the Emperor expected them to. Farming and mining the planet's resources. Procreate and keep the cycle going. The Shadow Empire got richer and more powerful. Knowledge increased along with the power of the Shadow Stone.

Apart from the younger generation that were taking part in the Joining Ceremony, the Hav Guard that had taken them in and the few standing guard in the Great Hall blocking the doors, the Colosseum was empty from residents of the Outer System. As each couple revealed themselves, they were ushered to the seats where they expected to see the faces of parents and neighbours but instead, empty spaces, slowly being filled pair by pair. The noise from outside of the room grew greater and greater as an armada of shuttles and transports arrived. The mumbling of confusion between the pairs began to increase,

"Silence!" screamed the Hav Guard. "Sit down and be silent."

Armies stood side by side. Filling the halls in front of the stage. Front and centre of each army stood their Captains. Thousands upon thousands facing the Turach Vro Aka, waiting for the Higher Powers to appear. Vexorian soldiers from across the Universe and the snarling and frothing warriors from Eissol waited alongside the legion of Hav Guard. Theron Magda standing front and centre of the army of Octdrevion Six.

He had been scanning the faces of his Troop Commanders and Lieutenants, noticing that Troop Commander Drathon Telema and his Hav Guard troop were not present. He had given no order other than what had been handed down to him. Commander Telema was one of his top Troop Commanders. Where was he? Why would he disobey him?

Chapter 5

"Your mind is filled with doubt, Captain." The voice of the Higher Powers echoed in his mind.

Theron Magda stood completely still as he conversed with the Higher Powers in his mind's eye.

"I do not doubt any command given to me. I am just questioning the whereabouts of one of my troop commanders."

When the Higher Powers used this tool to control the minds of their soldiers, it was as if they had taken them to a shadow room in their mind. They stood face to face with the person they were communicating with in the mind walking web. Theron Magda knelt down before the Higher Powers in this shadow room in his mind.

"We know where Troop Commander Telema is." The six shadowed figures of the Higher Powers echoed in unison. "There is no need to doubt the whereabouts of your soldiers. Everything is as it is meant to be."

"What is his mission, my Lords?" Theron Magda asked the dark figures.

The six Higher Powers moved closer, growing taller to tower above the Captain.

"You do not need to know his mission, Captain. Wait as you are. We shall reveal all very soon." Their voices grew louder as the dark shadowed figures engulfed Theron Magda, snapping him out of the mind walk he had just taken with the Higher Powers.

The Captain stood facing his army once again. Shaking his head gently. Feeling as though he had woken from a dream.

"Call the armies to attention." The final message was heard in his mind like a lingering thought.

"Soldiers and citizens of the Shadow Empire... ATTENTION!" His voice echoed through the halls.

The clatter of armour coming to attention on the marble floors and the roars from the beastly warriors, drowned out the echo of the command. The Captain then about-turned to face the stage. Swiftly followed by the rest of the Captains. Bending down onto one knee to welcome the Higher Powers onto their stage.

Like a haunting mist moving quickly across the stage, each throne taken by the darkened clouds, the shadows took the forms of the six Higher Powers, causing the Great Hall to fall silent. Even though the hall was filled with thousands of troops and citizens of Randtyph, a pin drop could have been heard over the silence of anticipation.

Marra El stood to address his subjects and soldiers. Up out of his throne he stepped, the dark metal of his armoured gauntlets gripping the arms of his seat. His deathly, spectral cloak floating as he towered over everyone below.

"My warriors and subjects of the Shadow Empire. What a beautiful sight of power I see before me." The voice carrying to the back of the hall, as clearly at the rear as right at the foot of the stage. "It has been a long time since the shadow has needed to fear the light. Well, brothers and sisters, we must once again fear the light. Even as we speak, they grow in numbers. Infesting all from the inside. Other planets are already under attack from this disease. The same virus that took our Emperor from us the last time we let it shine too bright."

There was a low rumble as questions began to be asked among the citizens and soldiers of the Shadow Empire. The Higher Powers had never addressed the missing status of the Emperor. Many of the soldiers had blamed the Higher Powers for not protecting the Emperor as they were the Havshad Knights.

Captain Theron Magda looked towards Marra El for answers, but was quickly hearing the voices of the Higher Powers in his mind once again.

"Silence the room immediately, Captain."

The Captain gave a slight nod to confirm he had understood the command.

"Silence!" Theron Magda ordered at the top of his voice.

The muttering of questions quickly came to a halt as everyone focussed on the stage once more.

"The Shadow Emperor shall return one day soon. He shall once again take the Shadow Hammer in hand and vanquish this cancer that threatens our Empire," Marra El continued.

With the pointed finger of his gauntlet, metallic knuckles ridging his finger to a pointed end like a talon, Marra El motioned towards the Shadow Hammer. Hanging against the Turach Vro Aka, above the other five of the Higher Powers.

"Take this message back to your planets, sectors and colonies: the Emperor will return. By the blood of the Light he shall return. On that day, his vengeance will be felt across the entirety of the Shadow Empire and beyond. No angel can hide forever."

All the armies of the Shadow Empire began to cheer in unison. Roaring, stamping and clattering of armour. Boom boom cha! Boom boom cha! The vibrations could be felt around the entire perimeter of the Great Wall of Randtyph.

"Shad. Shad. Shad," they chanted.

"Sacrifice every light, no matter how dull it may shine! Drown our enemies in their blood! Feed on their souls. Once again we shall be feared by those who defy us. With the power of the Shadow Stone we shall conquer all."

Marra El finished addressing the crowd and he broke into a maniacal laugh, joined by the other Higher Powers. The cloaked figures that sat in the thrones once again turned to shadows and disappeared into nothingness. Their laugh falling to an echoed whisper.

The Great Hall was filled with the roar of thousands of soldiers cheering the message they had just heard. The noise could be heard by those taking part in the Joining Ceremony. It caused the youngest of Outer System younglings sat in the hall to brace in fear as every roar and cheer caused the ground to vibrate.

Captain Theron Magda turned to face the armies.

"Go forth, in the name of the Shadow Empire. Octdrevion Hav Guard, get those Outer System skaffs back to their slums. The Joining Ceremony is over." He barked his orders.

He then watched as the other armies took their transporters up to the massive cruisers floating in the sky. Blocking out the blue sky of daylight with the colours of the night. The Vexorian armies, one by one they disappeared out of view, followed by the Eissolian battle cruisers, as they all travelled back to their planets with a blink of a blue light.

As the citizens of Randtyph watched the armies disappear into the sky, a loud crash followed by screaming, was heard as the Hav Guard stormed the Joining Ceremony. Dragging the newly formed couples from the seated area, barking orders in their ears, grabbing handfuls of long hair, dragging the females as though they were nothing. Beating and zapping the males with their batons to make them move quicker. Any that fell were dragged by the scruff or ankle. It did not matter to the Hav Guard. All of them pumped with adrenaline and tainted thoughts after the speech from Marra El. Waging war on the younglings as they forced them into the transporters waiting to take them back to the Outer System. Beaten and bloodied, the Outer System younglings cried out for help, only to be beaten again into silence.

The cries vanished with their transporters. Captain Theron Magda watched on with a forced smile as the chaos ensued. Blood and tears speckled the marble floors. Theron Magda knelt down, removed his gauntlet and dabbed two of his fingers onto a patch of blood, that lay pooling on the floor. He rubbed the blood against his fingers. The crimson dripping through his fingers seemed to resonate with a part of him thought lost.

"What have I just started? I think there's going to be some dark times for the skaffs ahead," he said aloud to himself.

A buzzing noise was heard from above as Theron Magda stood upright once more, replacing his gauntlet before looking to the sky for the source. The pad on his gauntlet let him know that it was was Troop Commander Telema's transporter back from the Outer System. Several members of the Hav Guard moved towards the Captain in preparation of the transporter landing in the Great Hall.

"Captain, what are your instructions?" the Hav Guard asked as they arrived at Captain Magda's side. "Do you know who is on the transporter?"

Theron Magda was too focused on the transporter as it hovered above, slowly descending towards them.

"Wh- what? You lot get in line behind me."

His concentration moved from the transporter to the Hav Guard and then straight back to the transporter.

"Let's see what Drathon has to say for himself," the Captain muttered to himself.

The transporter came to a halt less than a metre away from the small landing party that had formed beside the Captain. As the energy doors cleared way for the exit, Drathon Telema turned to the Hav Guard.

"You do not speak a word of what happened in the Outer System or about the prisoner to anybody," he hissed at his men before turning to shake Theron Magda's hand.

Chapter 5

"Captain, what a pleasant surprise. I see we have missed all the excitement."

The Troop Commander stood with his hand out as the Hav Guard walked past him and off the transporter. Theron Magda looked down at the outstretched arm and then back to Drathon Telema's face.

"Put that hand away. Where have you been?"

There was an anger to Theron's tone of voice. Unsure yet if he had been disrespected, disobeyed or undermined.

Troop Commander Telema braced up, startled by the response of his Captain.

"Captain, I was sent to find the agitator, Feroshi Enlit," Drathon assured him.

He pointed back towards the slumped figure on the floor in the transporter. Immediately, Theron Magda became filled with anxiety, too intense to tell if he was becoming excited or if this was a feeling of dread.

"Enlit? How did you know about him?" Theron mumbled. "Bring that beast to me...NOW!'

Drathon jumped as the Captain shouted the final command.

"Theron...I mean, Captain, I have instructions to–" He was cut short in his plea.

"I am your Captain. Now drag that skaff off that transporter and lay him at my feet now." The Captain took a step back and motioned towards the space of marble floor in front of his boots. "Drathon, do not test me."

The Troop Commander hesitated for a moment and then reluctantly made his way to the space on the transporter where Feroshi's unconscious body lay. Battered, bleeding and motionless apart from his chest moving slightly with every laboured breath. Dragging the body left a trail of dirt and blood scuffs behind it. Drathon Telema was having to squat down and pull with all his might to move Feroshi.

"Faster, faster!" Theron Magda barked.

After a few painful and exhausting minutes, Troop Commander Telema had managed to drag Feroshi's unconscious body onto the floor next to Theron.

Captain Magda removed his helmet and held it in his outstretched arm, holding it out for Drathon to collect as another sign of his dominance. Never making eye contact, as he reluctantly took the helmet from the Captain. Burning rage inside him sent wicked and evil thoughts souring through his mind. He was being made to feel so small and disrespected by his Captain in front of his troops. A dangerous game to play with a psychopathic sociopath that revelled in inflicting pain and humiliation on anyone that stood in his way.

Killing off his twin in the womb. Murdered his mother when his father disgraced the family name. Addicted to Quaba from a young age. Breaking his competitions legs in the day and by night, slitting their throats while the lay asleep in their bed. Only to fall at the final hurdle of making Captain when he faced Theron. One of the few that had always stood up to him. One of the few who believed that bullies needed to know they could hurt too. Now, Drathon took pleasure in pain and had a constant thirst for more. Never to be satisfied. A hunger never to be truly and fully gratified. Not while Captain Theron Magda survived.

Theron Magda, eyes still on the body of Feroshi, knelt down next to his head, gently stroking the hair out of Feroshi's face to reveal the bloodied and bruised closed eyes of his foe.

"I told you that you and I were going to be seeing a lot more of each other, worryingly for you, I didn't order this. Now that is troubling wouldn't you say, Feroshi?" He spoke softly.

"What are you doing, Captain?" Drathon still stood holding the helmet.

Theron took absolutely no notice of him.

"Hav Guard," the Captain called out.

A member of the Hav Guard contingent, stood behind the Captain, stepped forward and to attention.

"Yes, Captain?" he replied.

"Take this skaff filth to the Prison Zone. I want him locked in solitary on the upper levels until I arrive."

"Theron–" Drathon started.

Theron Magda snapped his head to look at the Troop Commander.

"Captain!" Theron corrected.

"Captain, I am supposed to take agitators to Karantha El," he argued, still trying to pass the helmet back to the Captain.

Theron Magda stood up and snatched the helmet from Drathon Telema. Then proceeded to turn and face his Hav Guard.

"Do as I said. I'll be along shortly, don't you worry." He reiterated his previous order.

Members of the Hav Guard descended onto Feroshi. Four of the Hav Guard dragged him back on the troop transporter.

As the transporter left, Captain Theron Magda paid no attention to it. Just keeping his eyes on Drathon Telema. Still locked in a mental battle of the ego.

"Pft," the Captain snarled and then walked away, leaving Drathon Telema stood there, all alone in the Great Hall.

Completely emasculated, he could feel the fire burning. Each flashing memory acting as a fuel to the violent fury of his internal inferno. Drathon felt nothing in the way of empathy for others, but he felt everything for himself. He was a god in his own mind. He should be ruling the Empire. No mere mortal would ever disrespect him the way Theron just had. He knew he would have to wait, but his time would come. His opportunity to make Theron bend and break, cringe and cry would present itself in one way or another. The storm of Drathon was building and the centre of the eye was heading straight for Theron.

"I'll be seeing you again, Captain," Drathon whispered under his breath, while he looked around to see if anybody had noticed the scolding.

Chapter 6

Daylight and sunshine faded over Randtyph as nightfall set in. Artificial rain fell from the curtain over the Outer System. The aisles and alleyways between the rows and columns of homes, began to pool with the tear drops of this shaded sky, causing splash marks to turn to dirt filled puddles, that trickled under the sheet doorways of the ground floor pop-up homes. The sound of the rain created an orchestra of noises as each droplet crashed and burst. Ringing out a different note, against each of the different materials used to form the ceilings and walls.

Ruevanlynn's home was located two storeys above the Enlits'. Safe from the minor flooding below, he looked upon Simeskey as she sat perched on the edge of his bed, staring at the doorway. Barely blinking in a distraught daze.

"Baby girl, you can't do this to yourself anymore. Mumma Rue has watched you sit there all day now."

He walked towards her and crouched down next to the bed.

"I need to get you to safety and then I'm going to round up the troops. Believe me when I say this..."

Ruevanlynn moved in front of her, still crouched down, placing one hand on her leg and the other gently against her face. Simeskey stared straight past him towards the doorway, motionless, eyes wide and still barely blinking.

"That man, your man, is gonna stop at nothing to keep your fine ass safe. If that means tearing down the whole God damn Empire in the process...Feroshi won't stop." Trying to use his smile as reassurance.

There was a few minutes of silence as Ruevanlynn stared at Simeskey, while she stared straight through him. As the tears began to fall and stream down her face, she made eye contact with Ruevanlynn, finally breaking her emotional trance.

"I know how this goes, Rue. They take you and then you're never seen again. Look at Zedary," she snarled with contempt.

Reinitiating her dead stare-off with distant space. The smile faded from Ruevanlynn's face as he let out a deep breath and shook his head.

"Bitch, I am not the enemy here!" He stood up and took a few paces away from Simeskey before turning to face her again after regaining his composure. "Girl, I'm sorry, I shouldn't have snapped, but Zed is not Feroshi. I spent every day protecting Zedary. Feroshi has spent every day protecting everybody in this hole. Including me and you, Mumma."

A smile reappeared on his face along with a raised eyebrow on his tilted head.

Chapter 6

"It's protecting everybody that's got him in this mess." Simeskey's voice was softer but still filled with emotion as she stared at the door, willing Feroshi to walk through at that moment. "Who protects the protector, Rue? Who!"

With that Simeskey broke down. Holding her face in her hands, uncontrollably sobbing. Nearly touching her forehead to her knees before throwing her head back, trying to take in air as she wailed.

It only took a couple of seconds of seeing Simeskey crying for Ruevanlynn to rush to her aid. Sitting on the bed beside her, he pulled her into his embrace. Holding her head against his chest he kissed her and rocked her gently.

"Baby girl, it's going to be ok. I promise."

He continued to rock her until her crying came under control. Ruevanlynn took the rag bandana from his head and wiped away the moisture from her cheeks and under her eyes.

"We are going to take a short trip. There's some place we need to go."

Taking her hand, Ruevanlynn helped Simeskey to her feet before ripping the sheet from his bed and placing it over Simeskey's head and shoulders. She grabbed a hold of the edges and pulled it tight as Ruevanlynn rubbed his hands over her head, making sure that she was protected from the pouring rain outside.

"Where are we going?" she asked.

"It's a surprise. Now get on Mumma Rue's back and make sure you tuck that sheet in so you stay dry. It's a whole lotta wet outside."

Ruevanlynn replaced the rag around his head and crouched down, to allow Simeskey to climb onto his back. With one arm she held the blanket and the other fell down Ruevanlynn's front for him to grab onto like a safety harness.

"Hold on tight, baby girl and keep those legs wrapped round me nice and tight." He stood tall with Simeskey wrapped tightly round his upper body. "You ready?"

Simeskey nodded with her head on his shoulder and gripped on even tighter.

"I'm ready," she assured him.

"Here we go."

Ruevanlynn made his way to the doorway and held the sheet off to the side. Staring from left to right, at the river of mud below, to make sure the aisle was clear of any Hav Guard. Seeing there was nobody around, Ruevanlynn dropped to the floor below, splashing the soiled water up over his legs and speckling the underside of Simeskey, that wasn't protected by the blanket.

"Nothing like a dirt bath to get the juices going," Ruevanlynn chuckled to his passenger.

Due to the darkness and downpour of the rain, Ruevanlynn didn't feel the need to shadow run and stuck to the middle of the aisle. With Simeskey gripping on tightly, he headed straight towards the markets at the end of the aisle. As the pair approached the final few columns, whistling could be heard from above.

"Rue, where's that coming from?" Simeskey cried.

Chapter 6

Slowing to a walk, Ruevanlynn pointed from one roof to the other.

"It's ok, baby girl. It's our people letting the Pit know we are friendlies."

"The Pit?" she replied.

Ruevanlynn let out a chuckle.

"I have no idea, baby girl. Thought it was just a tall tale. But it was a friend that asked us to come, so here we are."

Stopping in front of the final column of doors on the corner of their sector, he helped Simeskey dismount. Wanting to make sure she felt secure, Ruevanlynn pulled her in tight as he walked towards the sheet doorway on the ground floor door.

"Yo yo, Mumma Rue coming in." Announcing himself as they hurried in out of the rain.

Two men sat in the home at the table. Obviously workers of the Diamond Farm because of their muscular physique.

"Hello, Mr Grezzie. And who is this..." Ranoa paused, noticing who was under the soaking sheet. "Simeskey Enlit, I am so sorry about Feroshi. I am Ranoa Sevil Rumray and this is my partner Shajo Rumray. Whatever you need, we are here for you."

Ranoa took Simeskey's hand to shake it. His working hands swallowing her petite ones in his grasp.

Simeskey smiled back.

"Hello, Ranoa. Thank you."

She lifted her hand to wave to Shajo. He jumped to his feet and bowed at her as though she were royalty.

"It's an absolute honour to have you in our home." He turned to face Ruevanlynn. "Mr Rue, always a pleasure. What brings you here on this typically terrible Outer System evening?"

The four of them began to laugh at the question.

"Well, someone said something about getting our beauty here off planet..." Ruevanlynn started.

Simeskey grabbed at his wrist sharply and turned him to face her.

"Off planet! Are you joking me?" Rage filled her voice.

"Keskey, I told you, baby. Mumma Rue needs to keep you safe. The only way Feroshi will give in to them is if they get to you." He placed his hands onto her shoulders. "Keep you safe and he'll save us all, baby girl. Trust me, mumma, please."

There was a moment of silence as Simeskey tried to process what she was hearing and trying to run through all the different scenarios, of how this could play out, in her mind. She looked at Ruevanlynn, then to her two new acquaintances before returning her gaze to Ruevanlynn.

"Okay then. Tell me about The Pit," she said assertively.

"She knows about the Pit?" Shajo looked at Ruevanlynn in shock.

His smiling pout was back on his face.

"Oh baby, I don't even know what The Pit is." Ruevanlynn put his arm around Simeskey, "So come on then, boys, does somebody want to begin?"

Chapter 6

Ranoa placed his hand reassuringly on the shoulder of Shajo. Like a master recalling his attack dog.

"It's ok, beautiful, she's an Enlit. We are here to serve," Ranoa assured Shajo.

"What do you mean serve?" Simeskey gasped.

Ranoa looked towards Shajo.

"I guess we better get her down there quickly. Let's get the bed moved." Ranoa dismissed Simeskey's question, hoping time would reveal the answers she was searching for.

He ushered Shajo over towards their bed. Dragging it out the way revealed four large wooden slats on the floor. One by one the pair lifted the slats, placing them off to the side to allow access to a large wooden door with a circular metal handle. After placing the fourth and final slat to the side of the wooden door, Ranoa stood up, dusting himself down and looked towards Simeskey.

"We will always keep you safe and the answers you need are down there. I know we may be unfamiliar to you, but trust Ruevanlynn when he says that if we keep you safe, Feroshi will save us all."

Like a wave crashing over her, each word flooded her with fear. Fear of the unknown pulling her down. Simeskey moved up against Ruevanlynn so that he would hold and reassure her.

"I'm not going to lie, Rue, I'm a bit scared." She whimpered.

"Mumma's got you, baby. It might not seem like it, but right now, down there's gotta be safer for you than up here," Ruevanlynn replied.

He pulled her in close, as Ranoa stamped on the wooden door five times and then moved clear, waiting for a reply.

A few moments later the round metallic handle began to turn anti-clockwise. The sound of the locking mechanism gave a click and a clack as the internal pins unlocked. Simeskey's grip on Ruevanlynn began to tighten with nerves of anticipation. The sound of cheering and roaring could be heard as the wooden door creaked open. It had been unlocked from the inside by a short and stocky man. His long grey hair tied back into a ponytail, ended nearly halfway down his back. Scars covered his face and arms with his nose badly disfigured. Shoja helped lift the door as Ranoa knelt down to greet the old man.

"Hello, Father." With a smile on his face he threw his arm out to offer assistance to his parent.

"Put that arm away, Ranoa. I might be old but I'm still too fast for you." Jumping up out of the now open passageway. "Hello gentlemen. Oh Simeskey, I hoped we'd be seeing you after Feroshi being taken. It's an absolute pleasure to finally meet you."

The old war-torn man quickly made his way to Simeskey and pulled her away from Ruevanlynn and pulled her in to hug her. Her arms pinned by her sides as confusion covered her face.

"I am the keeper of The Pit, Lemra Sevil." He introduced himself.

It almost felt like a daze she was so perplexed.

Chapter 6

"Sorry, sir, as lovely as it is to meet you...how do you know who I am? How does everybody here, know who I am, but I only know Rue?" Simeskey demanded answers.

"My dear, I'm afraid that even though a question may be asked at any time, the answer has a time and only then can it can be given." Smiling as he moved her towards the open hatch in the ground. "What I can tell you is that we have always been here. Rebuilding. Waiting."

Lemra jumped down into the hole in the floor, with the doorway sitting at shoulder height, he extended his hand out to Simeskey. She hesitated for a moment to turn to Ruevanlynn. Looking for any sign of approval in his face. He smiled and nodded.

"I'll be right behind you, Mumma...every step of the way. I got you, boo."

Simeskey grabbed onto Lemra's hand, allowing him to take her weight as she hopped down onto the step where he stood. Looking down she saw a staircase going deep underground in the direction of the wall.

"When you say 'we', do you mean you and your son?" she continued to question.

The father and son began to laugh. Lemra put his arm around Simeskey and started her on her way down the wooden steps. Ruggedly imbedded into the dirt, a crude, manmade hole with light glowing from the archways that supported the ceiling. Only giving enough light to see the next, acting as checkpoints on the journey down.

"Like a hand with broken fingers we heal to once again hold the sword," Lemra answered.

With each step the roaring and cheering became louder and the sound of iron and steel clashing could be heard. Bodies slapping together and slamming against the floor, joined in with the chorus of noise.

"Why do you speak in riddles, Mr Sevil?"

"As kings stay safe in castles, I stay safe in lyrics, love. You never know who's listening. We've learnt that the hard way with loss." Lemra stopped as he spoke plainly. "Now, welcome to The Pit."

Lemra threw his arms open as they finished their descent deep underground. This subterranean area stretched for as far as the eye could see and beyond. There was a whole army underground training, sleeping and eating. Men were sparring with each other. Mastering hand-to-hand combat along with handheld weapons made from anything and everything. Men of all shapes, sizes and colour stood together. Their families, hidden safely on the lower levels. Simeskey was stuck in place, blown away by what she was seeing. The wave of negative emotion, that she had felt earlier, was being replaced with pure astonishment and awe at what was in front of her.

"Wow, just wow. This is absolutely incredible. How long have you been down here?" Simeskey gawked.

"Now, that, my dear, I can tell you. In the last days of the war, the Havshad Knights were taking swarms of Hav Guard going home to home massacring anybody in sight.

Didn't matter if you were old, young, male or female. Killing indiscriminately. The Hav Guard rolled into the Outer System with energy cannons and blew homes away." Lemra started to walk Simeskey through the crowds. "We knew it was over, so the commanding officers told us to retreat and get as many of the families as safe as possible. Next thing we knew...the Emperor was gone, our commanders were dead or disappeared, and the Hav Guard were recalled back to Centre City. We got as many women and children off planet as possible. Some stayed and live in the family quarters. What you see here is all the men that survived and believed that once again we would rise up. For us, the war never ended."

Simeskey followed and stared in amazement at what was going on around her.

"This is just incredible. Do you truly believe there will be another war though?" she asked.

"I know there will be. The prophecy has foretold it."

"The prophecy?" Her voice was filled with confusion.

Lemra smiled at her and pushed hair out of her face.

"I'm afraid that is one of the answers that must remain unknown at this time, dear."

"So, you want to get my girl off planet." Ruevanlynn approached the pair from the rear with Ranoa and Shajo either side of him. "Can you actually make that happen?"

"After the commotion over the past couple of days it should be pretty easy to get you to safety. You must be exhausted after today though. Let's get you some food and water." Without hesitation and while keeping eye contact with Simeskey, Lemra replied.

He smiled at Simeskey and then motioned to his son.

"Ranoa, take Shajo and get a bed set up for Simeskey please."

The pair quickly made their way towards the opposite end of the underground compound where there was access to the sleeping quarters. Simeskey watched as they walked away.

"Where will you be sending me, Lemra?" she asked.

"A journey through the Cosmic Web will set you free. You will be safe. Off to see one of the last Mages of Light. He has a safe haven, hidden in The Land of the Broken Wing, on the planet of Laborine. It's located in the Cosfordia Galaxy. Do not fret, even though it will not be with me, your journey shall be as a three." Lemra chuckled at his rhyme.

Panic covered the face of the soon to be planet-hopper.

"Okay okay okay, two questions...what the hell is a mage and what is the cosmic web?" Simeskey asked hysterically as she struggled to breathe from panic.

Lemra's head was thrown back as he began to roar with laughter.

"Ha ha ha." He laughed, choking as he attempted to reply. "One thing at a time, Simeskey. Let's get you rested and refuelled then we can discuss our plans tomorrow."

He patted Simeskey and Ruevanlynn on the back and headed off in the direction his son and partner had left in earlier. Shaking his head and laughing at the innocence of his guest.

Ruevanlynn put his arm around his friend, both sets of eyes watching as Lemra took his leave.

"He's a weird old dude, ain't he, Keskey? Absolute heart of gold, but totally tapped. Just remember you're safe with the mad man...supposedly," Ruevanlynn joked.

They both looked at each other, scrunched up their faces and out laughing. The pair moved through the underground compound, Ruevanlynn guiding Simeskey through the maze of training warriors. A few had recognised Ruevanlynn, approaching to greet him, then noticing Simeskey they fell silent, bowing their heads as if she were a queen.

"Rue, you really are going to have to explain this to me one day," she nervously said.

Lifting her hand slightly to return the gesture of respect and timidly muttering "hi, hello," to anyone that bowed or paused what they were doing to furnish a smile her way.

Molten metal filled the air from walls opening up to stairwells, masking any smell of sweat or blood from the melee of men. The stench became stronger as they arrived at the opposite end of the Outer System's underground stronghold.

"You'll probably be surprised to hear that I know exactly what you know now, Mumma. Hell, girl, when you get to Laborine you'll be more in the know than me." Ruevanlynn pushed open the door that gave access to the stairwell down to the living quarters. "You go and get that pretty little head of yours down now, okay? I've gotta get home while it's still dark and pouring down out there. Got to get my beautiful ass to the farm in the morning."

He winked and smiled before turning to make his way back to the poorly lit stairway.

"Rue..." Simeskey's voice cracked.

He turned to see Simeskey's eyes filled with tears but a smile grew across her face. A picture of vulnerability. Vulnerable from heartbreak and loss, but pure beauty radiated through.

"Thank you," she mouthed.

Chapter 7

Sunrise over the City of Randtyph was a spectacle for all to see. The Shadow Emperor, a master of annihilation, knew that to destroy a population you need to cut off its resources. Earth couldn't survive without the Sun. From the moment the planet was blessed with the birth of a Turach Vro Aka, the population and allied planets were sentenced to death.

Without their Solar Fusion they couldn't escape when the attack began. They couldn't fight back, as the sun powered all of their planetary defences. Their satellites, space stations and lunar hospital sites, all depended on the power of the Sun to fuel the fusion reactors that created their artificial atmosphere. Within the first few minutes of the Empire's Armada arriving in the galaxy, two Shadow Matter Mines were fired from the Emperor's Destroyer, poisoning the Sun, turning it an astonishing purple. Killing its ability to provide any vitality. Now, with the dawning of each new day, the sky turns a brilliant crimson, then turquoise before the radiant blue of the daylight hours.

Captain Theron Magda awoke to the morning muster call from the barracks. Sitting up in his bed revealing his naked torso, he swept his blond hair back and rubbed his face to feel the stubble that had grown overnight. Moving to the edge of the bed, he threw his white long-john-covered legs out from under his sheet and placed his bare feet on the warm marble floor. Theron stretched his back before rolling his neck, cracking the bones in the process, prior to pushing up off his thighs and making his way to the sink and mirror next to his window. Resting his hands on the edges, he felt the soft fabric against his palms and fingers while turning his head to gaze at the crimson sky. Smiling as he breathed in the morning air.

Staring into the mirror, he shifted his face from side to side as he stroked over his cheeks and chin.

"Magda, you need a shave," joking with his reflection.

He picked up the small golden handled blade in his hand, that sat on a glass ledge between the faucets and mirror. The blade followed the fingers of his opposite hand as he used it to pull the skin tight, allowing him to return himself to his clean cut state, in which he took so much pride. Water flowed from golden taps, enabling Theron Magda to splash water over his face. Washing away any rogue hairs that may still be masking even the smallest of areas on his perfect face.

Bang! Bang! Bang! The sound of a gauntlet banging up against the Captain's door reverberated through the room.

"Captain!" a muffled voice called from the other side.

Chapter 7

"Enter," the Captain yelled out while dabbing a towel to his face.

Theron's door swung open. Troop Commander Drathon Telema was stood waiting on the other side. Helmet under his arm, he stared towards Theron Magda.

"Captain, will you be travelling to the Prison Zone today? Enlit has been chained up without food or water as requested," Drathon asked.

"Yes, I should think so. I think it is time for me to pay Enlit a visit." He smiled as he threw the towel onto his bed.

"Will you be needing any of the Hav Guard with you?"

Theron looked towards Drathon and then hung his head and chortled.

"Is this your way of trying to apologise for the way in which you tried to undermine my authority and position?"

"Sir, I was just following orders from the High..."

"Stop. That's enough, Drathon." The Captain began to don his black, gold trimmed tunic. "I have known for some time that you want to replace me as Captain. I genuinely thought beating you to the finish line would have stopped your games. Trying to gain favour with the Higher Powers in the hope that they will place you straight at the top. It's not your right to be Captain. You have to earn it. I earned it by breaking you."

The colour drained from Drathon's face.

"Captain, I don't know what you mean." Drathon tried to hide his deception.

"Don't lie to me. You think I don't know that your savage ways have continued. I know everything that happened yesterday, Troop Commander. I know about your night-time visits to the Outer System with your 'boys', raping men and women for sport. Get your kicks that way, do you? Well let me make you this promise...cross me again and I will take you beyond the wall, past the Faded and straight into the path of the first Grandor we come across. It would give me great pleasure to watch you being ripped apart and watching your blood pour onto the floor."

Buttoning up his tunic while he stared at Drathon with a wicked look on his face.

"I would rather your Lieutenants replaced me than you. Doesn't even matter, I'm the youngest Captain in Octdrevion Six history. You'll be chasing me for a good while yet. Now, get me a transporter ready. No Hav Guard. Just the transporter."

Drathon's face turned a deep shade of red as he snarled and frothed. Clenching onto his helmet so tight that it began to warp, he finally brought his rage under control.

"Sir." Drathon about-turned and headed out the open doorway.

"And close that door behind you," Theron barked as he began to pull his black bottoms on over his long-johns.

Drathon closed the door and paused for a moment, filling with fire and hate. Nobody, absolutely nobody, would treat him like this. Menacing thoughts began to tick tick tick in his mind, bringing a sinister smile to his face. Staring at the door as though it was the Captain himself.

"You are right about one thing, you fool, I will be Captain, but there will be no long reign for you."

He turned and made his way down the marbled hallway. Large golden-framed paintings of the Emperor and prior Captains hung on the walls, Drathon Telema gazing up at each one as he passed. Pausing at the one of Derza Telema.

"The name Telema will be feared again," he muttered aloud before turning to walk away.

With Feroshi in chains, the Captain felt no need to be covered in armour, hoping that this would add insult to injury as he began his torment over the prisoner. Strapping his belt around his waist, he adjusted his baton to hang down the outside of his leg.

"Today is going to be a good day," Theron said to himself.

After pulling on his boots, he gave himself one final glance in the mirror, winking at himself before leaving his living quarters and heading for the transporter that waited for him outside.

By the time the Captain made it outside, the sky above was the radiant blue of day. The sun caused the transporter to shimmer, showing the distorted reflection of one of his Lieutenants approaching from behind him.

Captain Theron Magda found peace and happiness, watching the hustle of the Hav Guard as they moved around. Troop transporters buzzing through the air. The noise only being dampened by the Hav Guard calling out commands such as halt and turn. All the noise reminding him that this was his sanctuary. He found no enjoyment in leaving the shine of the Inner System to invade the dull Outer System.

"Captain," the Lieutenant called out.

He stopped a few paces from Theron. His slicked back brunette hair shining underneath the Octdrevion sky.

"Lieutenant Froch," Theron replied.

Lieutenants worked in Hav Command as analysts. Sifting through the abundance of data that poured in every day. Messages from other compounds on other planets. Chatter from the spies in the Outer System and from beyond the wall. Data constantly circulating that allowed the Empire to stay ahead of their enemies.

"Sir, there's something you need to see," Froch divulged.

He stood there in his dark grey tunic, with the purple trim showing his rank, enthusiasm pouring out.

"I can't just now, Froch. Come by my quarters this evening with your report," Theron replied in a hurry.

The Captain was trying to end the conversation quickly. He was beginning to think about the pain and suffering he was going to get to inflict on Feroshi Enlit.

"But, Captain Magda..."

"Lieutenant Saldo Froch, not now. The Prison Zone has a guest that is just dying to see me." Beginning to snigger, he made his way onto the transporter.

"Captain please," Saldo Froch pleaded.

Theron paused and held out his hand as he hung his head.

"Lieutenant, listen to the words coming from my mouth. NOT NOW!" he bellowed. Theron moved towards Saldo and placed his hand on his shoulder. "Look, Lieutenant, I really need to get going. Please come by my room this evening and we will discuss whatever it is."

Saldo Froch bowed his head in reluctant acknowledgement.

"As you wish, sir."

"Thank you. I promise that tonight you will have my undivided attention."

The Lieutenant stood to attention as the Captain boarded the transporter.

"Oh..." The Captain tilted backwards, both feet inside the transporter with his upper body suspended in the air as he grabbed onto the railing. "Under no circumstance are you to share your findings with anybody until we have debriefed. Especially, Troop Commander Telema. Even if he pulls rank...you wait. Got it?"

"Yes, sir."

The Lieutenant smiled awkwardly, almost a grimace. Feeling the pressure of being placed between his superior and the highest rank in the Hav Guard. No good would come from disobeying Captain Magda but, there would be pain involved if he was reprimanded by Drathon Telema for insubordination.

"What have I just walked myself into?" Saldo thought to himself as he walked away.

Watching the Lieutenant walk away, the energy doors reformed into a wall in front of him, Theron's focus unbroken as he stared out, eyes wide with his arms pulled tightly behind him. His mind, far too focussed on the task in hand, to be getting side tracked by any minor military mission that may be awaiting him, upon his return to his quarters in the evening.

The transporter ascended into the sky, high above the barracks and Hav Command below. Even from the sky, the Diamond Farm below was blinding to the eye. Like a burning hot river of energy encircling the Turach Vro Aka, the archive and the colosseum. Giving off a sheeted shadow, lifelessly shrouding the eight sections of the Outer System, killing off any hope. All bound together tightly by the dark enveloping ring of the Great Wall. Passing over the barricade revealed the arsenal of long and short range weaponry, defending this talisman of the Shadow Empire and monolith of Octdrevion Six.

Swarms of Faded slowly moved their way through a maze of bodies and remains that littered this breeding and feeding ground of the Grandors. The sight of the near motionless forms shuffling towards their death justifying the title of: the Dead Space. A Grandor pouncing and playing with the remains from last night's catch caused Theron Magda to look away before its jaws clamped down and obliterated this helpless, lower member of the food chain. Usually a sight that would cause the Hav Guard to break out in jubilation, but the Captain had grown tired of such cruelty long before he made rank. Even a small glimpse of a feeble citizen of the Outer System being unnecessarily harmed would cause him to intervene. Just as he had intended to do when he first saw the Hav Guard entering the home of Feroshi and Simeskey. Only to find himself an enemy that was now awaiting his arrival.

He may have stood tall before, but now, Feroshi Enlit would be hanging by his wrists from the ceiling. Lowered to his knees and made to gaze upward, towards the victor of their skirmish. The thoughts were running rampant through the Captain's mind, causing him to become riled up. Pumping his chest with his hand, psyching himself up, as though this meeting of the two would be settled in hand-to-hand combat. A battle to the death.

"The transporter will now be commencing with its descent to the destination, the Prison Zone. Please prepare for arrival." The announcement from the tannoy broke up the battle going on in Theron's mind.

He rushed over to the railing at the front of the transporter to stare out and see the immense Vexorion stone fortress of the sea. Artificial weather controls inside allowed the Prison Zone to constantly have storms, creating perilous conditions outside for anybody that considered the attempt at escape.

"It's time, Feroshi. Can you feel it." Theron spoke aloud to himself.

Sneering as his eyes twinkled with the reflection from all the spotlights shining down over the landing pad.

"You are Captain Theron Magda and he is nothing but a piece of shit on your shoe. You are Captain Theron Magda and he is nothing but a piece of shit on your shoe," he repeated to himself, over and over.

He was trying to put the self-doubt out of his mind, that had been forming ever since Troop Commander Telema had been given a mission without his input. To instil the fear from pain and suffering that he wanted to inject into Feroshi, would need his mind firing at nothing less than full speed.

"You will be arriving at your destination in a few moments. Be ready to depart shortly. Have a lovely day." The soft female voice once again breaking the mental battle Theron was having with himself.

Releasing the railing, Captain Magda stood tall, adjusting his attire before stepping out, onto the landing pad. Two black-masked Hav Guard waited to greet the Captain.

"Good day, Captain." They stood to attention as he disembarked the transporter.

"Good day, men. Where is my prisoner?" Beginning to walk towards darkened stone doors, that gave access to the control room, as soon as he was steady on his feet.

The two members of the welcome party were caught off guard by the Captain's immediate movement, having to extend their stride to catch up.

"Emm, sir, we need to sign you in. If you could give us a moment to scan you please."

Theron stopped in his tracks.

"Scan me. Scan me! I am your Captain, you insolent little prick!" Shocked at the request, mixing with the fire burning deep in his soul, caused rage to overcome him.

Chapter 7

Lunging at the darkened mask of the Hav Guard that had been foolish enough to try and get in his way, he ripped it over the Guard's head, revealing a terrified face below. With the other hand, Theron Magda viciously pulled at the guard by the collar of his armour, causing him to trip so Captain Magda released him, allowing the Guard to crash to the floor. Stepping back at the realisation of what he had done, he turned to face the Hav Guard that remained standing. Then back to the Guard on the floor. Before staring at the black mask in his hand and throwing it to the ground in panic.

"What just happened?" Sweat beaded on his forehead from the mental distress of trying to remember the past few moments of his life.

"Slow down, Captain!" The Hav Guard backed away, as Theron looked towards him, while throwing his arms out in defence in fear of being attacked next.

Theron Magda, with his mind in complete disarray, ran towards the doors with one of his hands holding the top of his forehead, attempting to compose himself and steady his mind. Arriving at the doors, Captain Magda paused to catch his breath and look back to check on the state of affairs behind him. The fallen Hav Guard was now crouched, rubbing at his face where it had slammed against the stone floor, with the second Guard aiding him to his feet. Turning to face the door once more, Theron rubbed the sweat from his face into his hair. Sliding all the loose hairs back into place, he took a deep breath, before exhaling and pulling the door open.

Troop Commander Niloc Ecurb, the Commanding Officer of the Prison Zone, stood up from his black marble throne, in the centre of the large spherical room. Screens, scattered with Vexorian Hyrogliphics, were being controlled by fifteen unarmoured female Hav Guard with holographic gloves and goggles on. All dressed in the same dark blue military uniform. Blue tunic. Blue trousers. Black boots and hair pulled back. Not a single finger movement was broken as the Captain entered the room. Only the Troop Commander broke from his screens that were live footage of all the prisoners.

"Captain, what a nice surprise. You're on your own? Are you here to see the latest agitator?" Niloc rushed to greet Theron.

Theron Magda had noticed that one of Niloc's screens was enlarged on Feroshi's live footage.

"Is that my prisoner?" Theron quizzed.

He flicked his head to show the Troop Commander that he had seen what he had been viewing prior to his arrival.

"Emm, well." Niloc turned quickly, pressing at a control pad on his forearm to close down his screens. "Yes well, when Troop Commander Telema dropped by to visit the prisoner last night, he told us the Higher Powers wanted us to make him aware of any visitors Feroshi had..."

"What?" Theron barked.

"...before you see him," Niloc awkwardly finished and attempted to force a smile, as he felt the conversation slipping away from him.

"Why was I not made aware of his visit?" Captain Magda began to make his way towards Troop Commander Ecurb.

"Once again, he said specifically that we were not to tell you," Niloc reiterated.

Theron stopped.

"Let me guess. By orders of the Higher Powers." He threw his hands out in disbelief.

"Sorry, Captain, just following orders." He began to lift his hand to his control pad, obviously to contact Troop Commander Telema.

"DON'T...even think about it. Stand down, Ecurb, I'm your superior and you will follow my orders," Theron ordered, resting his hand on top of his baton.

Pausing in a moment of uncertainty, Niloc dropped his arms in obedience.

"Would you like me to take you up, sir?" Niloc asked submissively.

"Yes. Thank you, Niloc." Grateful that somebody was following his command and restoring a bit of normality back to his life. "Now, what else was Drathon Telema telling you to do last night?"

Niloc walked over to where the Captain was stood.

"Not a lot, sir. You know how he is. Doesn't like to give too much away now when it benefits him, does he?" He chuckled. "Just those two orders and then went to see the Prisoner. Even left without saying goodbye."

"So, what did he want with the prisoner?" Captain Magda rolled his hands to try and put some haste into the Troop Commander.

Niloc looked back to where his screens had been, then back to the Captain.

"I can only see, not hear, sir."

Theron let out a large grunt of disapproval and rubbed his face with his hands.

"Just take me to see the prisoner, please." Theron sounded exhausted by the conversation.

"Ok, one moment please."

The Troop Commander pressed at graphics on his control panel, activating the personal teleport. Their bodies became engulfed in light, reappearing at the desired destination within the compound.

"And that's us here, Captain." He turned but there was no Captain. "Sir! Oh."

Niloc realised the Captain was on his knees retching outside the large stone wall separating themselves from the prisoner. Spitting excess saliva onto the floor, Theron once again ran his hands through his hair, making sure every hair was pulled back and pulling the excess fluid from his mouth.

"I'll never get used to teleporting."

"Ha ha ha, don't worry about it, Captain. Maybe avoid space jumping anytime soon, because that twists the stomach a lot worse. The new tech prevents the sickness now to be honest. Helped to design some of it myself."

Chapter 7

The Troop Commander smiled as he patted the Captain on the back in jest. Theron Magda squared up his tunic before nodding towards the Troop Commander so he knew he was ready for the wall to be unlocked. Looking around the small dark room they had arrived in, he noticed there were no doors and light was given by a single ember burning dimly above. Troop Commander Ecurb placed his hand against the wall causing it to shimmer and turn opaque. With the wall opened, Theron turned to Niloc.

"It's ok, Ecurb. I've got it from here," Theron insisted.

Hesitantly, the Troop Commander acknowledged the request. Without saying a word he looked towards his control pad, prodding at the graphics once more, before departing in a beam of light.

The Captain stood stationary for a moment as the wall reformed and took its natural state. He listened to the pitter patter of rain droplets leaking through from the ceiling. The shallow rasp of laboured breathing could be heard from the beaten prisoner, along with the slight rattle of his chains.

Entering the cell triggered the spotlights in the room. Feroshi, with his arms raised upwards, hung there, sluggishly swaying as his knees and feet dragged across the cold stone floor below. His rag shorts damp, filthy and blood-soaked.

"Feroshi Enlit, what a pleasure it is to see you again," Theron taunted.

Circling behind the beaten and bruised detainee, he watched as sweat, blood and rain drops ran over the muscular arms, shoulders and back of his enemy. Feeling enjoyment from watching his drooping and debilitated body hang there.

"I hope you are comfortable. Probably going to be here a long time."

Feroshi remained with his head hanging down into his chest. His dark hair, matted from dirt and bodily fluids, hung forward, oscillating with every motion backwards and forwards.

Continuing to circle, Theron removed his baton from his belt. Making sure to stay at a safe distance, he placed the tip of his baton under the chin of Feroshi, lifting his face, revealing the bruised, bashed and swollen flesh. Cuts, above and below his eyes, were trickling down his cheeks. The blood from his nose and lips had begun to dry into his beard.

"Now now, Feroshi, don't be rude. You had a lot to say earlier. Tell me why I shouldn't kill you right here and now," Theron continued to press.

A low, growling laugh began to sound from Feroshi.

"You have bigger problems than me it would seem." Feroshi forced a reply.

Coughing and spluttering as he tried to clear his throat and mouth, he smirked at Theron. Only his right eye was visible, as swelling had caused the left eye to clamp shut.

Energising the baton as he removed it from below Feroshi's head, Captain Magda stabbed the end into the torso of the prisoner. Zap! Snap! Skin sizzled from the electrocution.

"AHHHHH!" Feroshi let out a scream of distress.

Chapter 7

His scream echoed around the room.

"You will respect me. You will fear me. If you don't, I will kill everybody and anything you hold dear," Theron hissed.

Theron stared at the top of the prisoner's head as it fell forward once more.

"Maybe I'll bring your lovely Simeskey in here and have a few of the Hav Guard violate her. Would you like that?" The taunting increased.

The sound of her name caused Feroshi to tense up. Pulling on his chains, he attempted to throw a kick out at the Captain.

"Don't you speak her name!" Feroshi yelled out.

His voice bellowed out over the noise of the chains, clinking and clattering in his attempt to strike Captain Theron Magda.

"Oh well now, we seem to have hit a nerve. Turns out that you aren't as complex as I had started to think." Pacing from one side to the other, in front of Feroshi, Theron smiled at the revelation of the detainee's soft spot. "Sticking with that thought, what did Troop Commander Drathon Telema want with you last night?"

Feroshi remained silent, staring at the ground below, as he allowed his body to hang like a wet rag from his chains once again. This beacon of hope, now a picture of defeat.

Theron planted his feet in front of the helpless form.

"Feroshi, this needs to be a two-way conversation. Tell me what I want to know and I may just let your loved ones live. Stay silent and you will sign their death warrant."

Theron ran his baton along the cheek of Feroshi.

"What did Drathon Telema want with you last night?"

Slowly Feroshi lifted his head. Gritting his teeth, he stared towards the Captain. Tilting his head to allow his working eye to be unconcealed from shadow and hair.

"He wanted to know why you wanted me so badly. Wanted to know if I was some child or something like that. Then he beat me and told me I'd be seeing him again. Happy?" Feroshi snarled.

A look of bewilderment filled Theron's face.

"What?" Theron exclaimed.

"Turns out it's not just the Outer System that thinks you're a bitch."

Feroshi burst out laughing then wincing as the movement of his chest caused his battered body to writhe in pain.

THWACK! The loud noise of Theron's baton clobbering the side of Feroshi's face rang out. Blood sprayed out to the side and onto the floor. Breathing heavily, Theron glared at the lifeless form as Feroshi struggled to remain conscious.

"You will beg for death. Mark my words, you will scream out my name and ask for mercy as we break every little part of your worthless spirit."

THWACK! Theron brought the baton through a back handed swing, causing the crimson streams to fly in the opposite direction.

"And if you won't break...then we'll just have to suck the life force from you and toss you to the Grandors."

Chapter 7

Simeskey's voice, screaming his name, rang through Feroshi's head as he battled the fog of unconsciousness that was pouring through his body. Tears began to fall with the sweat that poured from his body.

"Simeskey..." Feroshi muttered to himself.

"What was that?" Theron rushed over.

Worrying he was missing important dialogue, he grabbed the back of Feroshi's limp neck, lifting his head to face his.

"Say it again. Tell me what you said."

An unintelligible gargling sound came from Feroshi as his head floated back.

The Captain moved in closer. He could feel the warm breath of Feroshi on his face.

"Yes, tell me," Theron encouraged.

Feroshi's head thundered forwards. THUD! SNAP! His forehead landing on the bridge of Theron's nose, destroying it as a result. Once again Feroshi's head fell lame, almost as though he had used the last of his energy, on the only opportunity he might get, to inflict pain on his captor.

Crumpling backwards onto the floor caused Theron's head to ricochet against the stone floor, forcing the blood pouring, from what seemed like his entire face, to drain and pool on the ground.

"What the fu..." Theron started.

Rubbing the blood from his eyes, whilst attempting to shake the daze from his head, slowly, he began to sit up. Unlike the events that had unfolded outside the control room, the memory of the attack came flooding back. He bounced to his feet.

"I am going to tear your heart out. You are de–" he screamed, lunging for Feroshi while his eyes throbbed with every erratic punch of his jugular adrenaline fuelled heart beats.

Dazzling light came from behind the Captain. Even in his half dead state, Feroshi attempted to lift his head, to check if the light was the afterlife calling him.

"Captain. No!" Troop Commander Niloc Ecurb yelled as he threw one arm around Theron's neck, the other under the left arm and pulled him back. "Captain!"

"Let me go." The Captain struggled and squirmed.

Niloc wrestled backwards to keep the Captain off balance.

"I will let go when you are calm."

"Get off me now!"

Theron became more and more agitated. His struggle becoming violent.

"Captain. No!"

Knowing that if he released Theron he would definitely kill the prisoner, Niloc tightened his grip around the Captain to allow him to press the graphics on his control pad. In a moment they were gone. Engulfed by light. Reappearing in one of the Prison Zone's hospital rooms.

The Captain jerked loose from the grip. Immediately throwing himself to the side, to be on his hands and knees, retching after the teleportation.

Chapter 7

"Bleurgh. I told you I hate teleporting." Continuing to retch.

"Sir, I had to do something. You were going to kill him," Niloc replied.

"If you're not careful I'll kill you, Niloc," Theron replied, attempting to get to his feet, while wiping the drool from his chin.

Hysterically laughing in hope that the last statement was just in jest, the Troop Commander attempted to help his superior.

"Come on, let's get you to your feet, sir."

Theron batted the help away.

"Get away. You've done enough."

Trying to stand up straight caused the Captain to become light headed and stumble back.

"Woah there." Nicol reached out and grabbed Theron, helping him backwards to rest up against the cold metal hospital bed. "We should get you fixed up before we stick you on the transporter back."

"Yes, I guess you're right," he said while hopping up onto the bed, finally conceding.

The electric purple sky of the sunset began to fade away into the darkness of night as Theron made his way onto the transporter. Nose reshaped, gashes cauterised, but his eyes and upper cheeks had become as dark as the tunic he was wearing, stained with blood all down his front. He gently caressed the new imperfections forming on the once perfect canvas that was his face.

"Feroshi, what have you done?" Theron began to weep as he boarded the transporter.

Sitting on the floor to allow him to wrap his arms around his legs and bury his head between his knees, he was completely lost in the dark thoughts of self-doubt and worthlessness.

Spotlights lit up the Inner System and Centre City of Randtyph. Only the torch lights shining from the Hav Guards' batons could be seen below the curtain, as they patrolled each arm of the Outer System. The tannoy of the transporter beginning to descend, finally snapped Theron out of his slump, lifting his head, revealing an over puffed face from swelling, bruising and crying.

"Come on, Magda. Pull yourself together." Standing up to stare out at the ground below. "What the..."

Gazing out, expecting to see a deserted space below, Theron was startled to see a troop of Hav Guard, forty deep, waiting outside his living quarters.

"You will be arriving at your destination in a few moments. Be ready to depart shortly. Have a lovely day."

Not even the tannoy could break the Captain's focus.

His eyes scanned across the white masks and dark armour of the troop. No purple or bronze trim in sight. Tensing up, head held high, Theron Magda exited the transporter. Bouncing with purpose as he approached the Hav Guard. The sight of them coming to attention for the Captain eased his mind slightly, parting in the middle to allow him access to the door of the living quarters.

Chapter 7

Once again Theron was filled with confusion.

"What is going on?" he thought to himself.

Entering his building and turning to walk down the marbled hall, outside his room, disclosed the reason for the large troop of Hav Guard. Lieutenant Saldo Froch, still in his dark grey, purple trimmed uniform, was sat with his back up against the Captain's door.

"Captain...you're here." Saldo jumped up, red faced after being caught daydreaming.

"What's going on, Lieutenant?" Theron asked.

He adjusted his tunic before addressing his superior. "Well, sir." Hesitating while anxiously trying to find the right words.

"Spit it out, man!" Theron barked.

"Okay, here it is. You know when I came to see you earlier?"

"Yes..."

Saldo swept his hand through his dark, greasy, slicked back hair, wiping away the nervous sweat that was beginning to stream from his forehead.

"Well, we have intercepted a planet-to-planet communication."

"And? Look, Lieutenant, as you can see by the state of my face, I've had a long day and I really need to get some rest." Trying to place his hand on the doorknob.

"There's a space jump happening and it's not one of ours...sir?"

Finally realising the severity of the situation Theron began to panic.

"Saldo, why didn't you say something sooner?" Theron roared.

He grabbed at the Lieutenant's arm and dragged him back down the hall to exit the building. Saldo's head whipped back as he was led away from the Captain's room.

"I tried, Theron," Saldo pleaded.

The platoon of Hav Guard jumped to attention as the doors to the living quarters opened. Theron turned to look into the distance.

"Lieutenant, when is that space jump happening?" he asked, noticing two flashing white lights, accompanied by a large, steady blue light below.

"Emm, that's the thing, Captain. It's happening now." Saldo's voice cracked under the pressure of the rapidly-unfolding seriousness of the Captain's shortcomings earlier.

Theron looked back at the Lieutenant and then back to the sky.

"Shoot the fucker down. Now, Saldo!"

The Captain's eccentric hand movements, supplemented by the pitch and volume of his voice, were a clear indication that his composure had been obliterated.

"Sir, the weapons are offline. We have no idea how this happened," Froch declared.

"What?"

Chapter 8

As the sun began to set over Randtyph, Ruevanlynn returned to the Outer System after a hard shift at the Diamond Farm. He felt very alone without his best friend at his side. The thoughts of what Feroshi might be going through started off as sadness and despair, but quickly turned to revenge, with the catalyst being the clang clang clang of pots and pans being bashed together, to signal the arrival of the Hav Guard patrol in his aisle of the Outer System. Breaking into a run, Ruevanlynn powered past his home, trying to put as much space and time between himself and the Hav Guard as possible. Slowing down as he reached his destination, the home of Ranoa and Shajo, Ruevanlynn began to whistle the call of the friend before entering.

"Yo yo yo, bitches. Mumma Rue coming through." Throwing the sheet door out of the way, as the two residents jumped up to greet him.

Shajo was wide eyed and tense.

"Shit, Rue, I nearly went for you. I didn't hear your whistle over that banging," Shajo warned.

"Don't worry, I heard you." Ranoa smiled as he stepped forward, opening up his arms to invite Ruevanlynn in for a welcoming hug.

"Missed you boys at the farm today." Squeezing his arms around Ranoa. "It's different without Feroshi there. Just had to talk to myself all motherfucking day. People still expecting a smile."

Ruevanlynn wiped a tear away as he broke the embrace.

"Well, we've had preparations to make for the show tonight. Hope you're ready, big boy," Shajo said.

He finally began to relax, smiling as he used his head to motion to Ranoa to help him lift the bed out of the way.

Ruevanlynn helped with the removal of the large wooden planks. With the Hav Guard on night patrol, time was of the essence.

"Hustle boys. I don't need any reason to cut those fools tonight. Their time will come. You best believe that," Ruevanlynn stated.

His cyclone of emotions making him rip the wood from Ranoa, having only just arrived and starting to take the weight of the opposite end from Ruevanlynn. Splinters sank deep into the hardened pads of Ranoa's fingers as it slipped from his grasp like soap out of wet hands. A souring missile with no plotted course or designated target. CRASH! The plank of wood landed on the table, throwing the beakers and bowls out like shrapnel from the explosion.

"Rue!" Ranoa bellowed out as he jumped backwards into Shajo. "Settle, brother. We've got a big night ahead and we need your head straight. Listen to the alarm, there's eight of them out there. It won't be long now. The day is coming where we'll all get the chance for real."

"Hey, Big Balls, want to help me lift the next one or do you just want to keep trashing our home, you lunatic," Shajo jeered while keeping a smile on his face.

The three friends burst out laughing, continuing to chuckle as they removed the final three wooden planks, covering the door to the underground compound. Once the final slat had been removed, Ranoa stamped on the door. There were a few moments of silence as the trio waited for the sound. Click. Clunk. Ranoa grabbed the handle to assist his father, with the opening of the large gateway to the underground. Lemra gave out a loud sigh of relief and smiled at the sight of the three men.

"Man are we glad to see you, boys. We heard the alarm going and half expected this to be a Hav Guard ambush. Come on then, they're still out there. Say goodbye to the Outer System, boys. If we survive this nothing will be the same," Lemra proclaimed, waving them down into the entry point, onto the step below.

"I love you, Dad." The moment his feet touched the steps, Ranoa launched his muscular arms round the thick neck of his father.

"Yes yes, get down those steps, boy." Lemra awkwardly patted Ranoa on his sides.

This battle-ready veteran of war was very apparent in how uncomfortable the show of emotion, from his son, was making him.

Second to jump down was Ruevanlynn, using his hand to spring down. Upon landing on the step he took a moment to look around the home, imagining his own: the thought of the nights he had spent with his love, Zedary Tawn. Kissing. Making love. Zedary smiling, as Ruevanlynn would arrive back from the Diamond Farm, excited to show off a new dress, fashioned out of fabric he'd found. Crimson light shining through the sheet door, the morning he heard the sound of Zed screaming in the distance, as the Hav Guard dragged him onto a transporter for "breaching the peace: by ways of dressing inappropriately". The beating Feroshi took for trying to stop it, due to Ruevanlynn taking too long to react. By the time he arrived, the crowd was too thick, of friends and neighbours, for such a large man to fight his way through quickly.

"Do you want to know something, there's a part of me that actually might miss this place. But fuck me, I'm going to enjoy stomping a Mumma Rue sized hole in the Empire."

Lemra let out a low chuckle at the sight of Ruevanlynn strutting down the steps as though there were mass crowds looking on.

"Right, your turn, Shoja."

Lemra made his way over to grab the inside handle, to begin pulling the door closed the moment all three were making their way below.

Shoja turned to face Lemra, totally disengaged from the home he was leaving behind.

Chapter 8

"Old man, if you thought that it could be the Hav Guard, why did you open the door?" Shajo enquired, making his way down a few steps, to allow Lemra to pull the door closed and lock it into place, before he looked for an answer.

Once again Lemra began to chuckle.

"You may not be blood, my boy and I may not show it with Ranoa, but I love you both very much and if there was even a slim chance it could be either one of you...I'd swing that door open every time. Now get your arse down there so I can brief the team."

Lemra smiled, watching his son lead the three newest recruits, to his underground army, enthusiastically down the steps of the manmade tunnel, filled with pride at the thought of fighting alongside his boys. Proud to die for them if need be.

The sound of weapons clashing, bodies slapping and commands being yelled came into earshot, as the group of four reached the coarse wooden doorway into the Pit. Ranoa smiled emphatically at the warriors in training. Waiting eagerly in anticipation of the other three arriving at the bottom of the tunnel.

"I know it might be a bit hypocritical saying this from the bunker of an underground army, but life just got a whole lot brighter," Ranoa yelled back up the tunnel.

"Bitch, it's only brighter cause Mumma Rue just arrived up in here...or...down..in here. Damn that was poor, I apologise peeps." Ruevanlynn pinched Ranoa's cheek as he arrived at the bottom of the steps.

Disembarking the final step like it was spring loaded, Shajo wrapped his arms around his partner and friend, filled with pure ecstasy at the thought of taking the fight to the enemy.

"The Hav Guard ain't going to know what hit 'em."

Laughing as his feet hit the floor, he began to jump up and down on the spot, keeping his arms around the necks of Ranoa and Ruevanlynn. Imbued with energy, the other two began to join in with Shajo's hysterically happy bounce. The sight of the three was enough to make Lemra chuckle while he attempted to show disapproval with a head shake.

"Come on now, lads. I need the three of you to pull it together and follow me through the training hall to the briefing room."

Brushing past the huddle to lead the way, Lemra returned himself to a picture of strength and poise. Shoulders back. Straight faced, with his chest high. As the three made the escorted walk through the mass of training men, Ruevanlynn made his way to the front of the three, so as to be closer to Lemra.

"Old man, when you say training hall...how big is this place of yours?" Ruevanlynn enquired.

"My boy, at this moment you know everything you need to know. More will be revealed shortly," Lemra replied, twisting his neck slightly to engage Ruevanlynn.

"Jeez, I thought when we brought ourselves down here that was it–"

Chapter 8

"Rue, it's ok. We're going to the briefing room. They will have to tell us some good stories in there." Ranoa grasped on to Ruevanlynn's wrist as he interrupted the conversation.

Ruevanlynn hung his head in disapproval, but deep down inside, in such a short time he had already come to understand that it was only through secrecy the stronghold had survived as long as this. Even Ranoa, Lemra's son, knew no more than himself.

"Yeah, you're right. Lead the way, boss man." Ruevanlynn took his telling and ceased with his questions.

Hedges constructed from the backs of the men facing inwards at the sparring pairs, formed a walkway, too narrow for Ruevanlynn, Ranoa and Shajo to stand shoulder to shoulder. Nearly straight enough to be a line of symmetry through the middle of the training hall. A line of symmetry in the kaleidoscope of shape and colour. A line of symmetry in a room of fractured lives waiting to become whole again by being unleashed.

Following closely behind Lemra, the three friends were far too excited about the thought of the new knowledge that awaited them, to take notice of the training going on around them. Men in armoured bottoms and thick leather boots, unlike the previous visit where the men had only been dressed in fabric shorts. Their torsos still bare, but the armoured lower half was a sign of a dress rehearsal for thriving in the opera of the harsh times ahead.

Reaching the opposite end of the training hall, Lemra took a moment to turn and address the arriving trio.

"Right, boys, before we head down to the briefing room there is something I need to say. Most of the men behind you and the families living below, have been here since the war. Secrecy and hiding are the only way we have managed to stay alive. Everyone here knows exactly what they need to, some more than others. With that in mind, what you are about to hear is for your ears only."

"Baby, we are yours. Signed up and ready to go," Ruevanlynn replied while meeting the eyes of his other two compatriots.

"Yeah, Dad. We are ready to get this show on the road." Ranoa smiled, buzzing with energy.

Lemra chuckled as he turned away from the men and forced open a partition in the wall, revealing a steel stairway that led even further below the grounds of the Outer System. The jaws of Ruevanlynn, Ranoa and Shajo dropped, almost in unison, at the sight of the stairway. Rusted metal walls dulled the reflection of the clean steel staircase.

"Suppose now's a good time to ask, where did you get all the materials and tools to build this place?" Ruevanlynn asked, moving his large frame past Lemra as he held the wall ajar.

"Just a little while longer and all will be revealed but for now, you know exactly what you need to know at this moment in time." Smiling as Ruevanlynn and the other two made their way into the stairwell. Once the final body had passed the threshold, Lemra followed them in, releasing his hold on the wall doorway, allowing it to slowly creep closed.

Chapter 8

"Follow me."

Scrutinising everything in astonishment, the three followed Lemra down two flights of stairs to the level below. The stairway continued down, but Lemra opted for the large metal door that sat at the end of the landing, adjacent to the stairway. After a twist of the doorknob, he pressed his weight against it, forcing it open. Behind the door was a large black oval table, surrounded by twelve seats, six on either side. One of the seats was already taken by Simeskey. Her attention was on screens at the top of the table, but the noise of the metal door pressing up against the darkened walls was enough to break her concentration.

"Rue, Ranoa, Shajo." Jumping up out of her chair with glee, she ran towards the trio of men. "It is so good to see you again."

"Baby girl, I didn't think I would see you again. At least I get to say goodbye this time." Ruevanlynn wrapped his bulging arms around Simeskey as her arms wrapped around his waist.

"I'm so happy to see you." Tears tumbled down her cheeks as she squeezed Ruevanlynn, burying her head into his chest.

"Let me take a look at you." Ruevanlynn unwrapped Simeskey's arm and moved backwards to be able to look her up and down.

Simeskey's attire had completely changed from the rag top and skirt she had been wearing. She was now dressed in an all-in-one, skin tight, white battle suit, sporting a utility belt, with her hair tied high on the crown of her head.

"You like?" she said while she spun around three hundred and sixty degrees. "Supposedly this is what they're all wearing on Laborine."

Lemra closed the large metal door before turning to address the room, allowing the friends to have a final moment of happiness and jubilation. Knowing that moments like this were going to be hard to come by during the struggle ahead.

"Right, everybody, take your seats. We still have a lot of ground to cover before we send Simeskey off on her travels."

Scraping from the seats being dragged out from under the table filled the room. One by one the group sat down.

"What is this?" Shajo asked while rubbing a small metal mound in the middle of the table.

"Not the project–" Lemra tried to lunge across the table to stop Shajo from touching the projector.

A blue hologram of Octdrevion Six appeared in the middle of the table above the projector, the moment that Shajo's hand registered against it.

"Whoops." His face turning scarlet with embarrassment at the same time.

"Holy shit, you've got Empire technology down here." Ruevanlynn's voice filled with wonder at how technology such as this, had managed to make its way below the derelict land of the Outer System.

"That we do, Rue." Lemra smiled as he replied and made his way to the hologram, glowing and slowly rotating above the table.

Chapter 8

"And how did you manage that, old man?" Ruevanlynn asked.

"Well, I suppose the time for you to know more is now..." Lemra began but was interrupted.

"About time," Ranoa joked. "Sorry, carry on," he said while lifting his hand apologetically, as his face drooped in reply to the stern look that his father was firing at him from across the room.

"As I was saying. It is time for me to bestow some information on you all. The planet you see in front of you is Octdrevion Six. This here..." he began to use his fingers and thumb to zoom in on the large space of land, while using his other hand to hold his weight as he stretched across the table, "...is Randtyph. To answer your question, Rue, during the war we began to steal what we could. We have people inside the Hav Guard that have helped us adapt the weapons and vehicles we took. The space transporters we have are adapted from the old troop transporters."

"What do you mean, we have people inside the Hav Guard?" barked Ruevanlynn.

Simeskey grabbed his arm with both hands. "It's ok, Rue. Sit down."

"Yes, we have people inside the Hav Guard. We can't act on anything they tell us because that would break their cover. They provide us with all the food, water, everything in this room...all provided by our inside people." Lemra smiled towards Ruevanlynn, looking for acknowledgement.

"I hope they can be trusted," Ruevanlynn stated, as he took his seat once more.

"Thank you." Simeskey smiled at Ruevanlynn as she whispered her thanks.

"Thank you, Rue. I truly believe they can. It's because of them that we are in the position we are today. Later this evening, Simeskey, Ranoa and Shajo will be travelling to Laborine. Rue, you will be staying behind and put through the training programmes. You need to start getting ready for our mission to save Feroshi."

Simeskey looked from Lemra to Ruevanlynn and then back to Lemra.

"What about Zedary?" she asked forcefully.

Lemra moved from the table to the screens.

"I'm sorry, Simeskey, Feroshi is the target of the mission. We get in and we get out. If we see Zed along the way we can try, but I can't risk the others. I hope you understand." The focus of Lemra's eye contact moved from Simeskey to Ruevanlynn.

Ruevanlynn nodded towards Lemra as he patted Simeskey's back in gratitude. Knowing that even though Feroshi, her partner, was going to be the target of the rescue mission, but she still cared enough about him to try for Zedary, filled him with love.

The nod was reciprocated by Lemra.

"Simeskey, the purity of your heart never goes unnoticed. Even from the underground levels of the Pit, your kindness shines through. Now if everyone could look towards the screens please." Lemra picked up a small remote from below the screens and brought up live feeds from outside the wall.

The city and planetary defences were visible. Different angles of the same patch of land showing on each of the six screens.

"Holy Grandor shit, that's the Octdrevion Six ground to air and space weaponry," Ruevanlynn gawked in admiration at the Empire's technology being in their hands.

A brief moment of laughter broke up the presentation.

"Ha ha ha. Yes, Rue, it is indeed. The area you're looking at there, opens up to allow our space transporters out."

"But, Dad, as soon as the transporter takes off those weapons will blow the three of us straight to Vexora." Confusion and worry filled Ranoa's voice.

"That would be true, my boy, if we didn't have people inside the Hav Guard. All the weaponry will be offline and you lot will fly on through. As soon as you're clear of the atmosphere, you'll trigger the Jump Drive and the next thing you know, bing bang boom, you'll be approaching Laborine." Whilst answering his son's worries, Lemra had noticed the perplexed expression forming on Ruevanlynn's face. "You hanging in there, Rue?"

Taking a moment to gauge the others' understanding of the information so far, Ruevanlynn realised he would need some clarity.

"I'ma be straight with you, Lemzey baby, I don't have a clue how this is all possible, but I believe in you, so I'll trust you. Just know this, old man, she may not have the same gorgeous complexion as me, but I love Simeskey like she's my own flesh and blood. If this doesn't work out and something happens to her, you won't need to worry about Feroshi. I'll kill you myself."

Lemra chuckled. "I love the fire, Rue. Believe me, all we have is our faith in each other, so please trust me. Okay?"

"I do trust you, it's your faith in the Hav Guard that I question," Ruevanlynn snarled.

A large sigh was heard from Lemra. "Rue, my son will be with her the whole way. The people we have inside the Hav Guard are spies for the Army of the Light. You are now all members of the army."

"Now that's what I'm talking about." Excitement had returned to Ruevanlynn's voice as he applauded, clapping his hands together. "I knew the army was real. Feroshi told me I was crazy...I cannot wait to rescue that bear and be like boom, bitch"

"Yes, the army is real. Every soul down here, male and female, is a Soldier of the Light. We once fought against the Empire and the day is fast approaching, where we will emerge from the shadows and fight again. Which brings us to post Space Jump." Lemra clicked the remote, changing the screens to show live feeds of the Prison Zone. "Ranoa, Simeskey and Shajo, the time for your information upload has ended. Everything you need to know at this moment in time, you now know."

There was a low grumble of disapproval from the group.

Chapter 8

"If we are all Soldiers of the Light, why do you need to cut us off?" Shajo asked.

Once again, Lemra let out a large sigh, knowing he was going to have to share more than he was supposed to, with the newest members of the army.

"Okay, okay. Look there's no riddles or half-truths here...you four probably don't remember what the Higher Powers were like as the Havshad Knights. Fierce and deadly warriors that had terrifyingly immense power. When the Emperor disappeared, they lost all that power. Now they float like shadows under their cloaks and armour. But now they're getting stronger. They have something or are very close. We feel it. But we cannot not fear it. Without us there will be, only fear. To keep everyone safe we only know what we need to know...in case somebody is taken."

"Is that why the fighting stopped?" Simeskey asked gently.

"All I can tell you is that the battle in the Great Hall of Centre City ended with a flash of light. After that, the Higher Powers recalled all the Hav Guard, but we knew it was only a matter of time before we would need to be ready again. Now, I've already told you too much so, if you three could just wait outside while I speak to Rue, thank you." Lemra made his way over to the door, opening it as a sign that the briefing was over for Ranoa, Shajo and Simeskey.

A row of four became one, as the three exiting soldiers pushed their seats out from under the oval table. Each one saying their goodbye to Ruevanlynn, accompanied with a handshake and hug. Even though the four friends would see each other on the opposite side of the door, there was a doubt in the future by all of them.

"You lot stay safe. Believe in one another and we will be together again. One way or another." Ruevanlynn wiped a tear from his eye as he watched his three friends leave. He turned to face Lemra as the door creaked closed behind. "Saying goodbye never gets any easier, does it?"

"I'm afraid not, Rue. Never lose hope or faith though, brother. The hope of seeing them again, is what will keep you going when things seem most bleak." Lemra moved towards the screens again, bringing up a live feed of Feroshi being quizzed by Captain Theron Magda.

Ruevanlynn let out a gasp in shock at what he was seeing.

"Oshi, what have they done to you. We need to get him out...now!"

"We need to wait until the dust settles after the Space Jump. Life could get very ugly for the people of the Outer System once the Sun rises. If we move too quickly then it could ruin our element of surprise. Timing is just as important as the secrets we hold." Finally, Lemra took a seat opposite Ruevanlynn, making the meeting more personal.

"Before we talk about the mission, I need answers to two questions that have been running around my pretty little mind; how did you become the big boss man down here and will you tell me what Feroshi's part is in all of this...pretty please?" His patented pouting smile ended the questions.

Chapter 8

Lemra broke his eye contact with Ruevanlynn, to look towards the screen which had the interrogation going on.

"Well, I guess it's time for me to tell you seeing as both of us could be dead very soon." He let out a loud nervous laugh, but catching the eye of Ruevanlynn, realising the laugh was unrequited, he stopped and composed himself. "Sorry, it's just a joke we have down here that we could all be dead soon. Both your questions can be answered very easily. Before I answer your questions, I need you to promise me something."

"Anything. Mumma Rue is one of you now." Ruevanlynn perched forward on his seat, pressing all his weight onto his forearms that were resting on the table.

There was a few seconds of silence as Lemra looked towards the video of Feroshi once more.

"If we manage to save Feroshi, he cannot know what I am about to tell you. It is not quite time for him to know just how important he is. Can you promise this to me?"

A worried look poured from the face of Ruevanlynn, looking towards Feroshi before turning back to Lemra.

"You're scaring me, old man, but you got it, I won't say anything." Nodding as he replied.

"Feroshi is more than just Octdrevion, he is the key to everything. He has the blood of Turach Vro Aka, as did his mother and grandmother. His father was Alenca Enlit. Our leader. He was fearless. Much like you and Feroshi fighting with the Hav Guard since you were young boys. He gave his life to protect the rest of us in the end. The home that Ranoa and Shajo stay in was once mine, a long time ago. Before Alenca went to face the Emperor, he gave me the order to start taking all the women, children and wounded down into the Pit. That's all it was then, the tunnel and big open space. The ceiling was held up with wooden beams and scrap metal. Before the eight arms moved as one, this was our sector's heart. I promised him that I would rebuild the Army of the Light and watch over Feroshi, until it was time for us to rise from the ashes." Lemra began to choke up as he remembered his fallen leader. "Everybody loved him, Rue. We still love him for the chance he gave us."

Ruevanlynn's jaw was dropped by what he had just heard.

"Well I've said it already but this seems like a more fitting time...holy Grandor shit. This is blowing Mumma Rue's mind."

"I can imagine that your head will tell you to ask a million more questions, but please just take some time to digest what you've learned. As soon as that Space Jump happens, we are all at risk. The Outer System will be overwhelmed with Hav Guard searching for answers and out for blood."

After rubbing sweat and tears from his face, Ruevanlynn pushed his chair out and walked over to the screens to get a closer look at his best friend.

"Do you think–" stopping mid sentence as Feroshi's head clattered against the face of Theron Magda's on the screen. "Woooooo. That's my boy. You're right about something, Lemra."

"What's that, Rue?"

"Feroshi is fearless. Let's get Simeskey safe and then rescue our boy." Ruevanlynn took a few paces towards Lemra, before offering his hand out to show that he was fully committed to the cause. "For the Army of the Light."

Lemra smiled as he took Ruevanlynn's in his. "For the Army of the Light."

After shaking hands, Lemra clicked at his remote, clearing the videos from the screens then turned to head for the door. Following closely behind, a thought began to form in Ruevanlynn's mind that he needed to let free.

"What's these training programmes you got me down for, old man?"

"Just you wait and see, dark stuff. You'll be sore after a few run throughs." Lemra laughed as he replied.

"Dark stuff? Getting a bit of sass about you, old man, but your flirting has a lot to be desired."

"Emmm...erg...ah..." Embarrassment filled Lemra as he was completely unprepared for Ruevanlynn's quip.

A loud roar of laughter bellowed from Ruevanlynn at the nervous state of Lemra.

"Ha ha ha. Be calm, old man. Mumma Rue is just messing with you." Patting the leader of the Army on the back, he exited the room through the opened door.

Simeskey, Ranoa and Shajo jumped up from where they had been sitting on the cold metal floor, patiently waiting for the private meeting of Ruevanlynn and Lemra to finish.

"Ah, finally. Thought you two had forgotten about us for a moment there," Ranoa joked.

Lemra helped the door close before turning to face the group of four.

"You'd be so lucky, son. Right, I need the three of you to follow me down to the armoury. All of the transporters and weaponry can be found down there. Rue, if you go through that door." Pointing towards the wall on the opposite side of the landing from the briefing room. "Take the stairs down to the simulation room. In there you'll find Joldak Volgan. He will be your best friend over the next few days while we put you through your paces."

"Yes, sir." Ruevanlynn nodded towards Lemra. He then turned to Simeskey. "Baby girl, you stay safe, okay. These two brutes will keep you safe. Once this is all over and done with, we will all dine together in one of the Great Halls, on a planet far from here."

Ruevanlynn placed his herculean hands on either side of Simeskey's face, using his thumbs to wipe the tears from her cheeks.

"We will see each other again. This isn't goodbye, it's just...it's just, I'll see you later. Now come and hug me before I start bubbling too."

The pair squeezed each other like it was their final goodbye. Thoughts circled both their minds about times past. All the dark memories had been forgotten in that moment of embrace. Times of laughter and happiness with Feroshi and Zedary. Supporting each other through the bad times. Protecting each other at all costs. Both of their trains of thought ended with the thoughts of a brighter future. A life without the shadow of the Empire. No Hav Guard. No Higher Powers. No Emperor. Hope was no longer something that needed to be feared. Hope could now be their driving force, whenever fear and helplessness tried to creep back in.

Ending the embrace by stepping backwards, Simeskey began to wipe the continuous flow of tears from her face.

"Okay, let's do this. If I don't go now, I don't think I will ever go." With that Simeskey started to make her way down to the armoury, following Lemra closely as he guided them down another two flights of stairs.

Ruevanlynn watched as the four disappeared below, not wanting to miss a single moment of gazing upon his departed friends. Almost as though he was making a memory bank full of his time with them, just in case he never saw them again. As the four reached the large double doors at the bottom of the stairwell, Ruevanlynn finally took his leave and headed for the simulation room.

"Well, I guess it's my turn to save you, Feroshi," he muttered to himself.

The large double doors to the armoury rattled from the draught driving through from the other side. Ranoa helped his father as the air caused the doors to fight back against their strength. All three of the travellers were completely dumfounded by what was unveiling in front of their eyes. Completely dwarfing the training hall in length, breadth and height, the armoury was a colossal space. Transporters, darkened cruisers and golden tear drop speeders sat in uniformed rows. All older technology, powered by Light Stones and not used by the Empire for decades. Weaponry, ranging from blasters to missiles, were placed in their hundreds in racks near the entrance. On the opposite wall, rested a monumental rolling door. It took up nearly the entire face. Soldiers, trained as Engineers and Weapons Specialists, flocked around their chosen apparatus. Servicing, calibrating and testing. Making sure that every system, no matter how small or insignificant, was fully functional and ready to go at a moment's notice.

"Well I'll be damned. Have you ever seen anything like this?" Shajo asked the group, looking around in wide eyed amazement.

This room, ready for war, made Shajo feel like he belonged.

"I don't think any of us have ever seen anything like this, my love," Ranoa replied as he took his partner's hand in his. The sight of the weaponry caused unease in him. Almost as though the realisation of the amount of lives that were going to be lost in the fight ahead, had just dawned on him. A heavy toll sensed in his soul.

Lemra watched over the three friends as they took in this spectacle of strength and power.

"Like I said before, Simeskey, this struggle has never slowed. We have been lying in wait. Rebuilding. Preparing. Now follow me to the flight room. Ranoa and Shajo, you will need to change out of those rags. We have golden flight suits for you both."

"White is definitely more my colour," Shajo joked.

"I'm afraid only the females get to wear white where you are going," Lemra replied.

"I'm going to ask why but I have a funny feeling that I already know the answer."

"You are learning, my boy. Everything you need to know at this exact moment in time..." Lemra paused as he looked to Shajo to complete his sentence.

There was a sense of disapproval as Shajo wobbled his head. Trying to resist the urge to finish the sentence. Simeskey and Ranoa started staring towards Shajo, knowing the silence wouldn't end until the sentence was finished.

"Okay okay. Everything we need to know we know. I understand. Let's get this over and done with."

Chuckling as they made their way to the flight room, Simeskey and Ranoa poked and prodded at Shajo in jest, over his downturn in mood, after once again hearing Lemra's favourite riddled phrase. The further the group moved into the armoury, the more breath-taking the size of the transporters and cruisers became. Vexorian metal covered space craft with a single hull mounted Space Jump Engine, cannibalised from the Empire's old style cruisers, was enough to blow the minds of anyone that had grown up and lived the sheltered life of the Outer System.

"After you." Lemra opened the door to the flight room to allow the others to enter. "Quickly please. We don't have long until take off."

"Ah, Lemra, this must be Ranoa, Shajo and Simeskey. I was starting to worry that you weren't going to make it on time." A frail old man stood up from behind his work station. Long white hair and cloudy cataract-filled eyes showed the age of the flight room operator.

"Wow, you're old." Without thinking, the words fell from Shajo's mouth.

There was a moment of awkward silence, before Lemra and the operator burst out in laughter.

"Yes, you are correct, Shajo, I am old. Coming up for my hundred and sixty-fourth birthday soon. Anyway, I'm Fendo Docheran. I am the flight operator here in the Pit. If you boys come over here, I'll give you your flight suits to change into. They'll stop your insides becoming your outsides during the jump. Simeskey, you look as beautiful as ever and that white really makes the blue of your eyes pop." It seemed like his whole body was vibrating as he slowly made his way over to the lockers next to his work station.

Simeskey blushed at the compliment. "Thank you, Fendo. It's very nice to meet you. I apologise for being asleep when you dropped off my flight suit."

"No need to apologise, my dear. I don't know if you know this, but you are the absolute double of your mother," Fendo replied as he removed the golden flight suits from their locker. "Boys, squeeze into these and grab boots that fit from the next locker please."

Chapter 8

"You knew my mother?" Simeskey was eager to hear stories and tales.

"And your father. I was there when he was beheaded in the street. What a horrible time it was. It fills me with joy to see what a strong woman you have turned into."

"It was a horrible time indeed. My mother died not long after my Joining Ceremony. She held on until I moved in with Feroshi and then just sort of slipped away."

"A broken heart never truly heals. She was never the same the poor dear." Fendo turned to check how Ranoa and Shajo were getting on with their costume change. "Are you two nearly ready?"

Shajo had managed to squeeze into his all-in-one flight suit but needed to assist his partner getting dressed. Using his knee in Ranoa's back as leverage, he was attempting to pull the skin-tight suit over the muscular arms and shoulders of Ranoa.

"Almost...got...it." Struggling with all his might, he managed to get the suit fastened at the back. "There. Ready."

"Well, this is snug." Ranoa began to bend and flex, amazed by how the material moved and moulded itself with every movement he made.

Lemra clapped his hands with joy at how the three travellers looked in their attire. He moved over to Ranoa and ran his hands over the shoulders of the flight suit, ironing out any imperfections until they moulded themselves around his upper body.

"I hope you know how proud you make me, son."

Rattling with every step, Fendo made his way back to his work station. He sat down at his wooden desk that was littered with scrap paper, lying in front of the flight screen he was operating.

"Well, I guess it's time to say your goodbyes, Lemra. It won't be long now until we get the signal that the weapons are offline. Once that happens, you'll only have a few moments to get into the air and activate the Jump Drive. Boys, don't forget the belts."

"You are right. Come on, you three, let's get you onto your transporter." Ushering Ranoa, Simeskey and Shajo to the door, Lemra led the group back into the armoury, weaving his way through the racks of weapons and flocks of soldiers gathered around their assigned piece of weaponry.

"You see that baby there?" Pointing towards the large transporter that was sat centre of the massive rolling door. "That's your ride out of this place."

"I can't believe this is actually happening," Simeskey said to Lemra, gawking in adoration at the size of the modified transporter.

"Better believe it, beautiful. We are off to the Land of the Broken Wing. Just need to hope we make it off this rock without being blown out of the sky," Ranoa said excitedly, as he placed his arm around Simeskey.

She fired a fearful look at Ranoa. Up until this point Simeskey hadn't considered the possibility of the mission failing.

"Lemra, this is going to work, isn't it?"

Chapter 8

"It has definitely been a substantial amount of time since we have sent anyone off planet, but you have nothing to worry about. Believe me when I say, we wouldn't be sending somebody so important to the cause off planet, without extensive planning. I am very aware of what goes wrong doing this without proper planning." Lemra looked towards his son.

"Dad?" Ranoa innocently hinted for more information.

"Son, there's something you need to know." Lemra began to weep as memories that were buried deep inside came flooding to the surface. "Your mother died trying to escape off planet. There was twenty-three women and children on board. They'd literally just activated their Jump Drive when the long range weapons locked on and took down their transporter."

"I knew my mother died during the war, but I didn't realise. I had no idea. They were trying to escape. Women and children, man. I cannot wait to see the Shadow Empire burn." Ranoa consoled his father, wrapping his arms around him. "I've never had a chance to say it and I don't know when I'll get another chance so here it is...I love you, Dad."

"I love you too, son." Lemra wiped the moisture away from under his eyes, breaking free from his son's embrace so he could move around to the entry point of the transporter. "If you climb up this ladder, the hatch will open up into the flight deck."

A makeshift rope ladder hung from the forward hull of the transporter. All three took a moment to say their goodbyes to Lemra and Shajo took a moment to think about what was going to happen.

"Boss man, I have a quick question. How are we supposed to fly this thing?"

"Ha ha, don't worry, Shajo, the coordinates are already entered. All you need to do is hit the Jump Drive once you've cleared the Octdrevion atmosphere. If you hit that button too early, there's a chance of the Space Jump Engine separating from the transporter, and we really do not want that." The words left Lemra's mouth and instantly put Simeskey, Ranoa and Shajo on edge.

"Woah woah woah. You're telling me that, apart from the chance of getting shot down, there's a chance the transporter will fall to pieces in the sky. Great. I'm feeling really confident about this. I don't know about you two, but I have a bad feeling about this." Shajo was very hesitant to approach the ladder first.

Instead, Simeskey approached the ladder first, knowing it was exactly what Feroshi would have done. After getting halfway up the ladder, she looked down to check on the other two.

"Come on, boys. You can't tell me you'd rather stay here." Immediately beginning to climb again.

"Come on, Shajo she's right, rather die in the sky than be crushed on the ground. See you on the other side, Dad." With a final pat of his dad's shoulder, Ranoa turned and began the climb.

Chapter 8

The pair of men still on the ground watched as Simeskey forced open the hatch and climbed inside. Once Ranoa was high enough for Shajo to be able to climb safely, without being thrown about from his movements, he turned and nodded to Lemra.

"I'll keep them safe. No matter what."

Lemra could only watch as the three made their way onto the transporter. He watched as the ladder swayed forwards and backwards from the movement of Shajo climbing. The picture of his wife climbing the ladder onto the transporter, many years ago, was vivid in his mind's eye. The look of happiness on her face as she helped the other women and children climb. Her final words to him, "I'll see you soon, Lemra. I love you." He hated that he had just watched instead of replying to her on that day. A pain that had never left him. Thinking that he wouldn't make that mistake again, he grabbed a hold of the ladder and looked up. Ranoa was preparing to pull himself through the hatch.

"I love you, son," he shouted.

Hearing the affection from his father, Ranoa paused and looked down to share a smile with Lemra. He knew that his dad had been hardened from battle and loss, so this rare show of love was special. In times of darkness, he knew he would use this memory for strength. With a final nod towards his father, Ranoa pulled himself through the hatch and into the transporter. Shajo and Simeskey were stood waiting for his arrival.

As the three made their way to the cockpit of the transporter, automatic lights activated, illuminating the controls and space around them.

"Hello, travellers." The voice of Fendo rang out causing Simeskey, Shajo and Ranoa to look around confused.

"Where is that coming from?" Simeskey asked.

"Down here." A screen on the controls showed Fendo waving, trying to get the attention of the three friends. "I need you all to take your seats and strap in."

With haste, Simeskey and Ranoa took the two seats nearest to the controls, while Shajo strapped in behind them.

"Fendo, it's now or never. Let's do this," Simeskey said, filled with nerves and excitement.

"I like the hustle, my sweet girl. Now here is the important part: when the alarm triggers it means that the weapons are offline and the rolling door will open. Can you see the big blue button just above the screen?" Fendo pointed towards the space above his head.

Simeskey followed his finger with her eyes to the guarded button.

"Yes, I see it, Fendo," she replied.

Fendo carried on with his address. "The transporter knows where it needs to go, but when that button begins to flash, hit it. For anybody that hasn't travelled by Space Jump before..."

"None of us have travelled by Space Jump before, old man," Shajo nervously snapped as he tried to tighten his harness.

"Yes, yes, well as I was say–" No sooner than Fendo had started again, a flicker of lights through the transporter was followed by a deafening siren. "Well I guess you'll just have to find out about the Space Jump in real time, ha ha."

Fendo's statement was drowned out by the noise of the alarm, but his laugh could be heard.

Every soldier, Engineer and Weapons Specialist cleared the armoury at the sound of the siren, all expertly drilled in the motions and movements that had to be carried out, at the sound of any alarm or siren. Just as Fendo had foretold, the massive rolling door began to open.

Still pulling at his harness to try and tighten its grip on him, Shajo began to panic.

"I'm starting to have second thoughts, guys. Maybe the Outer System isn't so bad after all. I mean maybe we just need to communicate better with the Hav Guard," he hysterically rambled as sweat began to pour down his face.

Simeskey turned her head to engage her panicking companion. "Shajo, it's all going to be alright. Close your eyes and breathe. I need you, Shajo. I need both of you."

The soft manner of her address acted as a calming blanket, falling over Shajo as he brought his breathing under control.

A cough and splutter from the engine caused the transporter to shudder as it shook free from its supports. Hovering gently, the sound of the Space Jump engine filled the armoury. Air cracking as it passed through the intake. Whirring and spinning up of the Light Stone technology caused a gentle hum of vibration of the cockpit floor.

"It is time for me to say goodbye, my young friends. Communication must be cut to avoid any detection once the weapons come back online. Remember, as soon as you clear the atmosphere, hit that button like your lives depend on it...because they do. May the power of the Light set you free. Until the next time. Stay safe." Fendo's farewell ended as the screen went dark.

Rocking gently from left to right, the transporter began to make its way through the opening. With every movement the three travellers gripped onto their harnesses a little tighter. The back of their heads pinned in anticipation of the unknown path they were about to take. Slowly they moved towards the ramp that led to an opening in the ceiling. Darkness was all that could be seen. No sooner than the hull-mounted engine had cleared the opening, the ground below reformed. Hiding the exit from sight.

"Did you ever think you'd make it outside the wall... guess there's always the Prison Zone?" Ranoa asked in sheer disbelief at the voyage they were beginning.

The transporter began to pick up pace as it ascended from the ground. Untroubled as it made its way past the offline weaponry. Picking up speed, the Space Jump engine gave off a trail of electric blue in its jet stream. Dense was the atmosphere that shrouded the night sky. Travelling through, caused the transporter to creak and wain.

"If anybody knows the prayer of the Lord of Light, now would be the time to step up...please." Fear had taken over

Shajo once more. Sweat pouring and knuckles white as his whole body clenched in apprehension.

Ranoa cleared his throat and threw his hand out to grab Simeskey's. "Oh Lord of Light, from the shadow we need you. Oh Lord of Light, in fire we find you. Oh Lord of Light..."

"Ranoa, the button. It's flashing." Simeskey interrupted the prayer. Her gaze became fixed on the continuous flash. Slowly she lifted the guard that covered the button.

"Shajo, my love, I hope you are holding on tight," Ranoa joked with his hyperventilating partner.

"Yeah, good one. Just hit the bloody button." A high pitched shrill of panic filled Shajo's voice.

For a moment, Ranoa's hand hesitantly lingered above the blinking activator of the Space Jump drive. Thoughts of memories and moments past flooded his mind's eye. In the last few days he had spent more time with his father than the rest of his life combined. He had missed the moments of him changing from young boy, to youngling and into the man he had become. Now to be leaving these memories behind, the expression of love his father had shown as he climbed the ladder, gave him reason to pause in a silent dream.

"Ranoa...the button." Simeskey could see the fear of the future and the melancholy of the past battling inside.

The soft voice of Simeskey was enough to snap Ranoa from his daze.

"Emm...yes...let's do this." Ranoa slammed his hand down on the flashing button, causing the blinking blue eye to shine constant.

Three rings formed around the transporter, the forward and rear spinning anticlockwise as the middle spun clockwise. Sparks of lightning began to snap and crackle as their speed intensified. "Oh dear, oh dear, oh dear," Shajo repeated over and over again. Eyes tightly shut as his grip moved from his harness to the cold steel of his chair.

A charged cloud of emerald and cerulean arcs of power formed in front of the transporter, like a doorway ripping into the fabrics of the dimension. Circulating into a twisted wormhole through Space.

For a split second Shajo unlocked his right eye, but seeing the thunderstorm of terror materialising in front of them only intensified his fear.

"No, no...let's go back. Ranoaaaa," Shajo screamed.

Twisting and warping as the lightning took a hold of the transporter. In the blink of a blue light they were gone. The lightning, the wormhole, the transporter...gone. Vanishing into the darkness of Space. Spotlights once again filled the sky above Randtyph. The weapons were back online and the hunt had begun.

Chapter 9

Thick clouds of smoke bellowed out from the chimneys of the factories behind the barracks of Hav Command. Higher Intellects watched from walkways above, whilst the chemical suit wearing workers below shovelled mounds of Light Stones, from the Diamond Farms, and small piles of Shadow Stones, from the dark mines below the city, onto conveyor belts. These belts led to the heating and liquidation galleries, breaking the stones down into a solution, so as to be forged into the technology and weaponry that could benefit the Shadow Empire and be feared by their enemies.

Alarms had been ringing through the barracks since the dark hours of the morning. Hav Guard, nearly a thousand deep, stood at attention waiting for the arrival of their Captain. The sea of cloaked black armour seemed highlighted by the rows of white masks and flashes of the waist-mounted energy batons. Whispers and rumours of the transporter escaping the planet, had spread through the ranks of the Guard. Any doubt that the whispers and rumours had caused, in the minds of the men, had quickly been drowned out by the excitement of knowing the Outer System would suffer. No proof of involvement was needed in their eyes. An example must be made, and the weakest would suffer the most.

Back in the Living quarters, Theron Magda paced backwards and forwards in his room. Helmet under his arm, the clatter from his armour echoed around the room with every step he took. He could not rest out of worry of the consequences that may be headed his way. Drathon Telema was already making a very obvious power play to undermine his command. Would this be the final nail in his coffin? How could he fix this? Questions and self-doubt began to swallow Theron whole. The negative judgements finally became too much for the Captain. He broke down, falling to his knees. Screaming into the face plate of his helmet.

"Ahhh!" he frothed, throwing his helmet at the wall. He watched as it clattered against the wall, down onto his bed and then onto the floor in front of him.

Bang! Bang! Bang! The thundering sound of the clatter of a gauntlet against his door snapped Theron back from his emotional turmoil.

"I'll be there in a moment."

He wiped away the pain from his eyes as he stood himself up from his knees. Before opening his door, Theron took a moment to check his face and hair in the mirror, storing his contemplations in a box at the back of his mind, as he picked his helmet up and placed it on his bed. With one final large inhale of air, he was ready to face whatever this day had in store for him. As he swung the door open, his large inhale of air became a lacklustre exhale seeing that it was Troop Commander Telema waiting for him.

"What could you possibly want right now, Drathon?"

"Captain, I merely come to receive orders. It is now light outside and the men are still waiting in the barracks for your address." A condescending tone polluted his words as he smirked. Ecstatic to see Theron Magda in such distress.

"I will be there soon," Theron barked as he attempted to slam the door on Drathon Telema.

Drathon used his armoured boot and helmet to block the door. "Just one more moment, Captain. Nothing to worry about, just a small word of warning. Carry on the way you're going and soon it will be me with those gold flashes."

Theron lunged forward, grabbed Drathon by the throat and slammed him up against the wall behind him, causing him to drop his helmet in the hallway. "I will be dead before I let another Telema disgrace the Hav Guard." Spit flew from his mouth as he snarled his threat at Drathon.

"That can be arranged," Drathon snarled.

While Drathon struggled to get his words out due to being choked, he had unsheathed his energy baton. Placing it gently against the unarmoured underarm of Theron's armour. BOOM! Energising his baton threw Theron Magda backwards on the floor in his room. Theron shook his head, trying to focus his vision and catch his breath, after the feeling of being kicked by a Grandor in the stomach had passed.

Drathon stood crouched over the Captain, with his foot on his chest. "Your time is coming to an end, Captain. Lay hands upon me again and it shall be you, Theron Magda, that is disgraced by the name of Telema."

He released the pressure on the Captain's chest and made his way out of the living quarters.

Bewildered and anxious by what had just played out, Theron waited a moment before following the Troop Commander. What was left of his dignity he would wear with pride. His soldiers would not know of the power struggle and the disdain that was forming between him and Drathon. If any of the men suspected weakness he would be cast out. Knowing Drathon Telema, he would be disgraced and murdered in the most public of fashions. A plan began to form in the Captain's mind. He would lead his men, as a strong Captain should, and when the opportunity presented itself, he would assassinate Drathon in the shadows.

A wicked smile formed on the face of Theron as he made his way out of the Living quarters. He could still see Drathon in the distance across the clearing. Theron placed his helmet over his head and began to run after the Troop Commander.

"Drathon. Drathon," he yelled.

Drathon turned at the sound of his name being yelled.

"What does he want?" he muttered to himself, seeing the Captain running in his direction.

He gripped his baton in preparation for another round of the altercation.

Chapter 9

"Drathon, thank you for waiting." Theron patted him on the shoulder as he arrived. "I apologise for my outburst in there. As you can tell, things have been getting to me lately. I hope you know how much I rely on you and your strength."

The Troop Commander released his grip on the baton, completely taken aback by how the Captain was acting. "Er... whatever. Just know not to test me and we'll be fine."

"Now let's go round up the Hav Guard and have a little fun, eh."

"Yes, Theron. Now that's an order I can get behind." Drathon smiled with joy at the thought of running rampant through the Outer System.

Turning back towards the barracks, Drathon walked with purpose in his step. Rubbing his hands together each time a new thought of how to inflict pain, suffering and humiliation upon the residents of the Outer System, fluttered across his mind.

Like a hunter stalking their prey, Theron followed Drathon closely. Taking peace in this emotionally painful moment, knowing that this pseudo power Drathon felt, would not last forever.

"I'm glad to hear it, Telema," Theron replied.

Entering the barracks, Drathon Telema took his place in front of the Hav Guard. Theron took a moment so as to not raise any suspicions of friendship by the pair arriving together. To everyone else, the hatred between the two was to seem very much alive. Happy that enough time had passed, Theron made his way front and centre of his army of Hav Guard. The loud crash and clatter of a thousand gauntlets smashing against their chest plates, rung out in respect of their Captain.

Raising his hand instructed silence in the barracks. "Hav Guard. My brothers, I have called you here with troubling news. An unauthorised Space Jump happened from right here on Octdrevion Six. Now, we cannot know for certain that the Outer System had anything to do with it, but, somebody needs to suffer for this petulant disregard for our authority."

Cheering rang out from the audience.

"Mag-da! Mag-da!" they chanted in unison.

Once again, Theron raised his hand for silence.

"Thank you, thank you. I want constant patrols in all eight of the Outer System's arms. Double the guards at the Diamond Farm. Any smiles, any glimpse of hope...we break it. Destroy their spirit but do not turn them into martyrs, my brothers."

There was a low whinge of dissatisfaction from the crowd.

"Listen to me, men. Peace is a fragile thing. The tension between the Light and the Shadow grows every day. We do not need another war for Randtyph. Keep them in line. Destroy their homes. Break their bones if you really have to... but do not kill anyone. That is my command to you. Now, go out and find the answers we seek." Theron looked around at the Hav Guard before making his way out of the barracks.

Their chanting resumed as he exited.

Chapter 9

The thundering noise of a swarm of troop transporters arriving to take the men to the Outer System, caused the ground of the clearing, between the barracks and living quarters, to resonate under foot.

"Captain!" Drathon Telema shouted as he tried to catch up to Theron.

Captain Theron Magda hung his head, recognising the voice that was approaching from the rear and expecting to have more time before seeing him again. Not even the sound of his armour clattering, as he ran after the Captain, could hide the tones of Telema's voice. Turning to face him, he watched on as the horde of Hav Guard rushed onto their transporters. Eager to get on with their mission.

"Yes, Drathon?" Forcing the enthusiasm into his voice as the Troop Commander arrived.

"I just wanted to know if you would be joining us in the Outer System?" Drathon enquired inquisitively.

"I will indeed, but my hunt will begin at the Diamond Farm," Theron replied.

"Would you like some company? You know I can get the answers you need nice and quickly."

"No, Drathon. I need you to lead the men in finding out who was on that transporter."

"As you wish, Captain." Menacing thoughts flooded into the head of the Troop Commander.

He didn't trust the show of respect and friendship from Theron. Heading for his transporter, Drathon took one final look back at the stationary Captain.

"I'm onto you, Theron," he muttered to himself.

Theron waited and watched as Drathon and his squad of eight Hav Guard boarded their transporter and headed for the Outer System. A single transporter waited patiently for the Captain. He stared upon the glistening energy prism, wondering what the correct next steps were to take. His conscience had become a burden. Why couldn't he switch it off like the others? Watching his men assault the men, women and children of the Outer System filled him with hesitancy and compassion, but they did it with such pleasure. Shaking the feeling of remorse from his mind, Theron finally made his way onto his transporter.

It only took a few moments from the transporter's wall of energy closing, to the tannoy of the transporter warning the Captain of his imminent arrival at the entrance to the Diamond Farm. Four Hav Guard stood waiting to greet the Captain as he disembarked.

"Captain Magda, what brings you to the Diamond Farm?" the Guard asked.

"I am looking for Ruevanlynn Grezzie, have you seen him?" Theron asked.

One of the Hav Guard removed a control pad from under his cloak and typed in the name. It flashed red before bringing up a hologram of Ruevanlynn.

"I'm sorry, sir. Grezzie didn't show up for work today. Would you like us to find him for you?"

"No, no. Thank you, but that won't be necessary. I shall find him, don't you worry." Theron removed his helmet and ran his gauntlet through his hair. "How are things on the farm today?"

"Emm...busy, sir. We've got them working double time, half rations, cold showers. The skaffs will feel the squeeze of the Shadow Empire. We will not have another incident like on Octdrevion Five."

Flabbergasted by what the Guard had said, Theron took a step back as his jaw dropped. "How do you know about Octdrevion Five?"

"Troop Commander Tel–" the Guard started.

"Drathon Telema?" Shaking his head before removing the scowl from his face, Theron paused, not wanting to show any weakness in his command. "Yes, you're right. We don't want another incident like that again. The whole planet is dead now, you know that don't you?"

"Don't worry, Captain, you can trust us to keep them in check." One of the Hav Guard that had been standing silent, jumped at his opportunity to address Theron Magda and show his passion for the Empire.

Keeping his eyes on the Hav Guard that had just spoken to him, Theron replaced his helmet over his head.

"Thank you. Now back to your posts. Keep up the good work." Bowing his head before stepping back on to his transporter.

"Where to, Captain?" The voice of one of the controllers from Hav Command, replaced the voice of the tannoy.

"To Sector Seven of the Outer System, please. Our new star prisoner has a friend I need to visit with," Theron replied zealously.

"As you wish, sir." Within seconds of the dialogue ending, the transporter departed from where it was standing and headed for the Outer System.

Flashing images of the altercation between Drathon Telema and himself, circled through Theron's mind. The impact of the energy from the baton sending him hurtling backwards. The threat that was made against the longevity of his captainship and life. Not even a year earlier the fear of mutiny would not even have entered his mind. No one, from the residents of the Outer System to the most obnoxious of Higher Intellects, would have challenged his command. Just when he thought his abyss of self-doubt couldn't get any deeper, the sight of the Outer System brought Feroshi to the front of his mind.

"You will be arriving at your destination in a few moments. Be ready to depart shortly. Have a lovely day." The voice of the tannoy caused the pools of sadness to evaporate against the fire of power and control he wanted to reclaim.

All the available Hav Guard were thrashing their way through the Outer System as Theron stepped off the transporter. Dirt-covered children wandered the aisles crying and screaming for their parents. Looking for help or a place to hide. A space of solitude in the carnage. Theron stared into the homes as he rushed to the ground outside Feroshi and Simeskey's home. Hoping to reach his destination before his soldiers, in an attempt to question Ruevanlynn in a peaceful and painless manner.

Chapter 9

"Ruevanlynn Grezzie. This is Captain Theron Magda. Come out for questioning," Theron shouted loudly and clearly at the top of his voice. Silence was the only reply that the Captain received. He looked around, feeling the eyes of the neighbours' burning into his back. "Mr Grezzie, if you do not come out, I will be forced to come to you."

With the Hav Guard fast approaching, Theron decided to make the climb to Ruevanlynn's home. Quickly he ascended knowing that at any moment his plan for a peaceful extraction of information would be in jeopardy, from the over-zealous soldiers using any means necessary to damage the hearts and minds of the population. The sound of the pots and pans alarm system was quickly being drowned out by the tsunami of bone chilling screams, soaring up the arms of the Outer System. Flooding all eight sections.

"Daddy!" a little girl screamed, throwing the sheet closed as Theron Magda passed their home.

"What the..." The sudden scream caused him to flinch and one of his boots to slip.

Pulling himself in dramatically, he looked down and paused as he caught his breath. He let out a chuckle at that the cold shock of fear he had felt.

Each gauntlet and boot movement was done with purposeful precision for the final few rungs. Theron Magda climbed through the doorway into Ruevanlynn's home. He inspected the space, confused.

"Where are you?" he spoke softly to himself.

There was no sign of Ruevanlynn and nothing to suggest he would be coming back anytime soon. Upon inspecting the room, he noticed an opened ration pack from the Diamond Farm was beginning to rot on the table. Swatting away the flies, Theron picked up a moulding piece of fruit, squishing it in the palm of his gauntlet to test the decomposition. From the darkness of the juice, it was easy to see that Ruevanlynn had been gone for at least a couple of days. The rations they were given would begin to rot by the setting of the next sun, just another simple method of psychological control over the people. Grabbing at the pillow that sat peacefully on the bed, Theron wiped away the sludge of fruit juice and sediment from his gauntlet. He cast it aside and made his way to the doorway, watching as Hav Guard closed in on his position.

"Captain, we have found nobody that will talk. What do you want us to do?" an approaching member of the Guard called up.

"Keep going. Somebody knows something," he ordered assertively.

"Yes, sir," the member of the Guard said excitedly, heading into the ground floor home below the Captain.

"No, not that one." But it was too late, the Hav Guard had already sloped into the home of Simeskey.

Panic overcame the Captain knowing Simeskey would be home alone, defenceless. He lept from Ruevanlynn's home to the ground below. Crouching down as he landed, he quickly jumped right up and rushed into the Enlit household.

Chapter 9

"Men, stop," he yelled.

The Hav Guard jumped back, startled by the entrance of the Captain.

"What's wrong, sir?" he asked.

Two other members of the Hav Guard had come rushing in behind, after seeing the Captain in such a hurry. Once again Theron looked around, bewildered by the vacant home.

"Er...emm...nothing, nothing's wrong," he stammered. "I...emm...didn't want you going in alone, that is all."

"Ha ha ha, don't need to worry about me, sir." The Hav Guard laughed, joined by his comrades standing behind the Captain.

Theron looked behind at the men chuckling. "Off you go, men. I need to inspect this home for clues. Thank you."

All three of the men quickly took their leave, eager to find a home with victims instead of the grunt work that went along with finding clues.

"Have fun, sir," they joked as they exited.

Following them out as they left, Theron pulled the door sheet closed. He wanted privacy. A few moments alone to imagine Simeskey in the home. Pulling the sheet over, his eyes were drawn to the handprint in the woodwork that he had noticed on his initial visit to the home.

"Feroshi, Feroshi, Feroshi. We know where you are but, where is your Queen?" Running his fingers over the recessed area.

Theron moved over to the bed, removing his helmet and dropping it on the floor as his eyes remained fixed on the pillow. He lay down on his side imagining Simeskey was there with him. Her natural perfumed scent still lingered on the pillow. He pulled it in close, smothering his face as he breathed her in. Becoming aroused, Theron began to press and squeeze his gauntlet against his crotch.

"Captain, you naughty boy," Drathon mocked sharply.

Theron bolted upright, startled to hear a voice in this compromising position.

"Drathon, what the hell are you doing in here?" Realising he still had the pillow in hand, Theron cast it off to the side.

Drathon chuckled as he let the sheet fall closed behind him.

"Well, I would ask you the same question, but it seems quite clear to me."

The Captain stood himself up off the bed, brushing himself down, trying to wash off the embarrassment.

"What I am doing is none of your concern. What do you want?" Theron barked.

"I want you to come with me, we've got a home ready to talk." Drathon started for the sheet doorway, but paused as he waited for the Captain to follow.

"Really? Take me there now." Theron reached for his helmet that lay on the floor.

Placing it over his head, he followed the Troop Commander outside.

Chapter 9

"Just across the street, Captain." Drathon pointed to a doorway that had Hav Guard spilling in and out. Heart-breaking screams from a male and female voice, accompanied by begging for their lives, were heard coming from inside.

"Drathon, what is going on in there?" Theron asked with worried curiosity. The bloodcurdling squeals causing the Captain to stop in his tracks. "Drathon!"

"Exactly what you said: not killing, just breaking the spirit of hope that plagues this skaff hole."

Another scream rang out, causing the Captain to rush past Drathon. He began to force his way through the crowd of Hav Guard stood in the doorway.

"Let me through! What is going on..." Theron stopped dead with horror.

Two Hav Guard were pinning a man and woman across their table while the others took turns raping and beating them with their batons. The pair were naked from the waist down. Blood trickling down the backs of their legs. Tears and saliva poured from their faces as the Hav Guard began to stuff rags in the pair's mouth to muffle the screams. The air was dense with the smell of horror. Cheers and adulation were all that could be heard from the Guards. The cheers only got louder as one of them removed himself from the man and started to adjust his armoured trousers.

"Stop this! Now!" Theron screamed in disgust at what he was seeing. Lunging for the men that were currently forcing their way inside the unwilling participants. "Get off!"

"Get him out," Drathon ordered the men.

"What?" Confusion filled the Captain's voice as the Hav Guard swarmed around, completely overpowering him.

Theron fought with all his might. His helmet was torn off in the process. Punching, kicking, tensing and squirming. Anything to break free but, it was to no avail. Each limb was taken under control and subdued, allowing the Guard to carry the Captain out into the aisle. Throwing him to ground once clear of the crowd. He immediately tried to charge the Hav Guard to get back inside.

"I am your Captain!" Theron screamed.

Four Hav Guard stood in defence, blocking Theron.

"They don't follow you anymore." Drathon moved in front of the barrier of men, holding the Captain's helmet in his hands.

"I will kill you." Launching his arm out, he attempted to grab at Drathon's throat.

Thump! Drathon slipped the attempted grapple and drove his armoured knee into the stomach of Theron. Smash! Followed up with a smashing gauntlet to the back. He watched as the Captain winced and grabbed at his abdomen after falling to his knees.

"You are too soft to lead the armies of the Shadow Empire, Theron. You belong here in the dirt with these skaff parasites," Drathon taunted.

Tears accompanied the look of pain and fear on Theron's face.

"I am not soft. I am the Captain. You can't kill me."

Chapter 9

"You are right, Captain, I won't kill you. I'll leave that to the Outer System." Drathon circled behind the Captain menacingly.

"You really want to follow him," Theron began to plead with the wall of Hav Guard in from of him.

Drathon approached Theron from the rear with the Captain's helmet in hand. SMASH! Straight to the back of Theron's head. Instant blunt force trauma with the helmet, knocking the Captain unconscious.

"Weak," Drathon scoffed, throwing the helmet into the blood that was beginning to pool around the Captain's head. "Come on, men, plenty more souls that need destroying."

The darkness of unconsciousness took Theron into a dark room that he recognised.

"Where am I?" he asked aloud, looking around for a door or a window.

A throne appeared in front of him, lit by burning purple flames slowly circling above. He took a step towards the throne but felt puddles beneath his feet.

"What the..." His feet were bare.

Theron was no longer dressed in his Captain's armour. He was dressed in a rag top and tattered shorts. The attire of the Outer System. Looking up, the throne was no longer clean and golden. It was a throne of shadows.

"Captain." A haunting voice sounded from behind him.

In panic, Theron looked around to see where the voice had come from.

"Who's there?" he screamed before turning back to face the throne.

Marra El sat proudly on the throne. His pointed steel gauntlets gripping the arms of the throne. The other five Higher Powers stood behind, cloaked and floating in the darkness.

"Captain, you have disappointed us."

Theron knelt in respect. "My Lords. I did not mean to disappoint. Drathon has–"

"Enough." Marra El came forward, his voice booming as he towered over Theron. "Drathon has embraced the Shadow, while you battle with feelings of the Light. An enemy craft left this planet, right under your nose."

"I apologise if I have offended you, my Lords. Tell me how I can make this right," he begged.

Falling back into his throne, the volume and sound of Marra El returned to a more settling level.

"There is only one way you can prove yourself to us."

"Anything..." Theron jumped to his feet.

"You know the answer." All six of the ghostly daunting voices of the Higher Powers spoke in unison.

"Please, tell me the answer."

The darkness once again engulfed the Captain, as the six shadowed figures of the Higher Powers crashed over him, causing Theron to wake in a cold frightened sweat. He went to jump up but the little movement of bracing to sit up caused searing pain to fill his head. Throwing his hand back, he felt the warmth of the blood on his hand. Bringing it forward, he looked as he rubbed the blood between his fingers.

"Wait a minute, where are my gauntlets?" Looking down he noticed that he was bare from the waist up.

"Young man, you need to lay still. It is a pretty hefty wound you have there." A voice that Theron did not recognise, came from the side of the bed.

Shaded light from a hole in the hall window allowed Theron to see the small frame of an elderly lady approaching him with a wet rag in hand.

"What are you doing? What is that?" Dazed and confused, Theron panicked, untrusting after his own men had turned on him.

"Theron Magda, be still. You need to rest to recover. You have been in and out of consciousness for over a day now and if I'm not mistaken, you have been mind walking with the Higher Powers. Well we will just have to make sure they cannot get to you here. Not anymore. Just know you are safe here," the old lady said as she cleaned the wound as gently as she could.

Every movement was watched and scrutinised closely by Theron.

"Over a day...I need to get out of here. Argh." The pain, once again, debilitating the Captain. He took a few breaths to get the pain under control before starting again. "Firstly, how do you know about mind walking? Who are you and why are you helping me?"

The old lady whipped her dreadlocked grey hair behind her head, before attempting to dab the sweat from Theron's face.

"I told you that you need to rest. I am Yvanny and it is because of me that you are still alive right now, so please, do as I say and just relax. Happiness and laughter shall dispel fear. I will answer all your questions when you are back to good health."

Finally, Theron began to relax into the bed, allowing Yvanny to dab freely at his sweat-soaked face. "Yvanny? I thought you were meant to be a crazy old lady that howls at the moon? You don't seem so crazy to me."

Yvanny chuckled at the premise that she was mentally unstable. "Ha ha ha. Theron, you make me laugh. I have not laughed in such a long time. Thank you."

"So you're not crazy?" Winking as he asked the question.

"I am old, very old...but not crazy." She smiled. "Now you get some rest and when you wake, I shall make you a nice hot cup of Vexorian tea."

"Thank you, Yvanny." Theron closed his eyes and drifted back into his delirious sleep.

It felt like only seconds had passed when his eyes opened again, but the poor lighting told him that it must be dark outside. The pain had begun to subside, but the dizziness was still very real. Sitting up onto the edge of the bed caused the Captain to feel like he was falling, so he gripped onto the bed tightly as he began to fall to the side.

Chapter 9

"Woah, woah, woah there, soldier. You got it? You okay now?" she said, holding onto the Captain as he found his centre of gravity sitting upright.

"Yeah, thank you. The pain seems better, just the dizziness to deal with now." He pressed at the back of his head, feeling the putty that was being used to close his wound. "A bit crude, but it seems to be doing the job."

"A bit crude, but it works. When you have lived for over three thousand years, you learn to make the smallest of things valuable." She lifted his chin gently with her hand. Yvanny's eyeline was only just above the sitting Captain's, so she barely had to lift his face at all to make eye contact.

"Wait a minute, you're three thousand years old," Theron gasped.

"And a few more." Yvanny turned and headed for the pot she had heating over a small woodburning fire.

"Wow, you really are an old lady." He chuckled. "So, do you want to tell me how you know about mind walking? Not even three thousand years on Octdrevion Six could give you the knowledge of mind walking. Not even in Centre City."

Yvanny filled a wooden beaker with hot liquid and brought it to Theron. "Octdrevion Six is only a couple of decades over one thousand years old. Before that it was Earth. I was not always here, I am Vexorian. I was a young woman, just coming into blossom when the House of El Radith gained control of the Home of the Shadows."

She ushered to Theron to drink up as he stared at her in disbelief.

"Wait...if this is true, why are you telling me? In all truth I should kill you and take your body back to the Higher Powers."

"Theron, my dear boy, a strong breeze would be too great of an adversary for you. More importantly, going by what happened yesterday, you would not be very welcome back at Hav Command. Would you...Captain?" Yvanny stood with a smile on her face.

No sign of fear or attempt to hold Theron against his will. To someone looking in, it may have even looked like she was caring for a friend or family member.

Theron started to speak with a facial expression full of venom, but stopped and began to repeat what had just been said to him in his head. His facial expression changing from angry, to surprised understanding, and then finally, ending with a soft smile towards Yvanny.

"You know what, I think you're right. I think the Higher Powers want me to kill Drathon Telema," Theron said.

"Yeah, that sounds like something they would do." Yvanny nodded.

"What do you mean?" he asked curiously between sips of his tea.

"They want you dead. They know you cannot beat Drathon, because he has beat you twice already..."

Theron spat his mouthful of tea to the side in shock, interrupting Yvanny. "How do you know he's beat me twice?"

"I have been watching you for a while, but I will get to that, do not worry. As I was saying, he has beat you twice already. With all the added pressure of "needing" to kill him, they know you will not be in your right mind. You can guarantee that they will make sure Drathon is ready. I have a long history with the House of El Radith. They can call themselves the Dark Mages of El, or the Havshad Knights, but before it all, they were just powerful men that lusted for more power." Yvanny climbed onto the bed beside Theron and let out a big sigh. "I have seen all manners of evil in my time. Not all evil comes from the dark. Evil can manifest itself in the light as well, but always remember, light can grow in the darkest of souls. You, Theron, are not evil and your light shines bright. That is why they want you dead."

Theron placed his head on the shoulder of Yvanny and began to weep. She seemed to be unbolting every emotion he had hidden deep down inside while Captain. All these fake morals now gone, he felt so much pain and remorse for what he couldn't stop.

"I really did try to change things for the better, but the strength of the Shadow is too great. Please forgive me."

She patted her hand against the back of Theron's head. "You cannot apologise for walking the path that has brought you right where you need to be. Now enough of those tears. Finish your tea and get some rest. I need you fighting fit. When you are feeling better, you are going to steal a scroll from the Havshad Archive."

"I'm going to what?" Theron barked, jumping to his feet. "No way. No way. No way. The Higher Powers will know I'm coming. They'll kill me before I even get my hands on the scroll."

"Trust in me, Theron. I will protect you from the Higher Powers. Hopefully, with a bit of luck, you will get through it without having to kill anyone." Yvanny hopped down off the bed.

Theron laughed at the height difference between the two, now that they were both standing.

"Laughter really does dispel fear." He sat himself down on the bed again, finally more relaxed about breaking into the Havshad Archive. "It will need to be at night. I can sneak in through the mines."

"Wonderful. At least one more day of rest, so take it easy tomorrow and stay out of sight. We are up high here so you should not be disturbed." Yvanny went to walk away, but stopped. "Oh and one last thing. Do not react to any of the sounds you may hear tomorrow. Goodnight." She sat down on the floor and began to chant quietly in tongues.

"Yvanny, you're not so bad for an ancient Vexorian," he joked for deaf ears due to Yvanny's ritualistic chant.

Theron felt more relaxed and at home in Yvanny's little, cold and damp one-roomed home than he had in a very long time. With his eyes clear and his heart full, Theron drifted off to sleep peacefully.

Chapter 10

Blood trickled from the gash below Ruevanlynn's right eye. Crouched down on one knee he wiped away the blood and sweat from his face, attempting to catch his breath.

"I need to take a break," Ruevanlynn gasped.

Joldack used his wooden training staff to flick Ruevanlynn's across the simulation room floor.

"We don't rest. We can't rest. You may have breezed through the simulations, but you know you need to defeat me to complete your training," Joldack replied, taking up a fighting stance with his staff held behind him in his right hand, smiling in anticipation. After a few moments of eyeballing, Ruevanlynn reached for his staff that lay on the floor in front of him. Rolling the handle into his hand with his fingers, he used the staff to take his weight as he pushed himself to his feet.

"You're enjoying this far too much," he snapped as he strained.

Sweat slowly dripped down the muscular and heavily scarred back of Joldack, a red rag ribbon acting as a sweat band, tied at the back and lying flush against his forehead.

"You have no idea." He smirked.

Twirling the staff through his fingers, looping it behind his body, Ruevanlynn brought the staff forward and charged.

"Ahhh," Ruevanlynn screamed.

Swishing and swooshing from Ruevanlynn's missed strikes could be heard. Joldack pivoted on his feet, dodging each swing of the staff, with his held tight along his back. Ducking down, his torso moved parallel to the wild horizontal swing, causing Ruevanlynn's momentum to take him to the floor. His leg muscles convulsing and collapsing, from the stress of the high intensity training. Slap! Joldack crashed his staff against the backside of Ruevanlynn, throwing him clambering on all fours, attempting to get to his feet.

"That's enough for today," Joldack stated.

Enraged, Ruevanlynn made one last unarmed attempt to charge his teacher. Anticipating the attack, Joldack stepped to the side, tripping Ruevanlynn with one leg. Slap! Crashing his staff against his back. Hurling Ruevanlynn splayed out, flat on his stomach, on the sweat-soaked floor.

"Yep, Mumma Rue is done now." Closing his eyes, his breathing was deep and fast.

Lactic acid in his muscles caused his whole body to feel like a dead weight. Placing his staff in the rack by the doorway, Joldack turned to face the exhausted and defeated Ruevnlynn. He looked around the black marbled cuboid simulation room. The orbs of light on the wall glowed blue as the shine of the black marble burst through. Although he could not show it, he was happy with the progress that had been made since the training had begun.

"Pick yourself up, Rue, I need to show you something."

Using his elbow pressed against the floor, Ruevanlynn rolled onto his side and rested his head in his hand.

"What's the point, boss man? I'm obvs not going to be ready in time." He jumped to his feet, anger and scorn bubbling and mixing together below the surface. "I ain't staying here when you go to save my best friend."

Joldack smiled, moving towards his student. "Do me a favour, put your staff in the rack and follow me. You'll be glad you did."

Drips of condensation could be heard bursting on the floor during the pause of silence, only broken by a scoff from Ruevanlynn.

"I will find a way." Picking up his training staff, he scuffed it along the floor as he made his way to the rack. "Ain't no way, no how, I'm being left behind."

"Talk, talk, talk. You love the sound of your own voice. Just hurry up and follow me." Disapproval filled Joldack's orders.

A clatter rang out as Ruevanlynn slammed his staff into the rack. "Lead the way then."

Joldack scoffed and shook his head before crashing his shoulder into the door, forcing the partition open to exit. Ruevanlynn walked closely behind with his head hung in shame. He disapproved of the way he had just acted towards

Joldack. Losing focus and attacking wildly. Judgement clouded when it needed to be clear. Too embarrassed to be the one to break the silence, he trailed behind like a shameful shadow. Even as the pair arrived at the entrance to the armoury, the silence remained.

Ruevanlynn, unlike his travelling friends, had not yet seen the full arsenal that hid beneath the dirt floor of the Outer System. The sight of the hustle and bustle of the workers and weaponry stopped him dead in his tracks. Reality poured into every fibre of the large, muscle-bound frame of Ruevanlynn. The reality of the war ahead. The loss that would be sustained. The fact that tomorrow was not guaranteed for any of them. All the training he had been suffering through with Joldack seemed so small in comparison now.

Light poured from the walls, illuminating everything in sight, reflecting off the sweat-soaked bodies of the two men.

"Welcome to the armoury, Rue. Amazing, isn't it?" Joldack asked.

No reply caused Joldack to turn to check on Ruevanlynn. He remained at the top of the steps, eyes wide, scanning from left to right, mouth open dumbstruck.

Joldack paused to allow Ruevanlynn a few more moments to take in what he was seeing. "It's a terrifyingly beautiful thing."

Ruevanlynn moved his focus to Joldack. "Mumma Rue is lost for words. Where did all this come from?" he asked as he made his way down the steps.

"Soldiers, scientists and engineers that turned away from the Empire. Many lost their lives to get us the materials and data we needed to be able to fight back. Do you know how we power everything down here? Lights, weapons, transporters...any idea?"

"Tell me," Ruevanlynn replied enthusiastically.

"Follow me." Joldack motioned to Ruevanlynn to follow him as he made his way through the armoury.

Ruevanlynn found himself running his fingers over everything he walked past, feeling the cold metal against his fingers. He strayed from the path that Joldack was taking to admire the speeders and transporters. Being dwarfed by the size of the transporters, Ruevanlynn could do nothing but stare in amazement. These old tech machines were enormous compared to their modern counterparts being used by the Hav Guard.

"Rue, you need to stay with me. Can't have you hurting yourself before I've managed to put you to good use," Joldack jeered.

There was a scoff of disdain from Ruevanlynn. He was still getting used to the jesting and teasing that the men of the Pit would partake in. These people did not know him, he had no bond with them. Ruevanlynn didn't mind his friends such as Feroshi, Ranoa and Shajo disrespecting and tricking him in fun, but he had a good relationship and level of respect for the ones that had struggled with him his whole life. New and random people trying to caper and jibe with him, still caused him to tense up anxiously, unsure of how to respond. In his head, he would fight alongside every single one of the people that had the same beliefs and feeling towards the Shadow Empire as him, but he didn't know them. He trusted Lemra and was slowly coming around to Joldack after spending the last few days with him. His bonds, with the ones he loved, had been formed in fire.

"So come on then, Joldey..." Ruevanlynn started.

"I've told you before, don't call me Joldey," Joldack interrupted, barking the statement as he whipped his head to look at Ruevanlynn.

Startled by the interruption, Ruevanlynn jumped back. "Woah, peace, brother. Keep your lid on, boss man, Rue's just playing."

"Hmmm. Well carry on, what were you saying?" Joldack started towards a small door that sat in the corner of the same wall as the enormous rolling door.

"What powers everything down here then?"

"Can you not guess?" Joldack smiled.

"Short of Hav Guard bodies, I have no idea," Ruevanlynn replied in jest.

Joldack removed the rope necklace that hung around his neck and opened the locket that sat in the middle of his chest to reveal a bright glowing gem.

"Light Stones."

"Well I'll be damned. I had been wondering how you powered the Space Jump. Next you'll be telling me we have a little Diamond Farm down here." Ruevanlynn held the locket in his hand and stared in marvel. "We don't, do we?"

Chapter 10

"Ha ha, no, we don't have a secret Diamond Farm hidden away down here. Just a forge for making weapons and fusing the stones. A couple of the farmers are sympathetic to our cause. I guess they remember the compassion they were shown when the farms were overrun by workers." Joldack gingerly took the locket from Ruevanlynn, closed the locket and replaced the rope over his head.

Ruevanlynn remained still, with his hands held out as though he was still holding the locket, while Joldack continued on his journey to the door. Reaching his destination, Joldack turned to watch Ruevanlynn hastily make his way to where he stood. A row of black tunics and cloaks hung to the left of the door. Joldack combed over the items of clothing, trying to find a good fit for their considerable frames.

"Here, put this on." Joldack handed the garments to Ruevanlynn.

Ruevanlynn held the attire at arm's length, inspecting the tunic and cloak. "Black definitely makes Mumma Rue's beautiful dark skin pop. Why are we putting these on?"

"We are going outside the wall. It's dark outside; the cloak and tunic will help us blend into the terrain," Joldack answered as he pulled open the door.

"Hold up, what about the Hav Guard and all their toys? We'll be dead as soon as we step foot outside." Caution filled the words from Ruevanlynn.

"The Hav Guard on the wall won't see us in the dark. They hardly pay any attention to anything other than the performance of the Grandors feeding on the Faded. Scanners and RADAR are programmed to pick up anything bigger than a fully grown male Grandor. Anything smaller and their systems would constantly be alerting them to threats. Their overconfidence will be their undoing one day."

The pair made their way into an uphill tunnel that was nearly identical to the entrance way they had taken into the Pit. Crudely made with wooden steps pressed into the floor and beams used to create archways to prevent the ceiling collapsing, and poorly lit by Light Stones pressed into the walls.

"You seem to know a lot about the inner workings of the Hav Guard and their defences." Ruevanlynn pried for more information. "Come on, Joldey...sorry I mean Joldack. Tell Rue how you know so much."

Joldack stopped with both feet on a step.

He took a moment to contemplate how much truth he was willing to share. "I was a Child of the Dark."

"A Child of what, sorry?"

"I wasn't born in one of the hospitals in the Inner System. I was born in the Outer System. You ever wondered where the younglings that enter the Joining Ceremony and don't walk out from under the curtain go? They end up in a compound, much like this one, below the barracks of Hav Command. The curtain senses shadow over light and searches for the one with the darkness within. I did a lot of wrong before I saw the evil I had become." Tears began to pool in the eyes of Joldack. The memories of the pain and suffering he had endured and dealt to others was hard for him to deal with. "Most of the Hav Guard aren't born hating the Outer System, it's burned and programmed into them."

"Oh lordy. Well what do you know, the younglings don't just spontaneously combust." Ruevanlynn clapped his hands together in glee. Very amused with his retort.

"Ha ha ha," Joldack chuckled. "No, they don't."

"What happened to make you come back?" Ruevanlynn asked.

"Alenca Enlit happened, but that's enough about my past if that is alright with you. Just know, the Hav Guard are but a small water droplet compared to the storm that is the Vexorian army or the assassins from Eissol."

"I've heard about the 'monsters' on Eissol. Nothing Mumma Rue can't handle," he joked as he patted Joldack on his back.

Joldack turned to give a disgruntled look as a reply. Finally the pair arrived at the shallow end of the tunnel where a hatch was positioned in the ceiling. Wasting no time, Joldack pushed open the hatch revealing the dark starlit sky above. Fresh air poured in and filled the lungs of Ruevanlynn.

"Once outside, stay close to me. I don't need to be explaining how I managed to allow you to get trampled by a Grandor, to Lemra," Joldack stated, issuing his final warnings about the world outside the wall.

"Sir, yes, sir!" Ruevanlynn said sarcastically while throwing up a fake salute while he skipped to attention.

A roll of the eyes was the only response Joldack could give. He had started to get used to the humour of Ruevanlynn. No sooner than he had finished rolling his eyes, Joldack grabbed a hold of the edges of the manhole. Using his strength he catapulted himself upward, landing crouched down on the balls of his feet. With his hand held out to signal for Ruevanlynn to wait, Joldack scanned the surrounding area, making sure it was clear of Grandors and Hav Guard prior to ordering his pupil to higher ground.

"We are all clear. Up you come," Joldack instructed, offering his hand out in assistance.

Putting one hand on the ledge and the other in the hand of Joldack, Ruevanlynn leaped out of the tunnel onto the grassy terrain above. The feeling of grass was not something that Ruevanlynn was used to. He ran his fingers across the blades, ripping a few from the ground and lifting them to his face to take in the scent. Behind him, Joldack closed over the camouflaged doorway in the floor.

"Do you see those markings on the wall?" Joldack pointed to etchings on the outside of the great wall, using his locket to illuminate the symbols. "It's the Sielfey symbol for safe haven. It was put there when the tunnels were first dug."

"Sielfey? What is a Sielfey?" Ruevanlynn asked.

"Sielfey is the ancient language of the Angels of the Light. They were once the sworn protectors of the Temple of Equilibrium, on Vexora, before being deceived by the Shadow Emperor and his Havshad Knights." Joldack closed his locket as he explained. "At the time of the war, there were six such tunnels. Only two remain. The others were discovered and destroyed by the Hav Guard."

"What happened to the Angels of the Light?"

"They tried to fight to protect the temple but, when the battle was lost, they retreated and fled. Their wings were bound to Vexora by dark magic. As soon as they left the planet's atmosphere, their wings died. Now they are hidden across the Universe. Most that survived ended up taking refuge on Laborine. They could be hidden there, from the Shadow Emperor, by the last surviving Mage of the Light," Joldack explained.

"Yep, okay...you've lost Mumma Rue now so I'll just nod, smile and look pretty." Ruevanlynn smiled as he overexaggerated his head nod and facial expressions.

The pair began to laugh under the magenta moonlight, as they made their way across the Dead Zone. Hundreds of thousands of hairless, mentally destroyed figures lethargically moved their way across the Pangean continent, towards the nearest family of Grandors.

"What's wrong with them?" Ruevanlynn asked while he waved his hand in front of the pale face of a female Faded. Her irises were grey. Skin drawn and tired. Her cheekbones and jawline driving through the epidermis.

"Their life force has been taken. Drowned in elixir made from Shadow Stones. If your light shines too bright for the elixir to bind, it destroys everything you are, or so they say. The truth is the elixir isn't designed to bind. Its purpose is to consume, poison and break. Until all that's left is what you see in front of you. Shells. Until they find the one they are looking for," Joldack replied. "If you removed the red cloaks you'd see burn marks and scarring all over their bodies from the torture."

"I hate the Empire. They are nothing but shit-covered monsters. It's unconscionable and for what...numbers? How many do you think there are?" Fury filled the words of Ruevanlynn.

"Too many to count, my friend. The population of Randtyph was nearly one billion before the war. Over three quarters of that was in the Outer System. Now the entire population is half of that, and I reckon the Faded outnumber us two to one, easily. That's even with the city stretching over two thousand miles wide."

Thunderous crashing and snapping noises began to fill the ears of Ruevanlynn and Joldack. Grandors were fighting in the distance, getting excited and ready for their night-time feed. The roars of the males increased as they whipped their tails and clambered over one another. With each roar and growl, Ruevanlynn jumped a little bit less.

"Do we need to worry about the Grandors?" Ruevanlynn asked tentatively.

"No, no. They only feed on emptiness and darkness. Saying that, they will absolutely crush you if they feel threatened. Grandors used to feed on vegetation on Vexora, but as the Emperor corrupted and poisoned the planet, the vegetation died off and they turned to the one food source there was left...the people. Two Mages of Light sacrificed themselves to curse the Grandor population, so they never feed on the light." Joldack opened his locket. "They won't harm us as long as we keep our distance, you're safe."

The two men waded their way through the ocean of red cloaks, solo gurgles from the figures becoming a humming chorus as they moved deeper and deeper into the flock. They moved closer and closer to the ever-growing pack of hunting Grandors. Their six dropped whiskers now stood on end like diamond spears, ready to protect them from a flank attack or skewer their prey. Crouching down, their ears pricked, they were ready to feed.

"We probably want to start heading back now. They may not try to eat us, but you don't want to be near them when they are feeding. Those whiskers are deadly," Joldack stated, turning to head back to the wall.

"Sweet. Let's head back to the Pit," Ruevanlynn replied. "I'm far too pretty to be a Grandor's late-night snack."

Ruevanlynn ran his fingers over the fabric of the cloaks as he passed each of the Faded, feeling the soft material in his hands. The crowd began to thin as they got closer to the wall. Once at a safe distance, Joldack turned to allow Ruevanlynn the opportunity to watch the Grandors feed.

"I hope you're not squeamish," he joked as the lead Grandor pounced on top of a group of the faded, crushing the ones below while they clamped their massive jaws down over their victim.

"Urgh." Ruevanlynn placed his left hand over his eyes, hiding them from the sight of the Faded being thrown into the air and beaten down with the enormous paws. "I'm just glad the ones on the farm are better behaved."

"Rue, there's a reason I took you out here. Do you know what that is?" Joldack asked.

"To teach me not to go near Grandors?" he joked.

"No. I took you out here to show you what we are fighting for. Look at this. Look at the Outer System. We are fighting...wait, what is that noise?" A warbling sound was coming from the opposite direction of the wall. "Get down! Get down!"

Both men dived onto the grass in the prone position. Flat on their stomachs. The noise was closing in on where they were.

"What is that? Where's it coming from?" Ruevanlynn queried.

Lights began to appear in the distance.

"It must be a troop transporter coming back from the Prison Zone. Just stay down and they'll pass over us soon enough," Joldack answered.

While they waited, they watched as the Grandors moved their attention from the Faded to the incoming craft, howling to alert the females and pups that danger was near. The fighting and feeding stopped so the Grandors could circle around their families. Although the males were covered in diamond skin and golden fur, the females and pups were soft and fluffy like golden clouds. This caused the males to rally anytime a threat presented itself. Once the protective ring was formed, the Grandors interlinked their spear-like whiskers, thus creating a razored barricade around vulnerable members of the pack.

Like a comet, the fogged pyramid tore through the sky on the way to its destination. Its speed rapidly decreased upon approach to the wall. Slowing to hover over the Dead Zone, not far from where Ruevanlynn and Joldack were lying in wait, attempting to hide.

"Joldack, have they spotted us?" Ruevanlynn yelled, nervously waiting to find out if there was trouble afoot.

"No, I don't think so. Stay low and follow me," Joldack ordered.

Joldack led the leopard crawl to cover. Dragging their elbows and knees along the cold, dry surface, they moved with purpose. Both sets of bare knees began to burn from the friction, but neither man batted an eyelid as they rapidly moved towards a mound of earth beside them. Piles of grass and dirt were heaped high where the Grandors had been wrestling amongst themselves. The soil mound was enough for the pair to hide in the dark and see what was happening. Catching their breath, they pressed their backs up against the knoll and listened as the troop transporter began its descent.

"They must be adding to the population of the Faded," Joldack stated.

Ruevanlynn pressed himself against the ground and peered around the mound, hoping to catch a glimpse of the unloading of the newest members of the Faded. The Grandors were worked up into a frenzy, growling and snarling as the transporter landed. Explosive clatters of the whiskers crashing together rang out in bursts, as the Grandors attempted to lunge forward to posture their position.

"Will the Grandors not attack the transporter?" Ruevanlynn queried with a smile on his face.

"Be careful!" Joldack grabbed at Ruevanlynn, pulling him back behind the knoll. "They'll see you if you're not cautious. There could be up to eight Hav Guard onboard and there's only two of us. You do the math. But to answer your question, no, they won't attack unless provoked. They are very protective of their packs."

Light from inside the transporter flooded the ground in front of it. The energy wall opened up, facing the direction of the mound hiding Ruevanlynn and Joldack. To avoid the light pouring in their direction, they shuffled around to the adjacent side of the knoll, attempting to stay concealed. A first set of footsteps were heard disembarking the transporter; very shortly after, a second set of boots landed on the ground.

"There must only be four Hav Guard onboard if there's only two lookouts. There will be another two onboard for unloading the Faded. Nothing we can do now but wait." Joldack exhaled loudly as he made himself comfortable against their cover.

Curiosity made the temptation to look, far too difficult to resist.

Chapter 10

"It's all clear. Unload the stiffs!" The command from the Hav Guard was loud and clear.

"Unload the stiffs!" The second lookout called back in reply.

Moments later, two large black-masked guards began to shuffle three broken souls, covered from the neck down in the red cloak of the Faded, to the doorway of the transporter. The two lookouts watched over for hostiles and over-eager Grandors, with their batons charged and ready in hand.

"One, two, three, lift," they yelled out in unison.

With one arm each wrapped around the torso, the two Guards lifted the first body from the transporter. They carried the Faded round the transporter and dumped them facing the direction of the Grandors, before heading back to unload the next lost being.

"Not going to lie to you, this is savage. We are just sitting here while they just send those people to their death," Ruevanlynn proclaimed, punching the ground in frustration.

"They're not people anymore, you need to realise that. Once shattered, there is no coming back." Joldack sounded frustrated. He understood the mental struggle that Ruevanlynn was feeling, but he needed him to realise that it was a lost cause to care.

"One, two, three, lift." Loud and clear, the command to lift the second hairless figure was heard.

Ruevanlynn shook his head, disgruntled and hurt by what he was allowing to happen. His whole life he had been fighting the Hav Guard and now, when the defenceless needed him the most, he could do nothing. Nothing but hide and save himself. He needed to look again. Assess the situation, seek and destroy. Evil thoughts polluted his mind. He imagined slowly feeding the Hav Guard to the Grandors. Listening to their screams as their bones snapped and cracked in the jaws of the solution, while being torn apart and their remains toyed with by the young.

"I thought we were supposed to be fighting against everything they stand for?" Ruevanlynn attempted to lean over Joldack to see that state of affairs.

"Will you sit down! Rue..." Joldack began to panic because Ruevanlynn had seen something that had caused him to break from the cover and stand bolt upright with tears in his eyes. "Rue, they're going to see you."

The Hav Guard were preparing to lift the final figure from the transporter. Ruevanlynn recognised the person. It was Zedary Tawn, his love. Once so full of life. Exuberant and happy. Now just a shell of skin. Frail and broken.

"Zed..." Ruevanlynn whispered, raising his hand as though he was reaching out to touch his lost love.

"Stop it. There's nothing you can do. He's gone." Joldack jumped to his feet and grabbed Ruevanlynn's arm.

"Get your hand off me!" Ruevanlynn snarled, ripping Joldack's hand from his arm. "Go back to the Pit, Joldack. This is my fight, not yours."

"Don't...be...stupid." Joldack wrapped both his arms around Ruevanlynn and attempted to drag him to cover.

"What use are you to Feroshi if you're–"

"Hey you!" One of the lookouts had noticed the commotion. "Hostiles! Contact front!"

"I'm really starting to dislike you." Joldack released Ruevanlynn and prepared to fight.

"Well I guess you're going to get a front row seat to Mumma Rue show." Ruevanlynn ripped the tunic and cloak from his body, rolled his shoulders and then tensed his upper body. "First one's mine."

The two lookouts charged towards Ruevanlynn, batons raised. He took a quick look behind him, but Joldack was gone. Ruevanlynn lowered his head with a menacing smile on his face.

SWOOSH! Ruevanlynn ducked under the wild over-arm swing of the first baton. Pivoting on the ball of his outside foot as he rolled out the way. WHOOSH! The second lookout sliced at Ruevanlynn. He felt the air rush past his stomach as he jumped back. CRASH! Joldack body-slammed from the top of the mound, throwing all four men to the floor. Ruevanlynn and Joldack began to wrestle with their foes, trying to gain control on the floor. Fear and adrenaline coursed through Ruevanlynn, empowering him to survive.

"Over here!" The two black-masked Hav Guard dropped Zed and headed for the skirmish.

Bang! Bang! With one hand Ruevanlynn pinned his lookout by the neck and rained down elbows and punches with the other. Punch. Elbow. Elbow. The white mask began to shatter, revealing a terrified face beneath. BOOM!

A black-masked Hav Guard struck Ruevanlynn in the face with his baton. Throwing him dazed onto his back. Blood poured from his nose and the gash under his eye. Ringing filled his ears. His vision double and blurred. The metallic taste of blood was so strong he could smell it.

The commotion was causing the defensive ring of Grandors to splinter. Growling low as they stalked.

"Argh." Joldack struggled, as he was rolled onto his back by the Hav Guard he was wrestling with. "Get...off..."

Joldack dug his fingers through the throat of the Hav Guard. Gargling and splurging blood poured from his mouth. Joldack ripped the windpipe and throat clean from the body, dropping him limp on top. He quickly threw his twitching body off and jumped up.

"Come on!" Joldack taunted the black-masked Hav Guard that headed his way.

Thud! Crash! He caught the swinging baton and crashed his fist into the gut of the Hav Guard. Thinking he had him beat, Joldack rushed in.

"Ah my eyes." The hunched over Hav Guard threw a handful of dirt in the face of Joldack.

BOOM! The winded Hav Guard energised his baton, hurling Joldack and the limp body of the dead lookout backwards. Joldack lay unconscious and motionless on the ground.

Ruevanlynn shook the daze out of his head, spitting a mouthful of blood onto the floor. Three Hav Guard formed an arc of assault in front of him. Batons outstretched.

Chapter 10

"If you're going to kill me, just do it!" Ruevanlynn screamed, standing tall and beating his chest.

The Hav Guard with the shattered mask ripped it off and stepped forward. "This is going to be slow. You won't enjoy it...but I am going to love every moment of peeling your skaff skin off. Strip by strip."

Death was guaranteed and imminent. At least he would be with Zedary once again. Knowing his fate, he went down on his knees. Arms stretched out wide, he closed his eyes and thought back to the days where Simeskey, Feroshi, Zedary and himself would joke, laugh and smile together.

"Ahhhh." Spinetingling shrieks caused Ruevanlynn's eyes to fire open.

Startling scenes were unfolding in front of him. Stalking Grandors had pounced and were ripping the Hav Guard into pieces. Two Grandors played tug of war with the unmasked Hav Guard's body. One with jaws clamped around his upper body, while the other tugged on a spare leg that was flopping around. Ruevanlynn remained on his knees. Mouth open but silent, in complete disbelief. All, bar one, of the Grandors dragged the remains of the three Hav Guard back to their pack.

"At least this will be over quickly." Ruevanlynn spoke aloud, preparing to feel the pain of the razor sharp teeth puncturing his skin.

He stared into the piercing blue eyes of the enormous golden figure. Growling with its head low, it moved its large paws forward. One paw and then the next. Slowly edging closer and closer to its victim. Ruevanlynn's heart raced. He could hear his pulse in his ears, while his neck throbbed as the blood rushed through his arteries.

Warm dense breath filled the atmosphere around Ruevanlynn, as the Grandor lowered to be at the same level as him. He could taste the flesh lingering in the Grandor's teeth. His breathing became short and sharp. The jaws were open. Ruevanlynn knew it was time.

"Ah..." His cry of defiance was cut before it started.

Ruevanlynn was in shock at the Grandor rubbing its face up against his. It began to purr so Ruevanlynn wrapped his arms around its neck and itched the side of his head.

"You're not so bad, are you?" He laughed as the Grandor rolled onto its back to allow Ruevanlynn to rub its belly.

"Rue...what's going on?" Joldack began to regain consciousness.

Turning to face Joldack caused the Grandor to jump.

"It's okay, baby, it's okay." Ruevanlynn spoke soothingly to the Grandor.

"Am I dead or are you talking to a Grandor?" Joldack remained on the ground, propping himself up on his elbows.

The Grandor looked past its new friend, straight at Joldack. Brushing up against Ruevanlynn, while it headed in the direction of Joldack, knocked him to the floor. It paused to look back and make sure Ruevanlynn was okay. Bringing its focus back to Joldack, it stared at him, before turning to the corpse next to him. Collecting the body gently in its fangs, it headed back to the pack. Ruevanlynn turned and winked at the dumfounded Joldack after waving goodbye to his rescuer.

"Are you going to explain to me what happened?" Joldack queried, trying to find reason in what he had just seen. "In my hundred and fifty years, I've never seen a Grandor approach somebody like that."

"You got your ass handed to you, so me and my new bae over there saved the day," Ruevanlynn jeered.

"Rubbish. No way no how. Really?"

"How about you get up and we get back to the Pit. I'll tell you all about it there." Ruevanlynn approached Joldack, holding his hand out in assistance.

"Argh." Joldack slumped back onto the ground in pain, his leg throbbing. "You're going to have to carry me, I think my ankle's broken."

"Give me a moment please. There's something Mumma Rue's got to do first."

Ruevanlynn headed back towards the transporter, wiping sweat and blood from his face and flicking it towards the ground. Zedary stood still where he had been left, staring into oblivion. Like a performer under a spotlight, the internal light of the transporter illuminated the ground where he waited for death. Seeing the dishevelled state of his love caused Ruevanlynn to burst out crying. He placed his hands on both of Zedary's cheeks and kissed him on the lips.

"I'm so sorry, baby." He sobbed. "There's no more pain, no more suffering where you're going. Please forgive me."

After gently laying Zedary on the ground, Ruevanlynn crouched down next to him.

"I'm so sorry. I love you." Ruevanlynn lay one final kiss on the forehead of Zedary, before placing his hand over the mouth and nose of the man he was supposed to spend the rest of his life with.

There was no struggle. No fighting for his life. Even though Zedary was not the man he once knew, Ruevanlynn's heart broke as he felt the life leaving him. Pure devastation caused Ruevanlynn to scream out in pain. In the distance, the Grandors began to howl towards the sky, joining in with the cry of an aching heart. Almost as though they could feel his pain.

"You're at peace now, baby. I'm going to kill them. I'm going to kill all of them." Ruevanlynn wiped the tears from his face and headed back to Joldack.

"Come here, you big baby." Ruevanlynn scooped Joldack up off the floor and took his weight, allowing Joldack to hobble on one leg.

"Are you okay? That was a brave and very selfless thing you did there." Joldack winced in pain as they made their way back to the entrance to the tunnel.

"I'll be fine. You know I'm going on that rescue mission. It's suicide and I have nothing to lose if I can't save my brother. You get me?"

"Rue, you were always going on that mission. I just needed you to know that this is bigger than you or me. Strength won't win this war. Hope will."

Chapter 11

The screams from outside, of all the pain and suffering, caused Theron's toes to curl. Trying to drown out the noise, he rolled from side to side in a cold sweat, hands pressed hard against his ears, but nothing could stop the commotion from breaking through. Flashing images of the pain he had seen, cries for help, the physical and mental abuse caused by soldiers under his command, filled his mind's eye. Theron sat up onto the edge of the bed, gripping onto his knees he rocked backwards and forwards in distress. Slapping his legs, he launched himself off the bed. He paced around the room, snatching in frustration at his blond hair.

"Will you calm down please? You are making the place look untidy," Yvanny asked softly.

"This is the Outer System, everything is untidy. Dirty, grimy, filthy..." Theron's hand gestures were becoming more eccentric with each word.

"Okay, Theron, that is enough. You are working yourself up and I need your nerves calm. Now, please sit down. I will bring you some water."

Theron scoffed and huffed in disapproval at being told what to do. Still used to commanding and demanding the respect of his soldiers, the manner in which Yvanny directed him was taking some time to get used to. Nursing his wounds, bathing him, clothing him and having him make the bed. It was almost the relationship of a mother and son. A relationship that Theron had been lacking in his life, since his mother had died within a few days of his birth. At one point in his life he would have enjoyed this relationship, but not now. Not as an exiled and disgraced ex-Captain. Not while he was likely to be killed on sight by the Hav Guard and any willing citizen of the Outer System.

"Look, it's not that I don't appreciate you taking me in, but I don't know if I can do this. I must be the most hated man in the Empire right now. I have no home. No friends. No family. I'm living on borrowed time and I think you know that." Anxiety and fear captivated Theron.

No response came from Yvanny. She remained sitting with her legs crossed and eyes closed. A smile on her face was the only reply for Theron to have.

"Yvanny, did you hear me? I can't do this." Theron moved closer to Yvanny. "Yvanny..."

With a smile on her face, Yvanny remained sitting with her legs crossed and eyes closed.

"Yva–" As Theron went to place his hand on Yvanny's shoulder his whole body was frozen.

Theron panicked, he was stuck in a state of paralysis. Suddenly his body was thrown bolt upright with his arms outspread and head back. He was in a dark room. A room he recognised. Not the home of Yvanny anymore but still a room he recognised. Looking around, the dark fog began to lift, revealing a black throne in the centre of the room. It was a mind walk.

"No no no no." Fear and anxiety turned to a feeling of pure terror. The Higher Powers had found him.

Theron collapsed onto the cold damp ground into the foetal position.

"Theron...Theron..." A soft angelic voice echoed around the room.

"No! Leave me alone!" he cried out.

"Theron..." The volume of the echo increased.

"Yvanny!" Theron screamed out for aid, grabbing tightly at his face. "It's not real. It's not real."

"Theron, look up. Theron..."

Slowly Theron opened his tightly clenched fingers, trying to sneak a glimpse of the owner of the voice. The room was no longer dark. The room was bright white and the throne was golden. A perfumed scent filled the air and the sound of laughing replaced the echoing sound of his name. He no longer adorned the tattered rags of the Outer System. Instead, a beautiful white robe with golden cuffs and collar. There were no cuts or bruises. No dirt on his hands. Running his hands through his hair, it felt washed and soft. The gash on the back of his head was gone as well.

"Ha ha." He chuckled aloud, feeling no abrasions or scars on his face.

"Theron," a voice called from behind him, causing him to whip his head round.

Bringing his gaze back forward, he jumped at the sight of a beautiful blonde woman standing naked in front of him. Pearly white wings stretched out from her back. Each feather, purer and whiter than the next. Porcelain skin covered her body. Her blonde hair was pleated and draped over her shoulder. She ran her fingers along the pleat and down the middle of her chest, gently brushing the underside of her unyielding breast before throwing her hair behind her. Not just beautiful, but powerful. Like she contained all the power of life in her hands.

"Simeskey? Is that you?" Theron gawked at the perfect form in front of him.

"No, my dear, it is me, Yvanny." Her piercing blue eyes looked up to meet the gaze of Theron.

"I don't understand. How can you be...oh I think I get... no, you'll have to explain it to me. Your eyes are blue and not purple."

"I told you, I am very old and have a few tricks up my sleeve. The eyes are a story for another time," Yvanny joked.

"But I mean, we are mind walking right now. How is that possible?" Theron thirsted to know more.

"I am an Angel of the Light. There is not much I cannot do. We take our truest form in this realm. The Higher Powers are consumed by the Shadow, which is why they do not take the form of men anymore." Yvonne moved closer to Theron. "I brought you here to ease your mind."

"Ease my mind? I thought they had found me," he replied.

"You were self-deprecating due to fear. Fear that the Light cannot match the power of the Shadow. You talked about no family, I got my family killed; my daughters, their loves...all gone. In the end, their sacrifice has brought us to where we are today. I will not lie to you, if you leave you will be dead within days. By whom...the possibilities are endless, but it will not be pretty."

With a large flap of her wings, Yvanny took flight and hovered in front of Theron. His eyes scanning her wing span and then her perfect hairless body. All the way down to the tips of her toes.

"With that in mind, are you ready to put your big boy pants on and fight for something real?" Yvanny queried.

Theron circled Yvanny, weighing up his options in his head. Would he die a coward on the run, or would he stand tall and fight for what was right and what he believed in? An exiled and dishonoured Captain of the Hav Guard that would be vilified across the entire Cosmic Web. Hunted wherever he went until his final breaths, or the chance to be a hero. Fighting and dying for a cause, or in the place of another, seemed like a better way to go.

Theron crouched down on one knee in front of the hovering Yvanny. "I pledge myself to you. Whatever you ask of me, I will do."

Yvanny began to spin, causing a whirlwind that pushed Theron and made him fall backwards. Falling made time feel like it had begun to slow down. Theron gasped and tensed up in anticipation of the crash, but it never came. He opened his eyes to see that he was back in Yvanny's home.

"Thank you," Yvanny said, standing behind Theron.

He turned to face her, his liberator. "Why are you thanking me? It should be me thanking you."

"Because without you, our fight would be a lot more difficult. Without the scroll, it will be nearly impossible to defeat the Higher Powers."

"You know that there are thousands of scrolls in the archive. Scrolls from planets that don't even exist anymore. It will be nearly impossible for me to find one single scroll without having days or help to look," Theron stated.

"What do all the scrolls have in common?"

"Emm, I don't know. They're all written on parchment from Vexora?"

"No, Theron, try again."

"They are all covered with either information or drawings?"

"Except..."

"The Keeper's Scroll, but that is blank. It hangs on the wall at the back of the archive." Theron was confused by the need for a blank scroll. "How can a blank piece of parchment defeat the stewards to the throne of the Empire?"

"I am afraid that everything you need to know at this moment in time, you now know. For now, the sun has gone down so it is time to go to work." Yvanny moved towards the doorway, to check for Hav Guard. "One last thing before you go off, you will need this."

Chapter 11

Yvanny pulled a locket from under tattered layers of cloth, lifting it up over her head. She handed it to Theron.

"What is this for?" Theron asked.

"What was once your home is now enemy territory, you will need some form of protection. This will stop you being detected by the Higher Powers," Yvanny replied.

"Thank you. Well, I guess it's time. I'll see you when I return."

"Stay safe." Yvanny patted Theron on the back as he headed for the doorway.

Theron gently moved the sheet out of the way, double checking there was no Hav Guard outside before leaving the premises. No lights were shining, so Theron made his move. He climbed out onto the roof. Staying low he scuttled towards the Inner System. Approaching the end of the pop-up homes, Theron lay flat on his stomach, checking the coast was clear once more. Two Hav Guard were loitering below. He waited a few moments to see if they would leave, but they stayed. He knew he could not just lie there and wait. The guards could be there for an indefinite amount of time. Theron had to act.

Silently, he scaled down the side of the building. Using the shadows as cover, he approached the two Hav Guard from the rear. They were joking amongst themselves. Laughing about the day's exploits and the damage they had done. The choice, in his mind, was simple: fight or hide.

He decided that the time for hiding was over. He searched the ground around him for a weapon. Nothing but a rock, no bigger than his hand. It would have to do. They were looking the opposite way. Thud! The first one dropped to the floor. Crash! Theron smashed his forehead into the white mask of the second Hav Guard. Shattering it with the force. He mounted the dazed man. Thump! Crash! Crash! With both hands holding the rock, he rained down on the guard. Blood sprayed and spurted, the warm crimson of the blood splashing against his face. Theron cast the blood-soaked rock to the side. Holding his chest high in ecstasy, breathing in the blood-filled mouthfuls of air into his lungs, calming himself, before he quickly dragged the two bodies into the shadows.

Knowing how difficult it would be for him to move freely, Theron had an idea. Snap! He broke the neck of the unconscious victim and stripped the body. The armour was too big for him, but it would do. At least the mask was still in one piece. Keeping his face covered would make this mission a lot easier. Holstering the baton, he made his way through the curtain and passed the Diamond Farms. Theron had never worn the white mask of the Hav Guard, he had gone straight in at the rank of Lieutenant after Officer Selection, before quickly rising to Troop Commander and then, finally, Captain.

In the hours of darkness, the Diamond Farms were deserted, so Theron moved through without any problems. Troop transporters whizzed overhead as he approached the barracks. He knew the only way into the mines, was through the forge behind Hav Command. Platoons of men buzzed around the clearing between the living quarters and the barracks. Theron put his head down. Moving quickly and with purpose, he hoped nobody would challenge him. Behind him, he heard a voice that instantly made his blood boil.

"Men, to the barracks for your briefing!" Drathon Telema yelled at the Hav Guard disembarking a transporter.

Theron found himself stuck, staring at his nemesis. Nothing could be done just now; he would have to wait for another opportunity to confront Drathon.

"Oi you, come here!" Drathon yelled at Theron.

"Nope," Theron muttered to himself as he turned and headed for the forge.

"Hav Guard, stop. Oi, you, I said stop!"

Theron halted. Sweat poured from his body. He could feel his hand start to shake from nerves. Turning to face the approaching Captain, Theron tried to think up a way to get out of this without being discovered.

"Why did you not stop when I told you? Are you fucking stupid!" Drathon screamed.

"Sorry, sir, I didn't realise you were talking to me." The mask muffled his words, disguising his voice.

"Not a good enough excuse. Why does your armour look like it's hanging off you?"

"I've been sick, sir. Haven't been able to eat for a week now. Too scared it comes flying out of me." Theron tried to lighten the mood to speed up his exit.

"Once again, not a good enough excuse. Remove your mask so I can see who I'm reprimanding." Drathon unholstered his baton.

This was it. Theron knew he was in trouble and there was nobody to save him. Nobody that would want to save him.

"Are you being serious? I haven't done anything wrong," Theron argued, knowing he was in an all-or-nothing situation now.

"I said now!" Drathon yelled as he poked Theron in chest with his baton.

"And I said no." Theron slowly started to reach for his baton, ready to fight for his life.

"Why you stupid–" Howling from beyond the wall broke Drathon's attention.

BOOM! Theron quickly drew his baton and energised it. Throwing Drathon flying backwards. He laughed, before realising he had better start running, due to Hav Guard turning to see who had energised their baton. By the time they had realised that somebody had just struck their Captain, Theron was gone.

Crashing through the door to the forge, Theron slammed the door behind him and caught his breath while leaning up against it.

"Wow, that was close, but it felt really good," he said happily to himself.

Normal soldiers were not allowed in the mines, only the Higher Intellects that specialised in Shadow Stones, officers and the Higher Powers were allowed down. Theron had only been down in the mines twice, but he knew where the passage was that would bring him under the archive. If he made it that far, he knew a couple of blasts from his baton would blow right through the floor. Blasting his way through would make too much noise though, so he knew his only other option was to take the passage that took him below the Akaveash Colosseum. There was a hatch that opened up in the waiting room, behind the curtain.

With his plan decided, he made his way through the forge. Attempting to avoid anybody working at all costs. The further he moved into the forge, the hotter it became. The air was dense from smelting of the Light and Shadow Stones. He could feel the sweat dripping down the back of his neck. As he reached the back of the forge, he took a quick look around to make sure there were no witnesses to him entering the restricted passageway, down into the mines. Nobody was watching. Quickly, he slipped through the door. Making sure to close it quietly behind him.

Once he was into the passageway to the mines he had to take a knee. He was overheating and dehydrating rapidly, leaving him feeling dizzy and nauseous.

"If I die from dehydration, I'm going to kill you, Yvanny," he said as he tore the mask from his head.

Theron removed the rest of the sweat-soaked armour he had hijacked. The tattered clothes below were saturated from the rate of perspiration caused by the heat and density of the forge. If the Hav Guard were not supposed to enter the mines, the disguise was obsolete. No need for his movements to be slowed or position to be given away, by the clattering of the oversized armour. Stealth in the quiet of the shadows would now be his ally.

Retaining the baton, Theron moved cautiously and methodically through the mines. Deeper and deeper he moved, until eventually he reached the Crying Cavern. The Shadow Stones resonated at a frequency that to an uneducated individual, would sound like the wailing of lost souls. Purple light, radiating from the stones that hung from the ceiling, complemented the cold forlorn air that sat stagnant in the chamber. Caution turned to temptation as the stones called to Theron. Pulling him closer and closer and closer, he could not resist. He was no longer in control of his actions. Thoughts of the power he could wield with the Shadow Stones flashed into his mind. With an outstretched arm, Theron reached out to touch the Shadow Stones.

"Theron!" Yvanny's voice boomed in his mind as the Light Stone in his locket burned into his chest and blasted him to the floor.

"Ahhhh..." He screamed as he crashed across the rubble and dirt below.

Theron shook his head and grabbed at the locket, but it was cool. Not a single blemish or bubble of burning skin could be felt. Confused, he continued to press and feel for a contusion.

"Did you hear that? It came from in there." A voice echoed through from one of the adjoining shafts.

Chapter 11

Panicking, Theron scrambled to his feet and dived into a shaft behind him. He peered around the corner and watched as two Higher Intellects, dressed from head to toe in chemical suits, rushed into the cavern.

"Are you sure it came from in here?" one asked the other.

"You know the stones play tricks on the mind, it's probably nothing."

"I am so sure I heard something." The two Higher Intellects looked around the room. "Oh you're probably right. At least it was just a noise and I didn't kill myself like the others."

Believing it was a trick of the mind, the two men exited the cavern, allowing Theron to let out a massive sigh of relief. Holding the locket tightly in his hand, while it hung around his neck, Theron headed for the passageway to the Joining Room. Terrified to be caught in the mind-altering pull of the Shadow Stones once more, he kept his gaze down.

The passageway was pitch black, so much so that Theron could not even see his feet below or his hands in front of his face. With one hand feeling for the coarse damp wall, he slowly moved one foot in front of the other. The ground felt uneven, and crunched and cracked with every step he took.

"What in the...argh!" he cried out as the unsteady varying heights of the floor caused him to stumble and fall.

Feeling around for stable ground to push up on, Theron fell again, dropping his baton as the rubble disintegrated under foot. When feeling around for his weapon failed, he opened up his locket to allow the Light Stone to illuminate the room.

"Oh my." He could not believe his eyes. Hundreds, maybe thousands of skulls and bones littered the passageway. "There you are."

Now with the baton back in hand and his path lit, Theron skipped through the tunnel as though he was running along hot rocks. The pathway made of bone seemed to carry on forever, but eventually he made it to the end. Light managed to break through the gaps in the slats of the hatch above. Theron closed the locket before carefully cracking open the hatch to check for any guards. No one was around. The Akaveash Colosseum was empty. He threw open the hatch and pulled himself out of the passageway. Theron was back where he never thought he would be again. Right back in the heart of Centre City. A flitting moment of melancholy was over and done in an instant.

Theron closed over the hatch and rushed to the doors to the Great Hall. Once again, he gently cracked open the door to check for company. Drunken Upper Citizens of Randtyph stumbled through the halls, on their way back to their living quarters, after a night of ale, Quaba and frivolity.

"Come on, I'll be here all night," he said to himself, anxiously waiting for a clear path to the archives.

Time passed, but there was no relief from the inebriated personnel passing through the halls in dribs and drabs. He could not wait any longer, so he slipped out from behind the door and rushed with his head down, across the hall to the ceiling-high golden doors of the Havshad Archive. As they were too focussed on flirting and laughing amongst themselves, Theron managed to transit the range of the journey and enter the archives undetected.

Eternal flames burned brightly above, lighting the walkway down the centre of the room. At the end of the walkway sat Keeper Thon's marble desk, and above it, the scroll. Theron beamed as he strolled between the sky high, knowledge-filled shelves. From the well-lit walkway to the shadowed wall where the scroll hung, his joy and pride were unfaltering. It only took a small jump for Theron to be able to rip down the large blank scroll. After rolling up the scroll, he ripped the top off a leather alchemist tube and packed the parchment neatly inside. Not wasting any time, he jammed the lid back on and threw the belt over his shoulder.

"That wasn't so bad." He chuckled to himself.

Full of gumption and feeling cocky, he was almost prancing as he strutted back towards the doorway.

"Vrack...vorf..." Theron counted down the last five rows of marble shelves in Sharish, the native tongue of old Vexora. "Rawn...troh...aka–"

The moment Theron stepped past the final row, the doors started to open. Somebody was coming. He had to hide. Attempting to spin and sprint in the opposite direction on the marble floor, caused Theron to slip and stumble. There was no other option, he would have to hide in the dark shadow at the end of the gap between the first two rows. Theron crouched down and found a gap between the scrolls and books to watch. Watch as the Higher Powers entered with Drathon Telema.

"My Lords, thank you for meeting me. We have a situation," Drathon announced.

Marra El stepped forward. "The problem is far greater than you think, Captain."

"That's exactly what I...wait a minute...what do you mean?"

Marra El did not reply. Only the rasp of the inhale and exhale of air was heard.

Drathon became infuriated with the act of disrespect. "Do not ignore me. I have done everything asked of me. I am the Captain of the Shadow Empire's Royal Guard. You make us live with no currency, no wealth, while you think I don't know the real reason you called that audience of the Empire. I know about the Quaba sales, so fuck y–"

His snarl was interrupted by a flick of Marra El's gauntlet finger. The flick throwing Drathon against the wall above the golden doors.

"You need to humble yourself, Captain. You would be keen to remember your place and show humility when in our presence." Opening his hand slowly as his words echoed around the room.

"Sorry...my...Lord..." Drathon struggled.

Nipping and searing pain bounced across the back of Drathon's head where it had burst open from colliding with the wall. Like a piece of fabric pulled tight, Marra El's opening gauntlet stretched Drathon's skeleton beneath his skin. Cricking and cracking as he attempted to scream out in agony. His face began to redden and blew under the stress and pressure. Bubbling and salivating at the mouth. Ringing bells in his head turned to cracks of pain, as the cataclysmic storm of torture tore through every fibre of his being.

Dropping his gauntlet back below his shadowed cloak, Marra El released Drathon, causing him to crash to the floor.

"Now kneel and speak," the demonic echo of Marra El's voice ordered.

Drathon got to his feet and marched with purpose to where his masters stood, before kneeling in front of them. Blood ran from the back of his head and trickled into his mouth. The metallic taste of the warm crimson droplets

"My Lords, the Grandors are killing Hav Guard. It's not safe to drop off stiffs anymore," Drathon whimpered.

"And what of the missions you were set?"

"Nothing. There's absolutely nothing in the city about where the transporter jumped to and the prisoner won't crack. No matter how much we beat him, he won't say a word." Drathon's head hung low, too afraid of what might happen should he look up.

"We have our suspicions on where it went. Our brothers on Eissol will clean up your mess. While the Hav Guard have grown to disappoint, they have grown to destroy and look likely to replace YOUR army, as the Hav Guard of the Shadow Empire." The eternal flames flickered from a gust of wind as Marra El raised his voice.

"My Lord, I would burn the Outer System to the ground for you. What can I do to prove this to you? Want me to kill the prisoner, just say," Drathon rambled as he panicked.

Karantha El eerily floated forward. "I have grown weary of his presence, let us take our leave, brother."

"The Grandors killed only three of the four. We are being blocked by another power, just as we are with your mute prisoner. No more raids. Begin the prisoner's conversion. If the elixir doesn't loosen his tongue, he will die RESISTING." Marra El's voice crashed like a thundering storm over Drathon.

With another gust of wind and flicker of flame, the Higher Powers disappeared into the darkness of the shadows, leaving Drathon on his knees, whimpering.

"AAAH!" he screamed at the top of his lungs.

Just as he had gained control, it was all slipping away. Everything Drathon had dreamed of, from Captain of the Hav Guard, to his chances of retiring on a planet far away from here. Maybe a planet with vast grassy plains, lots of jungles and wildlife like Barashanda. Or a planet of great wealth, where a retired Captain would be classed as royalty among the upper echelons of society. A planet such as Octdrevion One, the home of the Council of Courts. A spokesperson from each of the Shadow Empire's planets resided here. Bartering deals for weapons and provisions to keep their planet thriving and their luxurious pockets lined. Either way, he knew it was all slipping away and if things kept going this way, he would be retiring on Eissol.

Furious, Drathon jumped up and energised his baton in the direction of the rows of marble shelves. BOOM!

Chapter 11

The ceiling-high shelves disintegrated. Marble and golden shrapnel flew in all directions. Parchment and books exploded into the air. Theron was thrown, crashing into the wall.

"Argh–" he moaned, cut off as he was knocked unconscious and covered in rubble as it rained down.

BOOM! BOOM! BOOM! Again and again, Drathon energised his baton. Each bubble of energy ripping through the screen of dust and flying rubble, causing it to swirl and twirl into a vortex. Before initiating another round of chaos, with each crashing collision against another set of shelves.

After taking a few deep breaths and looking at the destruction he had caused, Drathon twirled his baton on the palm of his gauntlet and then holstered it and stormed out of the archives. Frothing with rage. The room fell silent, while the flames danced around in the dust that lingered in the air. Piles of debris now replaced the rows and rows of shelves. A lifeless space of callous desolation.

***

Yvanny watched from her doorway as the first hint of light attempted to break through the darkness of the night along the horizon. Gripping at her chest where her Light Stone locket had once sat.

"Where are you, Theron?" she muttered to herself.

Letting the sheet door fall back in place behind her, Yvanny walked back into the centre of her home. She dropped into a sitting position on the floor and closed her eyes. Channelling her mind to feel for any presence of Theron. Any sign of life. Even just a flicker or hint to give her hope. Her face reddened and beaded with sweat the more she struggled. Straining and toiling under the pressure of scouring through the pathways of the mind walking web. Person to person. Over and over. Again and again. From one person to the next. Without her Light Stone, her power was too weak to home in on Theron, so she had to adventitiously search with uncertainty.

"I can feel you, my love. It has been far too long. Come back to us and all will be forgiven." The demonic voice of Karantha El echoed through Yvanny's mind.

Dark storm clouds followed the voice. Rumbling and cracking, polluting the pathways of the mind walking web that Yvanny was channelling and searching for Theron.

"Karantha El, you never change. Still weak and insignificant next to your older brother?" Yvanny replied.

"Oh, quite the contrary." Karantha El's voice echoed into a maniacal chuckle.

Zap! Crash! A pulse of painful electricity tore through Yvanny's body before she was slammed and pinned against the ceiling.

"It is you that that seems to be the weak one, sister," Karantha El stated as he let Yvanny fall to the floor. "Pathetic how frail you have become since turning your back on us."

Chapter 11

Zap! Crack! Zap! With each bolt of electricity coursing through her body, Yvanny writhed and groaned. Her bones popping and cracking with every distorted position her body spasmed into.

"Blugh..." Yvanny coughed, spraying blood onto the ground in front of her. "You may kill me, but you are too late...the child born of light from shadow is coming. The prophecy that you think is over will be your end."

"Argh! I shall destroy your mind and then, I will come for your body," Karantha El's voice screamed out.

Zap! Crack! Zap! Over and over again, Karantha El caused Yvanny's body to twist and turn on the ground. Yelping in pain with every jolt. Blood poured from her mouth, ears and nose. Sinking into the deep creases of her wrinkled skin.

"Yvanny!" A voice broke through the dark storm clouds in Yvanny's mind.

Faint light started to appear, through the screen of dark decay and terrified screams, of loved ones calling out her name for help, reaching for her to save them, that now clogged, congested and choked the pathways.

Theron, battered and bruised, drenched in a clouded white paste of shards, splinters and chips mixed with sweat, tears and blood, had dragged himself back into Yvanny's home to find her writhing on the floor. He had no idea what was happening. Who or what was attacking her? Rushing to her aid, he attempted to hold her to stop her body contorting. Yvanny's spasming limbs were firing out like spears, but Theron would not give up. Broken or bruised, he would do anything for this woman who was quickly becoming a mother figure to him.

"Please Yvanny, tell me what to do? Please!" Theron cried out.

"Lock...lock...locket..." Yvanny struggled.

"You could have been the Shadow Queen," Karantha El's voice echoed in her mind. "Pitiful. I am going to enjoy this. Goodbye, Angel of the Light."

Theron ripped the locket off and placed it around the neck of Yvanny. The moment the locket touched her chest, the attack ended. Yvanny's body fell limp in his arms. Her face soaked in moisture and blood. Her eyes closed. Motionless.

"No, no, no. Please don't be dead. Please, Yvanny. Please don't be dead." Theron wept, pulling Yvanny's body in close to his.

"Looks like you got yourself into a bit of bother, my boy," Yvanny quietly rasped.

Theron pulled Yvanny's face away from his shoulder in disbelief that he had heard her voice.

"Yvanny!" he yelped, pulling her in tight into his embrace.

"Ow, ow...I am a bit delicate just now." Pressing her hands gently against Theron to signal him to release his grip. "Did you get it? Did you get the scroll?"

"Yes, it's over there, but there's something else. Feroshi will be one of them or one of the Faded very soon. His time for the elixir has come." Theron helped Yvanny sit up straight as he knelt in front of her. "Do you want to tell me what was going on just now? You looked like you were in real trouble."

Yvanny's eyes widened. Using Theron to support her weight, she forced herself to her feet. Groaning and wincing as she strained.

"What are you doing? You need to rest," Theron gasped.

"You walked in on Karantha El and I having a little disagreement. He is far more powerful than I feared. It will not be long before they come looking for me but, more importantly...we have to save Feroshi."

Slumping onto his backside, Theron was filled with fear. Like a dam bursting, the thought of the Higher Powers knowing where he was poured over him. Saturating him with anxiety and doubt. The soul breaking hell he had just gone through to get the scroll. The pain. The close calls. Near death by asphyxiation due to almost being buried alive. It all seemed so minor compared to facing the Higher Powers.

Chapter 12

Solar storms were a common occurrence in the Cosfordia. A galaxy with three suns sitting in the centre like three points of an equilateral triangle, each five hundred million kilometres away from the next. Gases given off by each sun would often mix, causing the storms in the galaxy. Breath-taking greens, oranges and purples would tear across the sky. Like a canvas being splashed with colours doing the dance of battle for all to see.

This galaxy, at one point in time, was home to thirteen planets, spinning on their axis, following the next corkscrewing around the suns. The fourteenth planet sat proudly in the centre of this trinity of stars: Laborine. Gravity from the three suns, pulling with just enough pressure to gently rotate the planet in an eternal ray of beautiful life-giving light.

Within days of every planet bound by the Akaveashen Cosmic Web Agreement, across the entire Universe, becoming the Shadow Empire, Laborine disappeared and Pharala, which was later annexed and renamed Octdrevion Five, was destroyed by the Emperor during the war for

Randtyph. Now all that remained of Laborine was the asteroid field that filled its space, like a graveyard of rock formed headstones. Or so the Shadow Empire thought.

Small sparks of electricity rippled and whipped, dancing about space in the Cosfordia. Ripples becoming waves. Building and building like a crescendo of energy. Spinning into a cyclone and opening up the exit.

"Ahhhhh," the trio screamed in adrenaline-filled fear as they came tearing out the other end of the Space Jump, through the Cosmic Web wormhole. Screaming to a halt while the exit dissipated.

"I'm going to be sick," yelled Simeskey, hurling her upper body to the side to vomit.

"Me too." Immediately followed by Ranoa.

"Me three." And finally Shajo.

Retching eventually turned to wiping spit and phlegm away from their mouths. Simeskey rested her head against the head-rest of her seat, looking at all the switches and dials that were directly above her head in the cockpit. The control panels had been illuminated previously. Now the once constant light, flickered intermittently. She wiped the tears and cold sweat away from her face, before turning to check on the state of her travelling companions.

"Are we all still alive?" Simeskey asked aloud.

Shajo pressed against his arm rest to sit upright in his seat. "Come back to me, I'm still not sure."

"Yes, I'm still here. Well, that was an experience," Ranoa said as he began to flick at switches randomly. "Just so you know, I have no idea what I'm doing here. Something has got to get us moving again."

CRACK! CLUNK! The two noises rang out, immediately followed by a great shudder of the transporter.

"What was that?" screamed Shajo, gripping onto his armrests for dear life. "We are going to die. I knew I shouldn't have got onto this transporter. I knew it. I knew it."

"Shajo!" Simeskey yelled. "We are going to be okay...I hope."

"Look." Ranoa pointed out the cockpit window to the underslung engine floating away into space.

Eyes bounced from one person to the next. Neither one of the trio knowing who to look at. All the faces were covered in fear and panic. But before any of them had a chance to question what to do next, a noise of metal being slightly compressed rocked the transporter. Gently the vessel started to yaw to the right.

"Can we panic now?" Shajo blurted out.

The marooned transporter creaked and groaned as it rotated, slowly bringing the galactic ocean of asteroids into view of the cockpit's windows. Suddenly a shunt initiated a pulling motion in the direction of the rocks.

"Yes, Shajo, I think we can start to panic now," Simeskey said through gritted teeth. Her knuckles white from the weight of her grip on the armrests of her chair.

"There's got to be something!" Ranoa exclaimed, swatting at buttons and switches.

Chapter 12

Slowly, but surely, the transporter was being pulled towards its certain destruction. With no training or understanding of the technology, Simeskey and Shajo joined in with the frantic attempt to save their lives. Small flickers of light around the consoles repeatedly raised hopes, but just as quickly as they would be raised, the blackout of the lighting would extinguish any optimism.

"Guys, please stop." Simeskey had given up panicking. If she was going to die here and now, she would not suffer twice by fearing death and the anticipation. "Hold my hands and close your eyes."

"We can't just give up. I didn't get off that prison to die in some heap of junk." Shajo spoke rapidly as his actions became frenzied.

"Shajo, stop!" Ranoa yelled, rushing up behind his partner and placing his hands on top of Shajo's.

Turning Shajo gently to face him, Ranoa embraced Shajo and kissed him on his cheek. A tender and sweet goodbye to the man he loved. His best friend. His life. The salty taste of the tears dripped through the cracks in Ranoa's lips.

"It's okay, my love. Just close your eyes and it will be over before you know it." Ranoa spoke softly as he wiped the tears away from Shajo's cheeks.

After a few deep breaths and wiping down his face, Shajo offered out his hands to Simeskey and Ranoa. The three looked from one set of eyes to the next. Each face covered with a smile but full of sadness.

"I'm sorry we failed you, Simeskey," Ranoa said.

"You didn't fail me, Ranoa. We are going to die free. Most of the Outer System never get that chance." Simeskey smiled and took one last look over her shoulder at the oncoming asteroid field, before closing her eyes and squeezing tightly on the hands of her companions.

It would only be a few more seconds until the transporter would collide with rocks and be obliterated. For a small moment, it seemed as though Simeskey's final words had helped them all find peace in their final moments. The quiet was not long lived though.

Shajo could not resist, he needed to open his eyes. "Ahhhhh!"

"Oh no..." Shajo's scream had caused the other two sets of eyes to bolt open, with Simeskey being the first to notice what was causing the terror.

An enormous rock was hurtling through the asteroid field, headed directly for the transporter. Faster and faster, it closed the space. Larger and larger it grew. Dwarfing the vessel a hundred times over. Here it was. The end. All options had been exhausted and their fate had been excepted.

"I love you, Feroshi!" Simeskey yelled as the planet sized rock collided with the transporter.

Her mind thought back to the first time she ever laid eyes on Feroshi. It hadn't been at the Joining Ceremony, but a few days before. Children from the Outer System were begging for food at the market while she had been collecting water. Two Hav Guard patrolling had noticed the children and began to belittle and bully. Pushing them to the ground.

Stepping on the backs of their heads to make them eat the dirt. All she could do was try and ignore it, until she saw a young Ruevanlynn peering round the side of the water pump shack, using his hands to signal to somebody she could not see.

Fascinated by this strange behaviour, she watched as the skinny Ruevanlynn, who even at a young age loved to have a rag bandana around his head, continued to signal as if to himself. What was he doing? And then she saw him... her Feroshi. With both Hav Guard heckling as they forced the starving children to eat dirt from the floor, Ruevanlynn whistled. Like a call to war the whistle unleashed Feroshi. From the shadows between the homes, he tore across the clearing with a wooden pot in each hand. CLANG! CLANG! Crashing the pots into the outside of each of the guards' masks. Knocking them to the ground.

"Run." Feroshi motioned to the two young children to follow him.

Paralysed with fear, they couldn't move. Simeskey looked around in disbelief at what she was seeing. Two younglings fighting back. She wanted to help, but as she started to head in the direction of the two frozen children, Ruevanlynn sprinted past her. In one motion he grabbed both children by the scruff of their tattered clothing, dragging them with him.

It wasn't the violence he had displayed that left her longing for him that night. It was his courage. For her as a girl, this was the first time she felt like a woman. He had stirred an emotion and hunger for another person that she had never felt before. Fate answered her prayers a few days later when she turned to see Feroshi on the other side of the curtain with her. He was hers and she was his. Simeskey gently sighed, finding peace in her memories.

Realising she had been caught up in her thoughts for longer than expected, Simeskey opened her eyes. "Guys, guys, look."

"Nope, I am quite happy to die with my eyes closed, thank you very much," Shajo cried out.

Ranoa glanced through one eye, then opened the other. "Well would you look at that."

The collision never happened. The asteroid field was no more. Now, their beautiful sanctuary was finally in view. Laborine was a mixture of beautiful masses of green, blue and orange. No curtains covering any of the land.

Entering the atmosphere, vast populations came into view. Men, women and children racing each other through the skies on Ravelons (a large four winged, hypogriff like creature. Covered in dark brown feathers, apart from the tips of their three tails, which never changed from pure pearly white. Two beautiful golden eyes and ears that retract in flight. As the ears retract the claws on the end of their four legs, extend to talons. The only thing sharper than their talons, the tip of their beaks).

Farms stretched further than the eye could see where magnificently bright vegetation grew. People waved from below as the transported zipped through the air. Simeskey,

Chapter 12

Ranoa and Shajo were all pressed hard against the cockpit windows trying to get a better look at a population that lived free.

"I'm going to take a wild guess here and say that's where we are headed." Ranoa pointed to a compound becoming visible in the distance.

Four large sand-coloured walls, with a grand archway for an entrance with a palm tree either side, surrounded a small town that looked very different from the rest of the planet they had seen on their descent. All three caught a glimpse of something very familiar inside the walls, right before the transporter lowered towards the ground outside the compound, Light Stones.

With no underslung engine, the bare flat hull of the transporter slammed against the golden sand below with a loud thud. Jarring and throwing the three passengers across the vessel.

"Oh, my head." Simeskey winced as she felt a raised bump where her head had crashed against the inside of the transporter.

"Is everyone ok?" Ranoa asked as he picked himself up off the ground.

"Yeah, we'll survive. Now then, what's the plan?" Shajo made his way to the cockpit window. "We've got company."

Simeskey and Ranoa rushed to the window. From between the two palm trees appeared three figures. At the rear, two females dressed in white warrior attire, both bearing pure white spears in hand. Leading the way was a small, skinny, frail man, dressed in white robes. Using a white wooden staff to help him hobble along. Even from a distance the roundness of his face was apparent.

"Come on, let's go and say hello," Simeskey said with a smile.

"Hold up." Shajo grasped Simeskey's arm gently. "How do we know they're friendly?"

"Shajo, let her go. This isn't Octdrevion Six anymore, we have to give them a chance." Ranoa placed his hand on Shajo's shoulder before heading for the exit hatch at the back of the transporter.

Simeskey gave a sympathetic smile as she passed the disgruntled Shajo. Lifting the safety panel to reveal the controls, Ranoa pulled on the escape leaver, causing jets of air to hiss before the door fired onto the ground a few metres away from the vessel. Without hesitation, Ranoa disembarked, hopping down onto the sand.

"Down you come, beautiful." Ranoa turned and offered his hand to Simeskey.

"Thank you." Simeskey gleefully accepted Ranoa's help. She turned back to the transporter and rested her chin on the step she had just leaped from and looked up at the one remaining passenger. "Please, Shajo."

"Fine then." With a roll of his eyes Shajo made his way off the transporter.

The moment Shajo's feet touched the ground, Simeskey wrapped her arms around him gratefully. Not even the distrusting and pessimistic thoughts running rampant in his mind, could stop Shajo from smiling as he was embraced. The moment of smiles was short lived as the footsteps of the approaching trio came into earshot.

"Get behind me," Shajo ordered.

The old man's gaze never left the ground, whereas the two females never broke eye contact with Shajo and Ranoa.

"That's close enough," Ranoa ordered, raising his hand. "Do you know why we are here?"

Step after hobbled step, the old man paid no attention to the commands from Ranoa.

"I said STO–" Ranoa took a step forward as he raised his voice.

Before he could finish his command, one of the females launched herself high into the air, like she had taken flight and came crashing down on top of Ranoa. Shajo pounced immediately, but like a flash of light, the tip of her spear was pressed against his windpipe, as her knee pinned Ranoa to the floor by his chest of his blue flight suit.

"You will watch your tongue when you speak, or I will feed it to you." Applying more pressure to Ranoa's chest as she stared into his eyes.

Simeskey stood stunned. Had she just convinced Shajo to leave the transporter just to get him killed? Was Ranoa bound for death for trying to protect her?

"Please, stop. Don't hurt them, they are only trying to protect me," Simeskey begged and pleaded.

"Thank you, Nalana, you can get off him now. They are friends." The old man stopped, only a few yards away from the downed Ranoa. "Please, help him to his feet and then if the three of you could follow me inside."

Nalana smirked at Ranoa as she dismounted him and offered her hand. Reluctantly he accepted once the point of her spear was no longer pressed against Shajo's throat.

"Hey, old man, we're not going anywhere with you until you tell us–" Shajo started.

SLAP! Nalana slapped her spear against the cheek of Shajo.

"That's twice you've raised your weapon to me. Next time–" Shajo caught the spear in his hand before it collided against his face once more. "You trying to get dead!"

"Enough!" The old man crashed his staff into the sand causing a shockwave to ripple through the ground. His gown gusting up over his ankles, showing his bare feet. "Now, follow me and we shall all get better acquainted over some tea and mountain boar. Oh, and by the way, welcome to Laborine."

There was a pause while Ranoa, Simeskey and Shajo looked at each other. Deciding what to do without words. Reading the slightest of facial cues. Finally they all nodded.

"Grand. Now do be careful when you enter the town. The market is always in full swing at this time, so stay close. Don't want you getting lost." The old man smiled and headed for the archway.

Walking behind the old man and his two compatriots, Ranoa analysed Nalana. From her tied back, braided dark brown hair, to her white skin-tight outfit, identical to the one Simeskey was wearing. The jangle of her golden bracelets. Skin, perfect and unblemished, yet she attacked like a seasoned warrior. In stature, he dwarfed her. How had she overpowered him? How had she managed to leap into the air like that?

The second female escorting the old man had long flowing brunette hair that fell freely down her back. Her only difference in attire was the white cloak attached at the shoulders to her suit. She had remained quiet and close to the old man during the commotion. Never leaving his side.

"Wow." Simeskey gazed up at the size of the two palm trees marking either side of the archway.

"I am going to guess that these two trees are the closest you have come to seeing the real beauty of nature," the old man said.

Scents of intoxicating perfumes, cooking meats and vegetables enchanted their sense of smell. The marketplace was set up in two rows, each one along the edge of the wall, leaving a clear walkway down the middle. Behind the stalls, growing along the wall line, the diamond formations of the Light Stones, standing tall and radiating light all around. Noises of people bartering, chuckling and discussing everyday life seemed so alien to the new arrivals. Never had they seen so many people, of different ways of life, conversing as one without the fear of consequence.

"This is incredible." Simeskey was in pure awe.

"It is a beautiful sight to behold. A population made of many that have become one," the old man replied.

"If it is so beautiful, then why do you stay so far away from the main group of the population? Wouldn't have anything to do with the fact you're growing the Empire's fuel here, would it?" Ranoa queried incredulously.

"We shall talk inside. Not here." The old man carried on down the path.

"Talk inside. You'll talk to me now."

"Inside there." The old man pointed, with his staff, to a large temple sat at the end of the pathway, ignoring any command given to him by Ranoa.

Eight white stone steps led up to six gigantic pillars supporting the front of the stone roof. Either side of each pillar stood two warriors. Beautiful women of all colours, shapes and sizes. Dressed in their skin-tight white suits and armed with their spears. Behind the pillars sat the entrance to the large hall of the temple. In the centre of the hall, a banquet table with four seats either side and a throne at the top. To be sat in throne, had you positioned front and centre of the point of worship, the statue of the Turach Vro Aka.

There was a dull clink with each arrival of the staff on the stone steps, supporting the weight of the old man making his way to the entrance of the temple. His two guards following closely, only a step behind. The moment his staff connected with the stone floor, after the final step, the twelve warriors came to attention. A harmonic crack of thunder rung out from the sound of twelve spears landing in unison.

Chapter 12

Reluctantly, Shajo and Ranoa followed their hosts into the temple. Constantly looking around and over their shoulders to check for a surprise attack or ambush. Even in the hustle and bustle of the crowded marketplace, everybody was smiling and bartering with no fear of an authority. Being born and raised on Octdrevion Six had caused a base layer of paranoia and distrust in the two men. Every little sound caused the hairs on the back of their necks to rise and small pulses of adrenaline to rush through their bodies. Simeskey did not seem to have this distrust. She happily followed. Not even the guards coming to attention caused her to jump.

"Please, take a seat. Food and drink will be out momentarily." The old man motioned to the table as he headed straight for his throne at the top of the table.

The two top seats, either side of the table, were taken by Nalana and the other female guard. There was no pause from Simeskey, who immediately took the first seat she could, followed by Shajo. The only seat remaining for Ranoa was next to Nalana.

Shajo let out a chuckle of laughter as Ranoa paced behind the available seat.

"Come now, you wouldn't be scared to sit next to me, would you?" Nalana jeered, patting the chair.

"Ugh." Ranoa scoffed before sitting on the seat and pulling himself into the table. "Happy?"

The old man rested his staff against the table and then plonked himself down on his throne. He then proceeded to remove five large golden chains from underneath his robe, and hung them on hooks at the end of the table. Each bearing a different symbol from the next.

Within seconds of the old man hanging his final medallion, servers, all adorned in white gowns with a golden rope belt tied around the waist, began to serve refreshments. It took four servers to carry the large mountain boar on its silver dish. Not one of the three new arrivals had ever seen anything like this. Freshly cooked meat. Flavoured teas. Fruit and vegetables, with more colour than a person from the Outer System of Randtyph would see in a hundred lifetimes. Shajo's mouth drooled from inhaling the intoxicating odours of the feast laid out.

"You all must be starving, so please, eat," the old man encouraged.

Shajo smiled as he ripped chunks of meat from the boar while Simeskey gently sipped her tea.

"Wow, this tastes amazing," Simeskey gasped.

"Ranoa, why won't you eat?" the old man asked, his head still low.

"You can't blame me for being a bit untrusting. You won't tell us who you are or what this place is. Worst of all, there's a damn statue of the Turach Vro Aka behind you." Ranoa's eyes were locked onto the old man. "We are supposed to be here to find a Mage of the Light in the Land of the Broken Wing. Can you help us or not?"

Finally the old man raised his head. His piercing blue eyes met the gaze of Ranoa's. He paused as he ran his hands through his long grey beard.

"Ranoa, please. They are just trying to help us," Simeskey pleaded from across the table.

"It is okay, my dear, he is right to be curious. After the life you have lived, I wouldn't trust you if you weren't." The old man chuckled. "Every answer you need is right here."

"Well, I guess you must be the mage then, because you speak in riddles the exact same way my father does." Trusting tones began to creep into Ranoa's voice.

"No riddles, my boy, but you are right, I am Scotunya the Wiseman. I am the final Mage of the Light." Scotunya bowed his bald head. "You and Nalana are already well acquainted, so no introductions are needed. This beautiful spirit here is Emla, and everything inside the four walls outside is the Land of the Broken Wing."

"Honestly, this is the best thing I've ever tasted," Shajo blurted, causing meat and liquid to spray out of his mouth. "Sorry, were you saying something?"

There was a united laugh around the table.

"Simeskey, how are you, my dear?" Scotunya asked softly.

Simeskey dabbed her hand against her lips to make sure she did not have any excess food or fluids around her mouth.

"I am just worried about Feroshi, sir. Can I ask how you know who we are?"

"There are eyes and ears all across the Cosmic Web and where there are eyes, I can see. We have waited for the child born of light from shadow to rise, for a very long time. Feroshi must battle the darkness on his own for now. You three are safe here." Scotunya hopped off the throne and grabbed his staff. "For now, I must take my leave. Nalana will show you to your living space in the temple. Emla my love, can you please carry my medallions for me."

Nalana stood up from her seat as Scotunya made his way behind the statue of the Turach Vro Aka.

"If you three are finished eating, let's get you off to bed," Nalana said.

Shajo stuffed a few more handfuls of boar meat into his mouth while pushing his chair back.

"Nalana, why do they call this place the Land of the Broken Wing?" Simeskey asked.

"We do not speak of it because of the pain we endured. That is why most of the inhabitants of this planet live away from the temple. Coming here only for the market. Nobody needs a reminder of the suffering they have had to endure to get here. If you read the golden plaque on the statue, it will hopefully explain more than I can." Nalana pointed to the golden rectangle near the base of the statue.

All three walked over to the statue as Nalana kept a watchful eye.

"Simeskey, you are the best at reading. Do you want to take this one?" Shajo asked.

"It reads, '*For the Angels that no longer feel the pain. For the Angels that did not lose their wings in vein. In an eternal sleep you watch. The prophecy we shall keep. We remember you and we wait for you. A child born of Light from Shadow, the odious masters of the darkness they shall smite.*' But, Nalana, why do you have such a beautiful memorial on a symbol of such evil?"

"The Turach Vro Aka is not a talisman of evil, Simeskey. Of power, yes, but not evil." Nalana shared a smile with Simeskey before turning away. "Now follow me please."

No sooner than Nalana had turned away, a flurry of servers made their way into the hall to clear away the banquet table and chairs. Leaving only the throne.

The quartet made their way to the rear of the statue, travelling down the opposite side to that which Scotunya and Emla had used to exit earlier. They walked down a long stone corridor with cherry wooden doors on either side. Each door with a name etched onto the exterior.

"You three will find your rooms at the end of this hall. As you can see your door will be marked with your name. Simeskey, tomorrow Scotunya would like to spend some time with you."

"What about us? The old man not wanting to spend some time with the two of us?" Shajo barked.

"You boys better get your rest. Tomorrow, you learn how to fight with the Angels. If you're good enough I might even teach you how to ride a Ravelon. Since you can't match me in combat, you might have a better chance at a game of Carou Dale." Nalana smiled and watched as Simeskey, Ranoa and Shajo made their way into their separate rooms.

"Can't match me in combat, meh meh meh," Shajo muttered to himself, mockingly imitating Nalana as he entered his room.

Bright light was pouring into Simeskey's room through her window. She was amazed by how clean and pure everything looked. From the soft bed to the faucets and wash pan. No damp. No dust. The natural smell of dirt she had become so accustomed to, had now been replaced with a beautiful perfumed scent. Even the still air that lingered in the room had a comforting warmth to it.

Taking it all in, she made her way to the window. Airborne wildlife flying free in the sky. Families joking and playing together. Everything about this place was filling her with joy. Rolling onto her bed, she let out a sigh of air. It was as though she was expelling all the bad energy from her past. Feeling at the quilted cover underneath she realised that she was alone. She had friends and allies around her, but she did not have her love. Sadness filled her heart as sleep took her.

Waking, the light was as bright as it was when she had fallen asleep. She sat up to see Scotunya sitting on a stool beside her bed.

"Morning, sleepy head. Would you do me the great honour of joining me on a walk?" he asked, offering her his hand.

"How long was I asleep for?" she asked, getting to her feet.

"You've been asleep for a couple of days. I sensed you stirring so I have been waiting here for this moment."

"Two days! Yeah, let's take that walk."

Walking out of the walled-off market revealed green pastures and beautiful waterfalls. Racing up and down were

Ravelons mounted by Ranoa, Shajo and Nalana. Throwing energy spears at targets that would explode and disappear when hit. Reforming at a different location.

"Looks like they all became the best of friends fast." Simeskey laughed. "So, can you be honest with me please. Will I ever see Feroshi again?"

Scotunya paused and brushed his hands through the grass, plucking a few blades to throw into the wind.

"My ability of foresight has long passed, I'm afraid, my dear. Hold onto hope." He let the blades of grass spin, whirl and twirl in his hand. "Hope can flicker a blinding light, even in the darkest of shadows, in the never ending, ominous corridors of the broken mind. All one needs to do is believe. Believe that there can be hope and the smallest spark can become a raging inferno of light. Just give yourself that chance to believe."

Chapter 13

Crashing waves, beating against the walls of the Prison Zone and the constant drip, drip, drip, of the condensation droplets falling, drowned out the slight clink of Feroshi's chains. Beaten, starved and dehydrated, there was no fight as he hung by his shackles. His knees were scabbed and wheeping from dragging against the ragged stone floor as he slightly swayed. Feroshi's long dark hair clung to the moisture and dried blood matted into his beard. His once dark brown eyes, now barely visible through the black and blue of bruising and swelling.

Drathon Telema had assigned a special detail of four Hav Guard to constantly torment Feroshi. Taking it in turns to enjoy their attempt to extract data or information from him. Very soon after the assignment of this detail, the men dispensed with the pleasantries of asking questions. Instead, they beat Feroshi until they were bored or tired, always making sure to leave him a few steps away from death. Once the Hav Guard were done with their torture for the day, Lieutenant Relta Brack, Troop Commander Niloc

Ecurb's most trusted Lieutenant, would tend to Feroshi. Feeding him water and injecting him with high dosages of nutrients, pain medications and sedatives. The Hav Guard had no idea that they may as well have been punching a stone wall, because Feroshi was obliviously unaware in his drug induced state of numbness. In a dream world far from the deplorable, dark, dingy, doorless hole that was now his home.

A dream of a land Feroshi did not know. Fresh clean air. Meadows of green grass. Beautiful mountain ranges and flowing rivers. Looking down at his feet they were bare, but he could feel every blade as though he was there.

"This can't be real. Where am I?" He spoke aloud, looking around in amazement.

Golden cuffs appeared on his wrists, along with soft white bottoms that tightened around the ankles. He felt at his face and then his head. His hair was tied back and beard soft and well kept. Large white birds cawed as they passed overhead. Feroshi began to run in the direction they were flying. Laughing at the feeling of freedom and strength.

"This can't be in my head, I've never seen anything like this."

Smiling and spinning around to gaze at the vast layers of beauty that were surrounding him. He had to know what the fresh flowing water would feel like. Making his way towards the graceful river, he felt a rumble through the ground under his feet. It faded so he took no notice. Moments later it returned and began to build. Turning to see what could be causing it, he stumbled back and fell to the ground at the sight of two Grandors sprinting in his direction.

"Oh no," Feroshi gasped as he scrambled to his feet.

His bare feet slipped as he tried to press off again. It was too late. Fear filled Feroshi. He could feel the rumble of the ground becoming impacts, as the Grandors' large paws thumped against the ground.

Closing his eyes he began to plead with himself. "Wake up. Wake up. Wake up, Feroshi!"

He felt the warm air of the Grandor's breath and heard the low growl right next to his ear.

"Wake up! Wake up!"

"Feroshi, look at me." A female voice spoke.

Feroshi opened one eye and then the next. A woman was atop one of the Grandors. Her skin-tight, sleeveless white suit was braided with gold across the front. A mixture of golden blonde and brunette hair flowed freely over her shoulders.

"Okay this definitely isn't real. Who are you meant to be?" Feroshi asked.

"Feroshi, I'm Jillezi, your mother," she said with soft hazel eyes and a smile on her face.

Feroshi paused as he processed what she had just said.

"Look, you're right, this is not the world you live in. I live in the light within you. You're a whole lot more than you think you are," Jillezi attempted to explain.

"Okay, so let's say I believe you. I guess since I'm speaking to a dead person that can only mean I'm dead,"

Feroshi replied.

"No. Pretty close, but you'll survive. Now if you get on top of Flower there's some things I need you show you before you go back."

"Flower, what sort of name is that for a Grandor?" he said, as the Grandor allowed him to use its whiskers like a ladder to climb aboard.

"You are so much like your father." She gleamed at Feroshi before turning to her Grandor. "Come on, Blue Moon, yah."

Thrusting her hips forward with her command sent her Grandor, Blue Moon, into an excited hop and skip before it took off, sprinting across the meadow.

"Woah," Feroshi gasped as he grabbed on for dear life as Flower took chase.

Tightening his thighs against the golden fur and leaning into his Grandor, Feroshi found his balance. Fresh, warm air caressed his cheeks as he took chase after his mother. With each gallop of these powerful beasts' legs, they soared through the air, clearing large spaces of ground with ease. Feroshi had never felt so free, so exhilarated.

"Woooo!" Feroshi howled in excitement.

In the distance, a white stone feature started to become visible. Closer and closer they got, bringing more and more details into view. It was a large temple, sitting alone in this pasture of green. Approaching the temple, Jillezi brought Blue Moon to a halt and jumped down. Cuddling into Blue Moon's face and itching under his chin.

"Good boy," she thanked her majestic friend.

Feroshi arrived moments later.

"What's in there?" he asked, dismounting Flower.

Before Jillezi had a chance to answer, Flower had knocked Feroshi to the ground with its enormous coarse tongue. Slobbering and purring with happiness.

"He likes you." Jillezi laughed.

"Yes, yes, you're a good boy." Feroshi patted the cheeks of Flower as he got to his feet.

Flower circled and bounded, crouching down, looking for Feroshi to engage him in play.

"Blue, it's time to take Flower home," she said softly to her Grandor.

With a low growl command, Flower broke from his playful excitement and followed Blue Moon as they made their way out of sight. Bouncing their bodies and heads against the other, attempting to entice the other into a mischievously merry and mirthful melee. These Grandors were nothing like the ones Feroshi had come to know. The savage beasts that fed on the Faded and dragged the large loads of Light Stones, harvested from the Diamond Farm.

"Amazing, aren't they?" Jillezi asked as she watched her son gawking in awe. "Come on, Feroshi, we don't have much time. Follow me please."

Feroshi's attention turned back to his mother. He watched as she made her way up the stone steps and passed the pillars to the entrance.

"Feroshi!" Jillezi yelled from the entrance to the temple.

Chapter 13

Striding up the steps, two at a time, he rushed to catch up with Jillezi. Entering the temple, he could see there was a large round marble table with twelve seats equally spaced around it. Half the table was a brilliant white. The other half, dark purple that seemed to roll like waves under the surface. At the rear of the temple, sat a statue of the Turach Vro Aka.

"What is this place?" Feroshi asked.

"This is the Temple of Equilibrium. A long time ago the Light and the Shadow lived in peace on Vexora. Six Mages from the School of Light and six Mages from the Home of Shadows sat in council. Learning from each other, growing together. Six medallions were made, one for each of the Mages of Light to wear around their necks, whenever they were sat around the table of council. Together the symbols tell the story of Light conquering the Shadow in ancient times, but instead of vanquishing their defeated foe, they showed mercy and agreed to live in harmony. Together as one. The Light gave life and themselves to the laws of nature, but the Shadow wanted more. Their magic was unnatural and in the cover of the darkness they grew in power," Jillezi began to explain, walking past the table and heading for the statue.

"But Mum, what does this have to do with me? I'm hanging from chains in the Prison Zone. I'll be dead soon if I'm not dead already, which I am still contemplating as an option."

"Do you know the significance of the Turach Vro Aka?"

"It's a symbol of the Shadow Empire so I don't understand why you would have a statue of it here."

Jillezi ran her fingers against the statue.

"The first known Turach Vro Aka was on Vexora. A gift from the Lords of Light in the time before time. But as I said, there cannot be one without the other. The gift for good and a symbol of life, gave birth to the darkness of the Shadow Stones. The more life that was given, the more unnatural evil grew in those stones, deep beneath the mantel of the planet. In a hope to shut out the darkness, the Turach Vro Aka was destroyed, but it was too late. The Shadow Stones were now a part of Vexora. The Temple of Equilibrium was built on the ruins once the council was formed, before life as we knew it was destroyed."

"You still haven't told me what any of this has to do with me," Feroshi pressed.

Jillezi's hand dropped from the statue.

"Feroshi, the Shadow Emperor harnessed the power of the Shadow while the Light flowed through him. Only the Lord of Light can defeat him." She walked over to Feroshi and took his hands in hers. "A prophecy was foretold of a child born of light from shadow. The birth of a new Lord of Light. You are that child, Feroshi."

"Firstly, the Shadow Emperor was defeated. I can attest to that because, unlike you, I've had to live under the rule of the Higher Powers my whole life. Secondly, as I've already told you, I'm hanging by chains. Doesn't seem like something a Lord of Light would be doing now, does it?"

Chapter 13

"Feroshi, there is so much I want to tell you but there just isn't–"

A crack of thunder and dark clouds polluting the clear blue sky above, broke Jillezi's conversation.

"Son, listen to me, you need to find the final Mage of the Light, he is the only one that can unleash your true potential. Without it, you cannot defeat the Emperor. Without it, you cannot defeat the one with the darkness within," Jillezi rushed her words. "Trust Niloc..."

SLAP! Feroshi's vision was clouded and he felt strange. Groggy and sore. There was a loud clink of chains as he attempted to move to feel where he had just been slapped.

"Feroshi...please wake up..." A muffled male voice managed to break through the fog.

He was back in his cell, hanging from his chains once again.

"Feroshi, are you in there? You have to wake up. Drathon Telema is on his way and I think they want me to start conversion. If you can hear me, I've injected you with adrenaline to wake you up. Stay alive and I will get you out of here, I promise."

With a flash of light the figure in the fog was gone. Feroshi's eyes rolled as he tried to bring his vision into focus. He could hear his heartbeat racing in his ears. His muscles began to contract and tense as the adrenaline coursed through his veins. Life poured back into his beaten and broken body. His bones popped and cracked back into alignment as he pulled on his chains.

"Ahhhh!" he screamed powerfully.

The rush of energy levelled out, allowing Feroshi to centre his thoughts. Was any of what just happened real? Had he really been speaking with his mother? Who had just been in his cell? Question after question fired through his mind, until his self-interrogation was interrupted by the beam of light signalling the arrival of a guest.

"Well, well, well, looks like somebody is awake today," Drathon Telema jeered. "First time you've got to see me in my Captain's uniform. What do you think? Decided that a Captain shouldn't have his face hidden, so I've scrapped the head gear. You agree with me, don't you? Of course you do."

Drathon circled Feroshi, gloating and running the cold metal of his gauntlet across Feroshi's skin. Coming back front and centre, Feroshi met his gaze and would not break eye contact.

"Do you want to say something? Looks like you've got something on your mind. Come on, Feroshi, we're all friends here."

Feroshi remained silent, staring into Drathon's eyes as though he was staring straight into the deepest parts of his soul. He could see the darkness inside of him. He could feel it radiating from every pore of Drathon's skin.

"Well, I have some good news for you. We are moving you today. You're going to get to make some new friends down there." Drathon laughed sadistically. "Oh, before we start the move, I want to show you the adjustments I've had made to the batons."

Chapter 13

Unholstering his baton, he squeezed at the handle causing a glistening white blade to extend from the base, causing a swish as it slit through the air.

"Cuts through flesh like air. Time to bring back the old ways. Once we're done with you, I'm going to find that little lady of yours and see how easily I can cut the clothes off her body. Might even use it to turn her skin into a nice flag once I'm bored of her."

Feroshi pounced from his knees in the direction of Drathon, his chains catching him before he could reach the Captain. Snarling and frothing with rage, Feroshi struggled against his shackles to reach Drathon.

"Yes, Feroshi, now that's more like it. Keep that energy where it's at. You're going to need it," Drathon taunted, staying just out of reach of his prisoner.

Laughing at Feroshi as he struggled to get to him, Drathon prodded at the control panel on his forearm and disappeared into the beam of light.

"Ahhhh!" Feroshi yelled, pulling and jerking wildly against the chains.

Tiring from the extreme exertion of energy, Feroshi dropped back to his knees, allowing the chains to once again hold his weight. Hanging there like a dead weight, he looked to the hole in the ceiling. Staring at the darkness above, he felt the droplets of water burst with each collision against his battered and beaten face. Thinking of his mother and the things she had said. Real or not, it had left him wondering. Wondering if he was more than just a slave to the Shadow

Empire. The wonder turned to hopeful thought. The thought that he would not die here. He would survive and he would make them suffer.

Refusing to look weak any longer, Feroshi got to his feet. Standing tall, with his chest and head high, he waited for the Hav Guard to come and move him. He knew, from the overconfident gloating, that the Captain would want his new form of torture, whatever form it may take, to begin while he was present.

Predictable as Drathon was, Feroshi had not been stood tall and proud for too long before two beams of light appeared in front of him. From each stepped a black-masked Hav Guard. One with his baton out ready to strike for any reason he deemed worthy. The other a syringe by its handle.

"Hope this hurts, you skaffy bastard," the Hav Guard taunted, sticking the needle into Feroshi's neck and pulling the trigger to fire the liquid into his body. "Nighty night."

No matter how hard Feroshi fought, he could not fight the fog taking over. He blinked over and over, shaking his head but nothing worked. He felt it spread throughout his extremities, until finally his legs wobbled and gave way, his body and mind consumed by the darkness of unconsciousness. There were no meadows of green or blue skies this time. Just ominous silence, darkness and the face that haunted his dreams. Purple flames burning from the eyes.

"Who are you?" Feroshi screamed in the darkness.

"You know who I am, Feroshi," the low growl replied.

Chapter 13

SLAP! SLAP! Startled, Feroshi regained consciousness. He had to squint at first due to the intensity of the lights overhead. The stinging sensation in his face had finally registered, causing him to attempt to reach for his cheek. Trying with one hand and then the next. They were stuck. His legs also. He tried to look to see what was going on, but his head would not move either. Struggling harder and harder, but he couldn't do it. His eyes began to adjust to the light, allowing Feroshi to open his eyes. Straight ahead ran a red floor. Either side of the floor looked like glass windows. It was too hard to tell from where he was stuck.

"You can stop struggling now," Drathon Telema said, coming into view. "You were injected with a minor sedative and not so minor paralytic. Don't worry, you'll be able to move soon enough...well I say move, you're clamped to that chair so maybe not so much."

Feroshi attempted to speak, but was only able to produce a gargle and slight twitch of his upper lip.

"Buh, buh, buh," Drathon mockingly imitated Feroshi's attempts at verbal communication. "Would you like me to tell you where you are? Of course you would. We are in the lower levels of the Prison Zone. This is where we do our testing of mixing your skaffs with different elixirs made from the Shadow Stone. We may from time to time throw in a bit of genetic splicing with some of our less friendly of allies. But remember, you can't tell anybody...it's a secret."

Feroshi's fingers started to come back to life again. The euphoria that Drathon was exuding while he taunted

Feroshi, filled him with fierce feelings of wrath. Clenching his fists so tight his knuckles began to crack.

"Now on to where you fit in. You see, we have four cells here. All of them are taken by one of our 'freaks'. So, here's the rules: I'll release you and open their cells at the same time. This is now our VIP section, so out of the five of you, there will only be one survivor. I could find you a cell somewhere else, but this seems like so more fun." Drathon clapped his hands together in merciless glee.

"No," Feroshi mumbled as he unclenched his fists.

"What did you say? Speak up." Drathon moved in closer to Feroshi.

"I...said...no." Feroshi struggled.

"Release his clamps," Drathon ordered the two Hav Guard stood behind Feroshi. "Now!"

The Hav Guard pressed at a button on the back of the dark metallic seated gurney, releasing the clamps from around Feroshi's head, arms, chest, waist, legs and ankles. The clamps retracting back into the gurney.

"Get up. Get up!" Drathon moved his weight from left to right, his uncontrollable rage triggered by this act of defiance.

Pressing against the armrests, Feroshi tried with all his might to lift his body, but his legs were still dead weight. He managed to shuffle himself to the edge of the gurney before crumpling to the floor. Feroshi would not give up though. Still determined to show no weakness, he pressed his hands against the floor. His arms shaking under the pressure. The muscles bulging and twitching while the veins swelled because of the force. With his back arched at nearly ninety degrees, arms fully extended and head high, Feroshi could look Drathon in the eyes.

"No!" Feroshi shouted through gritted teeth.

Enraged, Drathon kicked Feroshi's arms out from under him. Thump! Thud! He stamped on Feroshi's back twice.

"Leave him, the freaks must be getting hungry about now," Drathon said, motioning to the door behind the gurney.

"Argh," Feroshi grunted, pushing his body up again, refusing to give in. "No!"

Drathon had nearly been out the door, but the grunt had stopped him in his tracks. Shaking with rage, he unholstered his baton, holding it tightly in hand. He stood over Feroshi, his fury only heightened by the smile on Feroshi's face. THWACK! He smashed his baton across Feroshi's face. Thud! Thump! Stamping on him twice more to make sure he stayed down.

"What do you think you're doing with my prisoner?" Troop Commander Niloc Ecurb came bursting through the door.

"Your prisoner? Your Prisoner! How about I lock you two in a cell together and see what happens. Would you like that?" Poking his baton into the chest of Niloc. "Would you? Would you?"

"Captain or not, this is my house. Only the Higher Powers can overrule me here." Niloc spoke with no fear.

"Is that so?" Drathon triggered the blade and pressed it against Niloc's face.

"What are you going to do? Kill a Troop Commander in the Prison Zone and be put to death? Go back to Randtyph and I'll let you know when he's ready to begin...sir."

Drathon removed the blade from Niloc's face. Moving in so close that Niloc could taste the bitter smell of ale on his breath. With his face so close, Niloc noticed lilac burn marks around the inside of the Captain's nostrils.

"You better watch your step, Ecurb. Wouldn't want your lovely ladies up there to have some synchronised accidents," Drathon threatened with a menacing smile on his face.

In a final show of authority, Drathon sent Niloc stumbling back into the gurney with a shoulder barge on his way past.

"Probably want to stop sniffing that Quaba. Think it's starting to cloud your judgement, sir." Niloc watched as Drathon walked away, ignoring his comments.

The two Hav Guard were stood outside the doorway awkwardly, not knowing whether to stay or go.

"Make sure the Captain gets off safely and return to your posts. No more special detail. It's done," Niloc ordered.

Nodding in acknowledgement, the Hav Guard scarpered. Glad to be free of the awkward entanglement of the higher ranks.

Once certain the Hav Guard were out of sight, Niloc started to help Feorshi to his feet. Straining to get the muscle-bound torso elevated, his hands dug into the skin of Feroshi. Crack! Feroshi threw back his elbow, crashing it into Niloc's jaw. Sending him crashing onto his back. Like a beast pouncing on its prey, Feroshi flew on top of Niloc and wrapped his hands around his neck. Throttling him tighter and tighter. Niloc flailed his arms about wildly, grabbing at Feroshi's face and eyes. His face changing shades of red and then blue. Niloc's hands began to grab with less and less will as his brain function started to slow from lack of oxygen.

Realising it was not Drathon, Feroshi released his grip instantly and slumped back against the gurney. He watched as Niloc lay still, before his body jerked and then he coughed and spluttered trying to catch his breath. Sharp and shallow to deeper and slower.

"I told you, Niloc, you need to watch your step." Drathon's voice rebounded around the room. "I can't be punished if it's not me that kills you."

The swooshing noise of a cell door disappearing caused Niloc and Feroshi both to jump to their feet. Niloc still rubbing at his rapidly bruising throat.

"Hopefully you survive, Niloc. If you don't, I'll take good care of Relta for you. Show her what a Captain feels like. Bye bye." The feedback of the microphone snapped from Drathon disconnecting it on his end.

At the sound of Niloc's name, Feroshi's eyes fired in his direction. Maybe there was more reality, to the meeting with his mother, than Feroshi had originally thought.

"Niloc, what's in that cell?" Feroshi asked nervously, still not completely steady on his legs yet.

"There's no easy way to put this...monster, abomination or officially it's called Lakasha," Niloc said whilst unholstering his baton.

"Easy to kill?"

"Nope."

"Well at least tell me you have that new upgrade for your baton."

"Emmm, nope."

"I don't know why you are still here. You know if you stay there's a chance you'll die."

"You need to trust that I want to help you."

The weight of the Lakasha was obvious by the loud thuds each footstep made. Shaking the rest of the numbness out of his limbs, Feroshi rolled his neck and shoulders as Niloc energised his baton in preparation.

The loud rasping cry of the Lakasha preparing to hunt sent a shiver of fear down Niloc's spine, whereas Feroshi began to thrive. Ready to take on this abomination of the Empire. Crouching down as it exited the cell, the Lakasha came into view. Tree trunk legs that went straight down with stumps for feet. Overhanging stomach and each of its four arms layered in gristly, oozing fat. All the way down to each of its bladed hands. No eyes. Just stitched crosses where they would have been and its mouth full of razor blades.

"Give me your baton," Feroshi ordered.

"What? No, I need it," Niloc replied.

"Give me the baton and get behind the gurney. I'll end this quickly and I'm going to trust you're going to help me."

"They're blind but their hearing and smell is unmatched," he said, passing the baton to Feroshi.

Taking a deep breath, Feroshi settled his nerves. The tingling in his hands began and seemed to ignite the burning in his chest. Instead of fighting it, this time, he would embrace it. No fear. Power. He spun the baton on the palm of his hand and caught it by the handle again. Feroshi watched as the Lakasha turned to face his direction, sniffing at the air for his scent. He knew his stench would be intoxicating to the beast, as he had not been washed since he had been taken prisoner. Feroshi was right. The Lakasha screamed out as it thundered towards Feroshi.

"Come on, ugly, come and get me," Feroshi taunted.

With it barrelling towards him and gaining immense momentum, Feroshi took two strides before sliding under the slashing arms and then legs of the Lakasha. Its head followed his odour, causing it to crash and roll as it face-planted the floor. Taking the baton in both hands, Feroshi jumped into the air, bringing the weapon screaming down. Crunch! Squelch! Plunging it straight through the bottom of the Lakasha's skull, causing the other end to come out through the mouth. Crack! Smashing the teeth into the ground. The beast spasmed and then flopped.

"Typical, Shadow. All brawn," Feroshi said to Niloc.

With one strong yank he pulled the baton from the Lakasha, soaked in its black putrid blood and brain matter.

"And no brains. It's your turn, I hope I don't regret this," Feroshi said, throwing the baton onto the floor next to the gurney.

As soon as the baton hit the floor, Feroshi turned and headed for the empty cell. Bare from wall to wall and floor to ceiling, apart from a lavatory bucket in the corner. He walked over to the wall at the back and placed his hands against it. Catching his breath and thinking over what his mother had said, "Trust Niloc."

Chapter H

"Come on, come on. Stop dragging your heels, you cannot still be tired. You lay in bed for more than a day," Yvanny moaned at Theron.

"I'm sorry I nearly died and then saved your life. Why couldn't we have done this under the cover of dark? It's nearly there, but we couldn't wait? If anybody sees me they'll butcher me on sight," Theron replied, pulling the grey fabric sheet tighter over his face and shoulders. "Yvanny, you still haven't told me where we are going."

Even under the shade of the curtain, in the tight alleyways between the cramped rows of the Outer System homes, squeezed together en masse between the eight aisles, it was difficult to move Theron without him being spotted. Due to Yvanny having the reputation of being a mentally unstable old lady that howled at the moon, children followed, taunting and making howling noises. Approaching the home, that until recently had belonged to Ranoa and Shajo, Yvanny turned to hiss at the children, causing them to run off screaming. She chuckled as they checked around for prying eyes. With no unwanted onlookers, Yvanny rushed Theron out of the shadows, into the aisle and through the sheet doorway to the home.

The room had been reassembled, with the planks and bed replaced, covering the entrance to the Pit.

"Yvanny, can you tell me what the plan is please?" Theron asked, casting the fabric cover to the floor.

"I need you to drag that bed out of the way and remove the planks of wood below," she replied.

"Yvanny!"

"Do as I ask and you shall see."

After a scoff and roll of his eyes, Theron dragged the bed out of the way. Breathing heavily and sweating from clearing the doorway himself, Theron fell onto the floor once the final slat of wood had cleared the entrance.

"Why am I getting a really bad feeling about this?" Theron spoke aloud.

Yvanny crouched down, closed her eyes and placed her hand on the door. Clink. Clunk. The locking mechanism was opening.

"You should be able to open that now. Watch, it is quite heavy," Yvanny said, moving back away from the large wooden door in the floor.

Not wanting to spend any more time out in the open, Theron gripped onto the edges of the door and threw it open.

"Theron, I need you to stay behind me. Things might get a bit tense but no matter what happens, stay behind me," Yvanny said before hopping down into the tunnel.

Chapter 14

"You are really good at filling me with confidence, you know that," Theron replied sarcastically, following Yvanny into the hole. "What about the bed and the wood?"

"Just pull the door closed and leave the rest to the Outer System."

Reaching the entrance to the training hall of the Pit, Theron remained a few steps back from Yvanny, attempting to remain in the shadows for as long as possible. He could tell by the crescendos of sound that there was a very large body of warriors training. The sounds of crashing bodies and clashing steel were noises that Theron knew far too well, from his time with the Hav Guard.

WHACK! Yvanny clapped her hands together. The clap ricocheted around all four corners of the hall, stopping everybody and turning their attention her way.

"Gentlemen, I am looking for Lemra," Yvanny announced.

"Hello Yvanny." Lemra's voice carried from the opposite side of the hall.

Lemra made his way through the wall of warriors. All stood staring at Yvanny, the unannounced guest. Nobody ever entered the Pit without Lemra welcoming them at the door.

"My old friend," Yvanny said as Lemra wrapped his arms around her.

"Why are you here? The light still glows dull in the dark crown of the sea..." Lemra queried.

"I know, that is why I am here."

"He's been moved from his extraction cell. You need to act now or, Feroshi will be dead within a few days," Theron stated, walking out of the shadows of the tunnel and into the light of the hall.

The gasp of a hundred warriors turned into a disgruntled rumble of disdain. He was the enemy. He was the living embodiment of the mortal wing of the Shadow Empire.

"An angel walks a mutt of the Empire into our haven. Yet you dress him as one of us?" Lemra was sickened.

"YOU!" Ruevanlynn bellowed, finally managing to make his way through the crowd, only to see Theron standing there.

Shoving and barging through anybody blocking the way between him and his target, picking up pace as his stride opened up, his thigh muscles tensing and expanding with every explosive thrust.

"Here we go," Theron muttered.

There was an almighty clash of bodies as Ruevanlynn speared Theron to the floor. All the warriors began to cheer and yell chants of encouragement.

"Yes, kill him," they yelled.

"Break him, Rue," others shouted.

Theron struggled to defend himself from Ruevanlynn's fists, parrying and blocking with his hands and forearms.

"Ahhhh," Ruevanlynn yelped as Yvanny dragged him off Theron by his ear.

Theron got to his feet, bouncing his gaze between Ruevanlynn and Lemra.

Chapter 14

"Right, are we going to talk like adults now?" Theron asked.

"Somebody want to tell me why he's here, and, bitch, why you not howling at the sky?" Ruvanlynn snarled at Yvanny, rubbing at his throbbing ear.

The room had fallen silent as everyone waited eagerly to hear what was happening and why the previous Captain of the Hav Guard was now in the underground barracks of the Army of the Light.

"Ruevanlynn, I would not curse at her, but Yvanny, I am confused as to why you have brought our sworn enemy down here." Lemra turned his attention from Ruevanlynn to Yvanny.

"Breaking from your usual riddles, Lemra. Theron is one of us. The reason he looks so battered and bruised is because he risked his life to retrieve the Keeper's Scroll...for us. If I say he is one of us, he is one of us. Do you understand me, Ruevanlynn Grezzie?" Yvanny spoke with confidence as she closed the gap and stared up at Ruevanlynn.

"Who are *you* to tell me, Mumma Rue, that Theron Magda, HAV GUARD CAPTAIN, is one of us?" he replied.

Yvanny looked at Lemra and then back to Ruevanlynn. The tension in the room was so high, that the chance of it exploding was becoming more and more likely.

"What? What am I missing?" Ruevanlynn demanded answers.

"Rue, she's Feroshi's grandmother," Lemra unveiled.

Shock reverberated through the hall like the tremor of an earthquake. Gasps and mutters of disbelief silently circled.

"You're...you're...you're an Angel of the Light then," Ruevanlynn babbled.

"Well now, I didn't think I would ever see the day that Mumma Rue was speechless," Lemra teased. "Follow me to the briefing room. Let us hear what Theron has to say."

Like the good leader he was, Lemra led the group. Eyes may not have been on him, but the men still parted, clearing a path for Lemra before tightening the passage for Theron.

Their eyes, filled with fierce contempt, condemnation and disgust, followed Theron as he shadowed Lemra's footsteps through the crowd. To avoid antagonising any of the snarling men, Theron kept his gaze low. Even when provoked by the sweaty shoulder charge of a warrior, whose life had been torn apart by the Hav Guard, he did not engage.

He believed in their cause. Walking across the hall, feeling the hatred and foul intent towards him, Theron accepted and even appreciated, that they would have to see it for themselves. See that he was willing to die, not just for their cause, but be willing to put his body and soul on the line for each and every member of the Outer System. Every person, planet and galaxy that had been beat down, decimated and destroyed by the Shadow Empire. Theron was one of them, and he would put his dignity and pride aside, until he was accepted.

"I'm going to save our boy, you know that, don't you? Mumma Rue is gonna do what he do," Ruevanlynn assured

Yvanny, placing his arm around her with pride.

"You are a good boy, Ruevanlynn. It has been a pleasure to watch you and Feroshi grow into the fine young men you are today." She cheekily patted Ruevanlynn on the backside.

Sitting around the oval table, Ruevanlynn fixed his eyes on Theron.

"Do you remember Zed?" Ruevanlynn snarled.

"Who? Look I know I've–" Theron started.

"Zedary Tawn!" Ruevanlynn slammed his hand against the dark marble of the table. "The love of my life that I had to kill. Straight dead. No coming back. Never, because of YOU and the rest of your Hav Guard."

"Rue," Lemra pleaded, grabbing him by the arm.

"Best believe you're marked, fool," Ruevanlynn threatened, ripping his arm from Lemra's grip. "I'm sorry, Yvanny, but Mumma Rue ain't nothing if I ain't honest."

Theron grew more uncomfortable and uneasy. He looked around, confused by the level of technology, but also wondering if he had made the wrong decision to follow Yvanny into the abyss.

"Right, now that's out the way. You. Talk," Lemra ordered, pointing at Theron.

But as Theron opened his mouth to begin speaking, the door to the briefing room slowly crept open. The injured Joldack was using his body to force the door open, his arms being used to support his weight on his crutches. His leg covered in a glass tube with blue beams circling and travelling the interior, producing shocks of energy, being used to manipulate the injury and speed up the healing.

Ruevanlynn jumped up and eagerly rushed over to help his mentor and now friend.

"Joldey baby, you're supposed to be downstairs with the families," Ruevanlynn said, helping Joldack to a seat, the same side as Lemra and himself.

"I heard we had an unwelcome guest and I did not actually believe it to be true. Heard your mother died choking on the Empero–" Joldack's ability to throw insults towards Theron, or even speak, was failing because of Yvanny's abilities.

"There will be no more of this discourteous, disrespectful, derisive defamation in my presence. Lemra, you will make everyone aware that Theron should be treated as an equal. You, Mr high and mighty, do not forget that I know every single one of your atrocities in the name of the Shadow Emperor." Yvanny eyeballed Joldack whilst she held his tongue, until he bowed his head in submission and released him. "Now, Ruevanlynn, my dear, please allow Theron the chance to reveal what he knows."

"Proceed," Ruevanlynn jeered whilst giving a quaint flick of his hand.

"Look, whether we like it or not, without me you stand no chance of getting Feroshi out alive."

"Have you seen the amount of men out there? That's not even a half of the ground force," Joldack barked.

"Controlling the environment makes a victory by numbers impossible. If by some miracle, a few of you make it through...then what? It's a maze. Half the levels can't be reached without one of the Prison Panels. It allows you to enter sensitive floors and enclosed rooms. Troop Commander Niloc Ecurb is no joke either," Theron began to explain.

Joldack couldn't hold back a laugh that broke through his control before he could stop it.

"What's that supposed to mean?" Theron asked.

"You'll find out soon enough. Carry on...Captain," Joldack said, mocking his previous rank.

"Joldack, stop being facetious," Lemra ordered. "We had eyes on Feroshi but they've moved him. Do you have any idea where?"

"Feroshi has been sent for conversion. Knowing Drathon, he's probably moved him down to the testing area and is just leaving him there to rot until he's got no fight left in him. If we can find a way to travel across the Dead Zone and water at speed, I can do this on my own, but it would be much easier with another. We'd be in quickly and quietly. Couple dead Hav Guard and a safe Feroshi," Theron suggested.

"No way I'm letting you anywhere near my Feroshi without being there. Mumma Rue will go with you." Ruevanlynn jumped up out of his seat.

"We've got the mode of transport sorted. What you do you think, Yvanny? You are the angel after all," Lemra asked.

"I believe in Theron, stealth it is. You two need to get going. Ruevanlynn, can you take Theron down to the armoury please. We will alert Fendo Docheran of your pending arrival. I would like you to both be issued a locket and an O'Bohare blade. Off you pop."

Theron smiled and gave a reassuring squeeze of Yvanny's before heading towards the door now being held open by an unimpressed Ruevanlynn.

"Boys," Yvanny called out. "Trust each other. I mean it, Ruevanlynn, he saved my life so you play nice with Theron. You cannot succeed otherwise. Stay safe and bring our boy home. It is time to come out from the dark once more. It is time to let our light burn bright and blind."

Ruevanlynn winked at Yvanny, before blowing her a kiss and then letting the door fall freely as he led the way to the armoury.

"You know we only have three of those swords, Yvanny," Lemra grumbled.

"Yes, and mine shall be presented to my grandson upon his return. Mere steel will not be enough for our trinity of hope in the struggle ahead. More importantly, the O'Bohare are the birth right of all angelic descendants. Simeskey, Feroshi, Ruevanlynn, Theron...there is a reason they were all drawn together." Yvanny stood up and headed for the door. "Both Ruevanlynn and Theron were born to wield their power. Talking of which, I will be needing my blade please."

The pair travelled the flights of stairs silently. Acting as though he was taking the journey alone. Reaching the entrance to the armoury, Ruevanlynn pulled the door open himself, straining against the draught sucking the door closed.

Chapter 14

"Let me help," Theron offered, hurrying to aid with the weight.

Ruevanlynn released the door, letting the suction slam it closed.

"Let's get one thing straight. I love Feroshi like blood, you feel me? If Mumma Rue gets the smallest hint, the tiniest tingle in my massive black balls, that you're up to something...I will rip your spine out while you're forced to stay alive until I believe you're ready to die. Good?" Ruevanlynn declared.

"Yeah, we're good. Rue, I am sorry. I hope one day you'll believe that," Theron assured.

"If we survive and your plan works, I will think about stopping my boo tearing your arms off. Oh...and then beating you like a big old drum with them," Ruevanlynn gibed.

Tools clattered, being dropped in reaction to the sight of Theron walking down the steps behind Ruevanlynn. Scurrying workers, pushing trollies piled high with spare parts and tooling, theatrically slammed the brakes on, causing a comical scene. Momentum throwing their bodies distorting and contorting over the handlebars and into their load. Theron knew not to engage and kept his head low, focussing on matching the path of Ruevanlynn.

"After you," Ruevanalynn said whilst holding open the flight room door for Theron.

"Hello," Theron voiced, walking through the doorway.

"Hello to you too, Theron," Fendo replied, standing up from his desk to greet the men. "Here are your weapons. I have waited a long time to see who these would go to. Got to say, I am a bit surprised to see an O'Bohare go to you though, Theron."

Two identical swords were placed out in front of the men. A small set of golden, outspread wings sat at the bottom of the hilt. The slight curve of the grip was pearly white with two golden streams, starting as one, running and criss-crossing from the pommel. Until finally finishing their journey, together united once more, at the base of the one-sided cross guard. A single-edged blade followed the bend of the handle like an extended reflection.

"You'll be needing these," Fendo said, placing two leather belts, with sheaths attached, next to the swords.

"What do you mean a bit surprised? It's a sword," Theron challenged.

"Well, that's just it, isn't it...is it just a sword? These now belong to you as well," Fendo reported, handing over the lockets. "I have been told to inform you that everything issued to you here and now, is for you to keep. They must remain on your person at all times. Even when travelling around the family quarters of the Pit. Your speeders have been prepped and are ready for launch."

"Speeders?"

"There's technology out there from before you were born, few things you might recognise."

"Time to come see the toys," Ruevanlynn announced, adjusting the locket to sit in the centre of his chest and then sheathing his sword.

Chapter 14

Walking out of the flight room was the first time Theron actually managed to take in the brilliance of this underground hangar. Old technology missiles, blasters, planet to planet transporters and the two golden speeders sat front and centre, where Simeskey, Ranoa and Shajo's transporter had been, in front of the massive rolling door. The normal level of banging, grinding and clanging had resumed, but eyes remained to follow Theron from the workstations.

"This is incredible," Theron gawked in amazement.

Even with all the evil looks coming his way from all directions, Theron could not help but smile in marvel and astonishment.

"Turns out it was your lot that helped build this," Ruevanlynn taunted.

"That doesn't annoy me, Rue, it makes me happy to know there were others like me–" Theron began to reason.

"Like you!" Ruevanlynn fumed as he spun round, getting into Theron's face.

Even with his muscular and toned physique, Theron's frame looked average next to that of Ruevanlynn. Almost the exact same height, they were nearly nose to nose, eye to eye.

"Yeah, like me. Hated what the Empire stood for when we opened our eyes." Theron refused to back down anymore. "*Were* my lot!"

Theron barged passed Ruevanlynn. Reacting straight away, Ruevanlynn grabbed Theron's arm.

"What'd you say?" he snarled.

"Were my lot," Theron snapped back, ripping his arm free. "You are all my lot now, maybe you always have been. So stop being such a bitch and let's go and save your boo."

Ruevanlynn's evil stare turned to a pout and then he began to laugh, patting Theron on the side of his arm.

"Ooooo, Mumma Rue might've been wrong 'bout you, boy. Let's go cause some trouble." Ruevanlynn buzzed as he mounted his speeder. "You know how to ride one of these babies?"

"It has been a while, but I think so," Theron responded.

Sitting back into the seat and lowering down behind the protective glass, Theron gripped onto the handles and watched as the exit to the Dead Zone opened up.

"Remember, right pedal will make you fly, left is to rest those heavy feet. Oh and Mumma Rue's top tip...don't lean too hard or a turn becomes a roll," Ruevanlynn jested.

Voosh. Ruevanlynn tore off on his speeder. Whipping a stream of dust and vapour behind the streamlined blur of gold. Voosh. The race was on, Theron took off after Ruevanlynn. Any Hav Guard monitoring the wall, that happened to be looking in their direction, would have just imagined it was a trick of the eye. A blink and the object would have been gone in the dark, with no noise, just stirred-up dust floating in the air. Hovering long enough to make them question, but not long enough to care. Just another gust of wind in the night.

This gust of wind was not just like any other though. Both men could not help but smile as the fresh open air, of the world beyond the wall, brushed over the tops of their bodies. The red cloaks of the Faded looked like crimson bloodstains on the black wall of the night. Dropping off the edge of the land, each speeder began to free fall. Ruevanlynn, having already had this prank played on him by Joldack, laughed as Theron screamed hysterically.

He had not seen the edge because of sticking as close to the rear of Ruevanlynn's speeder as possible. Seeing it as a challenge between the two. Ruevanlynn would strafe right, Theron would shadow, go left and he would follow. When Ruevanlynn went over the edge, Theron only had a split second to realise and panic before he began to fall. Not knowing if he was falling to his death, he yelled out in fear. Only to bounce against the water below. A shockwave of water rippling out and then becoming a jet stream as the speeder raced forward once more.

"Get a little fright, baby boy," Ruevanlynn joked, bursting out laughing after circling back to check on Theron's post-impact reaction.

"Yeah, good one." Theron's reply turned from cold to happiness, after his immediate adrenaline burst and shock had subsided.

The protective layer of monstrous, life-threatening storms could be felt before it could be seen. Ripples from the crashing waves carried into the calm. Before crashing straight into the sinister cloud of catastrophic weather, Ruevanlynn pulled to a halt, hovering a few feet above the ever-growing surges of swell of the water below. Swiftly followed by Theron.

"So, new friend, what's the plan? Cause Mumma Rue sees a problem with your original instructions," Ruevanlynn jeered, pointing at the deadly barrier. "Ain't no way we're making it through that."

"You're right, we don't go through it, we go under it," Theron revealed.

"I'm starting to think your arms may not get ripped off by Feroshi...because we'll be on the bottom of the sea."

"The only way in without being spotted by a guard or camera is through the underwater landing pad. Transporters land outside so nobody is watching what's coming from below. I told the Prison Zone's Troop Commander to get rid of it after one of my security audits–"

"Bored!" Ruevanlynn yelled at the top of his voice. "You'll need to lead the way. Really hope you know where you're going. Cause if we get lost down there, probably gonna drown. Drown equals dead. Dead equals drown. Basically, drowning does not get Mumma Rue's vote."

"Yeah, I get it, drowning is bad. Trust me," Theron reassured, before diving his speeder into the water.

As soon as the speeder fully submerged in water, a film of energy spread from the windshield, engulfing Theron's body. He could see. He could breathe. Turning round to check on Ruevanlynn, he chuckled to see he was going through the exact same shock, in the same stages that he had just gone through. Looking back towards the Prison Zone, the underwater landing pad was well lit and it was a clear path.

Chapter 14

Taking a steady pace on approach, both men stayed vigilant for any safety measures the Hav Guard may have in place. Closer and closer they got without any obstacles or deterrents. Untouched and unharmed, like wandering into friendly territory, the two speeders arrived at the landing pad with the access hatch above.

"Stay on your speeder. Let me check there's nobody on guard. If it's clear, follow me up," Theron instructed.

Dismounting his vehicle, he pushed off from his speeder, propelling himself to the surface level. Slowly he let his eye and then nose float above the surface. Gently he treaded water, rotating to get a clear view of the entrance. It was clear. He motioned with his hand to Ruevanlynn to join him.

Theron dragged himself up out of the water, keeping watch to make sure Ruevanlynn could safely exit the water. One wall was filled with large glass windows, looking onto one of the walkways through the lower levels of the Prison Zone. He kept a close eye out for any sign of movement at either end.

"Did that all seem a bit easy to you?" Theron queried.

"Yeah, let's just take it as a good sign," Ruevanlynn replied, drawing his O'Bohare blade.

Following Ruevanlynn's lead, Theron unsheathed his sword. They quickly headed over to the door. Checking quickly, the coast was clear. Hugging the wall, they crept into the walkway. Swoosh. A door had opened behind them. Two Hav Guard were stood there. Both pairs were stuck in a momentary stand-off. Neither quite sure what to do. The leading Hav Guard slowly began to reach for his baton.

"Uh uh uh. Don't do it," Ruevanlynn warned.

There was no listening: the Hav Guard snapped for his baton.

"Gugh..." he gasped as Ruevanlynn plunged his blade straight through his heart.

The handle was clean but the protruding blade was soaked in blood. Ruevanlynn wrenched the blade up. Cracking and crunching as it tore through the chest plate.

"Help!" the second Hav Guard shouted, turning and running in the opposite direction.

"Get him!" Ruevanlynn ordered, letting the slumped body slide off his blade.

Sprinting after the Hav Guard, Theron threw himself round corners. Getting closer, the Hav Guard panicked and prodded at his control panel. WOO! WOO! PRISON BREACH. PRISON BREACH. The deafening alarm rang out across the entire Prison Zone. With nothing left to lose and the others warned, the remaining Hav Guard stopped running, unholstered his baton and waited for Theron to attack.

"Let's do this, traitor," the Hav Guard sniped.

Theron charged at the Hav Guard. BOOM! The Hav Guard energised his baton, sending Theron flying backwards and crashing to the floor with his sword sliding out of reach. Rolling over to reach for the sword, Theron's body began to throb in pain from the impact. His vision bounced in and out of focus while loud ringing filled his ears. BOOM!

Chapter 14

The Hav Guard energised his baton at the ceiling, causing rubble to fall down onto Theron. WOO! WOO! PRISON BREACH! PRISON BREACH! The alarm continued to ring out as Theron attempted to crawl for his sword. BOOM! The blast threw Theron against the wall. Blood poured from the wound on his head from the collision.

"If you're going to live like a skaff, you'll die like a skaff," the Hav Guard taunted as he stalked Theron, who was crumpled against the wall. "Goodbye, Captain Mag–"

SWISH! Theron spun round; the sword had been thrown with him against the wall, slicing straight through the baton.

"Goodbye!" Theron screamed, stabbing through the Hav Guard's throat.

The Hav Guard gargled and grabbed at his throat. Blood sprayed out to the side whilst it poured from under his mask. Dropping to his knees and then flat on his front, blood pooled as every drop leaked from the severed arteries. WOO! WOO! PRISON BREACH! PRISON BREACH! The alarm continued.

"Where the hell is Rue?" Theron inquired aloud.

Retracing his steps along the route he had taken to chase down his target, he arrived back at the body of Ruevanlynn's victim. He looked ahead, down the straight walkway but there was no sign of him.

"Rue. Rue!" Theron called out for him.

"In here, Theron!" a voice, not Ruevanlynn's, called out.

The alarm had finally stopped, but all Theron could hear was his heartbeat. If Ruevanlynn was in trouble and there was a chance of death, then Theron would die alongside him. Holding his sword above his head as a sign of yielding, he walked into the entrance of the underwater landing pad.

"I'm here," he said, dropping the sword on the floor.

Drathon was stood behind a crouched Ruevanlynn, O'Bohare blade against his throat. Lilac powder covered Drathon's nostrils and upper lip. Pupils dilated. His support, eight Hav Guard, all stood with blades extended from their batons. Theron and Ruevanlynn were outmanned. It was all over. He had failed Ruevanlynn, not keeping him alive. What hurt him even more, was the thought that he had failed Yvanny.

"Come over and crouch down here next to your skaff brother." Drathon's voice was different, darker and he twitched as he spoke.

"Okay, okay. I'm coming over." Theron said cooperatively. "Drathon, look what that stuff is doing to you."

THUD! Drathon crashed the handle of the O'Bohare blade into Theron's face. Bursting open the skin on impact.

"Did I ask you to talk, no I didn't. If the Higher Powers want to use Quaba to gain favour with enemy governments whenever they want, and I'm the Captain of the Shadow Empire's Royal Guard, best believe I'll be getting what's mine," Drathon rapidly rambled.

"Looks like what's yours is really working for you," Theron taunted.

"You know what, it doesn't even matter. Boys," Drathon commanded.

Chapter 14

Six of the Hav Guard left and disappeared out of sight.

"Show them."

On Drathon's command one of the remaining Hav Guard stepped in front of crouched Theron and Ruevanlynn and held up a screen. On the screen, Feroshi strapped to a gurney. Immediately Ruevanlynn attempted to jump to his feet. ZAP! He was tased with a baton from behind. He twitched and groaned on the floor.

"This is going to be fun. Like the good buddies we are, we are going to watch your boy's first elixir insemination. Theron can back me up here, Rue, the first stages make for the best viewing material. You'll see. You'll love it. Oh, look, here they come."

The Hav Guard that had recently departed the room, had just walked into the picture. One of them holding a syringe full of a purple solution with black ripples rolling through it.

"I am so sorry, Rue. I failed you," Theron sobbed.

"It's all good, baby. Mumma Rue saw the real you, can't ask for much more than that," Ruevanlynn groaned from the ground.

"Blah blah blah, what a load of weak skaffy bastard shit," Drathon hissed while pulling a sachet from inside his gauntlet.

Using his teeth he ripped open the sachet and poured the powdered substance into his nostrils, snorting hard at the same time.

"You two should thank me. Once you've watched this I'm just going to cut both your heads off." Drathon laughed maniacally.

"Sir, we are ready to begin," a voice came from the control panel on Drathon's forearm.

"Ooohhh I'm so excited. The talisman of the Outer System. The king skaff, never to be the same again. You are clear to begin," Drathon sneered.

On the video, Feroshi struggled against the restraints, but the excess Hav Guard helped pin him down while he was injected. Pulling the trigger and removing the needle from Feroshi's neck, all six Hav Guard backed off to monitor.

"Administration of the Elixir complete. Monitoring of the subject beginning," the voice from the control pad informed.

"Any second now and...wait, that's not right. What's going on?" Drathon yelled into his control pad.

Feroshi had begun to vibrate uncontrollably. The restraints were warping, cracking and snapping under the strain of his body jerking.

"Watch them!" Drathon ordered, running out of the room.

"What's happening? Hey, tell us what's happening," Ruevanlynn screamed.

"This isn't supposed to happen, Rue, I promise you," Theron said, confused.

Feroshi's body went rigid. Breaking free through all the restraints. Metal went flying around the room like shrapnel, bounding off the armour of the Hav Guard. His eyes and mouth open and glowing. His chest. His hands. All began to glow. Brighter and brighter. The video feed began to jump and glitch. The screen went white. BOOM! BOOM! SMASH! CRASH! BOOM! Explosions ripped through the Prison Zone. Light filled every corner. Vibrations, jolting and extreme shuddering threw Ruevanlynn, Theron and the Hav Guard flying through the air. The screams of prisoners being buried or burned alive, in their cells, rivalled the blaring fire alarm.

Ruevanlynn could smell burning but his vision was taking a moment to come back into focus. He could move all of his body and wasn't in too much pain, apart from the burns from being electrocuted by the Hav Guard's baton. He sat up, looking around. The bright light that had burst through the entire Prison Zone had finally subsided. All that was left now was flickering light and light from the flames.

"Theron, you alive?" Ruevanlynn called out.

"Ugh..." A groan was heard.

Ruevanlynn hurried to the source of the noise. It was the Hav Guard regaining consciousness.

"Oh now then, we have ourselves a party," Ruevanlynn stated menacingly.

Grabbing the Hav Guard by the scruff of his armour with both hands, he dragged him over to the entrance to the underwater landing pad. Once at the water, Ruevanlynn ripped off the Hav Guard's mask and forced his face into the water. Immediately he began to flail and struggle. Placing a hand into the water and then onto the floor, the Hav Guard tried to push up.

"Blurgh..." the Hav Guard gargled as his face broke free momentarily.

Ruevanlynn ripped the supporting arm away from the floor and round. Up behind his back. SNAP! He broke the arm and forced the head underwater again. He thrashed about wildly and his screams could be heard from above the water. Until he began to slow. Then until finally he went limp. Ruevanlynn pushed the rest of the body into the water and watched as the armour weighed it down and out of sight.

"Rue...help..." Theron struggled to yell for aid.

A part of the wall had collapsed and a concrete beam was lying across Theron's stomach.

"Got yourself into a spot of bother there," Ruevanlynn joked, pressing down on the beam.

"Please...Rue...I can't...breathe..."

"I'm only playing, you'll be ok," Ruevanlynn said, lifting the beam enough to allow Theron to escape.

There was a load crash once Ruevanlynn released his grip.

"I actually thought you were being serious there," Theron gasped as he tried to catch his breath.

"Nah, you're my boy now. I got you. We need to find Feroshi."

"I know where he is. Grab your sword and follow me."

Running back through the corridors, there were scenes of carnage everywhere. Fire bursting out from the walls. Escaped prisoners and test subjects ripping each other apart whilst skirmishing with the Hav Guard. Bodies lay sprawled out battered, beaten, bloodied and broken. Flickering light and the screams of terrified victims, death guaranteed, disorientated the pair. Losing their bearings. Sure they had already travelled these corridors before.

"We're going round in circles and this place is falling apart," Ruevanlynn stated.

"It is just down here, the test cells are through there," Theron reassured him. "Listen, Rue, we don't know what we're going to find through that door. I just need to know you are prepared."

Without a second thought, Ruevanlynn charged for the door. It did not matter what was on the other side. Dead or alive, Feroshi's body would not be staying in the Prison Zone.

"Feroshi..." Ruevanlynn softly cried.

Steps away from the door, it had slid open. Lieutenant Relta Brack, dishevelled and bleeding, her usual perfectly pressed dark blue uniform torn and shredded, was leading two Hav Guard. Carrying cargo, the most valuable of cargo. Draped across their shoulders and dragging along the floor. Limp, lame and lifeless, Feroshi's body was trailing behind as they stepped over bodies and rubble and climbed through the open doorway.

Relta Brack jumped back, startled at the sight of Theron and Ruevanlynn.

"It's about damn time," Relta proclaimed toward Ruevanlynn.

Flipping a small a blade from a short handle in her hand: Shwip. Shwip. THUD! Feroshi's body collapsed onto the floor. Crumpled. Motionless. Fractured and fallen. Ruevanlynn and Theron had been fixated and focused on their target, from the moment they had dragged him through the doorway. Watching him fall made their stomachs sink more vehemently than they had done from the cliffside on their speeders.

Wading slowly towards his fallen brother, Ruevanlynn's legs wobbled, as though his entire world was breaking underfoot. This had only ever been about Feroshi. From the very moment he knew Simeskey was safe, his every breath has been for Feroshi. All the noise of alarms and explosions, cries for help and screams begging for death were drowned out. Drowned out by the paralysing prison of the devastated essence, only a person with nobody left could know. His hypnotic trance only broken by the jettison of warm liquid soaking his face. Slapping him back to reality.

Each of the Hav Guard dropped to the ground. Blood soaking the floor and walls with every arterial spray. In the blink of an eye, Relta had slashed the jugulars of both men, causing them to drop Feroshi to the ground.

"Don't just stand there. Get him up, we need to get you three out of here right now," Relta ordered.

"Relta...wh...wait...what is happening?" Theron blabbered in confusion.

"Think we've found our inside woman. Thank you, baby girl." Ruevanlynn expressed his gratitude, kissing Relta on the cheek. "Mumma Rue's strong, but this beast is going to take two soldier boys."

"Glad to see you've joined us, Theron," Relta proclaimed. "I'll watch ahead, make sure it's clear."

"Here, take this." Theron offered his sword.

"I don't have that honour, I'm afraid. Thank you though."

Keeping her blade hidden behind her wrist, Relta scanned ahead and peaked around corners before signalling to the men to proceed.

"Stop," she whispered, holding her hand up in case the command was not heard.

Outside the exit stood a black-masked Hav Guard with two blade extended batons, one in each hand. Obviously placed on sentry to raise the alarm and kill any prisoners or intruders on sight. Feigning injury, Relta grabbed at her stomach and hobbled towards the guard.

"Help, I tried to stop them. Please help!" she cried.

Hearing his superior's calls for help he rushed to her aid. He put his arm around her in support. She dropped to one knee and spun. Swip. She sliced through the weak point behind the knee. Straight through the tendons and tissue.

"Argh!" he cried, grabbing his leg as he dropped.

Relta got to her feet behind the disabled Hav Guard. CRACK! She snapped his neck then dropped the body to the floor. Blood still pooling around the leg of the corpse, pouring from the wound. Lying on the floor lifeless, he was still holding his leg as though dying before his brain was able to give the command to let go. Relta helped Ruevanlynn with Feroshi, allowing Theron to climb into the water.

"Are you two going to manage to get him out of here okay, because this is as far as I can go, I'm afraid?" Relta queried.

"Yeah, we've got this, Brack. Turns out the speeders allow you to breathe under water," Theron explained.

"That was Niloc that designed that submersion system."

Theron could not help but smile. Questions he had asked himself during his tenure as Captain. Answers he could never get. Things were becoming a little clearer now. Both men treaded water, pulling on Feroshi, while Relta guided him into the water.

"You traitorous little whore," Drathon screamed.

"Get out of here. I've got this," she assured her allies.

Watching them sink below the surface, she turned to face Drathon. There was no hiding her straight blade this time. Handle gripped tightly in hand, Relta had the blade outstretched. No fear to show. In a return show of force Drathon extended the blade from his baton.

"Can't wait to let your little boyfriend see your flayed corpse hung from the Shadow Hammer. What would he say if he could see you now, eh?" Drathon ranted.

"Will you just shut up. You're disgusting and the Empire deserves you."

"Bitch," Drathon screamed whilst lunging forward.

Swoosh. Swoosh. Drathon swung wildly, Relta ducking and diving, avoiding the chopping and slicing blade. Ting. She parried the blade with her own. Thump! Followed by a punch to the jaw. The punch snapped his neck to the side, but he recoiled quickly, looking Relta straight in her eyes with venomous intent. Relta thrust her blade towards the abdomen. Drathon caught her wrist. SMASH! He threw his head straight into her face. Blood bursting across her face from her nose and mouth.

"Theron, where are you going? We gots to get our sweet behinds out of here, sweetness," Ruevanlynn exclaimed.

He was fastened into his speeder with Feroshi balanced between himself and the handles. Theron was originally mounted and ready to go but stopped, not wanting to leave Relta alone to face Drathon. If anybody knew how dangerous the newest Captain of the Hav Guard was, it was him.

"We stand as one, I won't leave her with him. You get our boy to safety. If I don't make it, tell Feroshi I'm sorry," Theron asked, before pushing off from the speeder and free from the protective film.

Clambering to her feet. Whack! Drathon punched Relta's face. Stamp. Stamp. Stamp. Every thundering stomp sent mouthfuls of blood spraying out of the mouth of Relta.

"Oi, Drathon. Leave her. Go one more round with me," Theron yelled from the water.

Stopping mid stomp with his heavy steel boot in the air, Drathon smiled wickedly as he turned to see Theron half out of the water leaning on the edge. Flipping the baton round he prepared to impale.

"Oh, I've woke up hard after dreaming about this moment," he snarled.

"Theron, get out of here," Relta screamed, launching her broken body towards Drathon.

Shunk! Rip!

"Noooo!" Theron screamed.

Looking out, he could see Relta was skewered on Drathon's blade. He had thrust back as she attempted her attack. Ripping up for maximum damage. Drathon turned round, staying eye height with Relta. Watching her fight to breathe. Slowly he removed the blade. It sawed through her ribs and organs, causing blood to teem from her mouth. She dropped to her knees, the life quickly leaving her. Swish! Thump! With one clean swipe he sent Relta's head soaring across the room while the rest of her body fell limp. Drathon threw his head back in extreme euphoria – it seemed as though he was almost at the point of climax, from the sight of the savage scene.

"Did you enjoy that, Magda?" Drathon asked sadistically.

"I will kill you, Drathon," Theron stated before disappearing under the water.

Swimming to his speeder he could not help but cry. His muffled wailing became clear as the speeder registered the rider. He had gone back to help her, but instead she had died so he could live to fight another day. Relta had died for him.

Taking one last look up at the entrance, Theron's sadness turned to pride that yet another person of the Light had put their life on the line for him. It was time for him to return to the Pit. No longer the outsider. No longer the Captain or ex-Captain of the Hav Guard. To them he was now a brother. He just had one last heart to win, the most difficult and dangerous of them yet: Feroshi Enlit.

Chapter 15

Cheers, clapping, whooping and wooing erupted as Ruevanlynn's speeder skidded to a halt in front of the jubilant crowd. Technicians, warriors, women and children. Young and old, it did not matter, the hangar was absolutely packed to the limits. People clambering on top of weaponry, staging and vehicles just to be able to see if the rescue mission had been successful. Having lain dormant for so long, the nerves and excitement of war were burning. The fire of hope spreading through every single person.

The rolling door had started to close behind Ruevanlynn. He took a quick glance back, but his feeling of wonder and concern for Theron was broken by Lemra slapping him on the back.

"You did it, Rue, well done. Really well done," Lemra yelled ecstatically. "Get me some water and nutrient solution."

Spectators clambered over each other, desperate to help Lemra lift Feroshi's body from the front of the speeder, placing him gently on the floor.

"Rue, you beautiful man." Joldack laughed, hobbling over to the speeder on his crutches. "Where's Theron? Did you kill him?"

"Sorry, Joldack, he's got Mumma Rue's vote. I just hope he knows what he's doing," Ruevanlynn replied, dismounting his speeder.

Workers wasted no time clearing the vehicle out of the area and into a service bay.

The crowd fell quiet as Feroshi's battered body was laid flat out on the floor.

"He's going to be all good, isn't he, Lemra?" Ruevanlynn asked, crouching down next to him.

Lemra pointed to Feroshi's torso raising and lowering with the inhale and exhale of air.

"Sure is, my boy," he stated while smiling.

The crowd erupted once again. The leader they had been promised was alive. Hope was alive. The dream of freedom was reborn. Clapping and elated cries fell to murmurs as the rolling doors began to open once more. Everyone watched on in silence as Theron's speeder pulled to a halt in front of Ruevanlynn and Lemra, crouched down beside Feroshi. Ruevanlynn got to his feet and headed in the direction of Theron.

"You made it," Ruevanlynn shouted in glee.

He scooped Theron from his speeder, dragging him off into his embrace.

"Did you doubt me?" Theron replied cheekily.

Overjoyed to see him, Ruevanlynn pulled Theron in again for another hug before raising his hand. This time, the crowd celebrated Theron. Patting him on the back. Greeting them as one of their own.

"Where's Yvanny?" Theron queried, looking around, unable to see her.

"Okay, everybody, back to work!" Lemra ordered, causing the crowd to disperse. "Did something happen when you were over there?"

"We were hoping you could tell us. There was a massive explosion, light shining everywhere. Nearly took down the whole Prison Zone," Theron explained. "What's that got to do with Yvanny?"

"The world shook, just like it did before. The day Feroshi was born. We sent out a scout and a great beam of light was radiating into the sky from the prison zone...and the Turach Vro Aka. We sent for Yvanny, for any insight, but when we found her, she was floating in the air, completely rigid. She's still alive but bare–"

"Rue...is...that..." Feroshi struggled, attempting to raise his hand to Ruevanlynn's cheek.

"Boo, who else gonna risk their ass for you," Ruevanlynn answered. "You're safe now, Mumma Rue's got you now."

Feroshi rubbed at his face, clearing the haze of unconsciousness. He tried to push himself upright, but his body was weak, too weak, flopping back with wide eyes.

"Yeah, you just take it easy, son," Lemra said, supporting Feroshi's head back to the ground.

"I know you," Feroshi mumbled.

"It's been a long time, but yes, my boy, you know me," Lemra gently spoke.

Two younglings rushed to where Feroshi was lay. The boy cradled a large glass bottle splishing, splashing and sploshing the water inside. His knuckles white from gripping with the force of a vice. Excited and eager to please, he refused to drop the bottle, very much like his life depended on it. Pulling it into his chest, as though it was a forbidden treasure, not to be shared with or seen by anybody. The female was carrying a small container, protecting the syringe. Hugging it to her chest as if a newborn. Carefully and securely. Terrified their opportunity to make a good impression in front of this godly figure, could be stolen away by another.

"Here's your water, sir," the boy said, handing the bottle to Lemra but looking deep into Feroshi's eyes.

"Here's the nutrients, sir," the female youngling blurted, dropping the small case onto Feroshi's stomach. "Sorry, Feroshi."

"That's ok, Seema. Thank you both, now you two get back to the family-quarters. There will be time to meet Feroshi later," Lemra nattered to the pair.

With all the strength he could muster, Feroshi lifted his head to smile and wave at his new admirers.

"Feroshi, this might nip a little, but it will start to give you your strength back," Lemra explained, before injecting the needle into his neck and pulling the trigger, forcing the nutrient solution into his body.

"Feroshi, what caused the explosion?" Theron appealed for more information, worried about Yvanny.

Chapter 15

Whether the nutrients were taking effect rapidly or a massive surge of life, Feroshi threw his upper body and hands at Theron in a possessed rage. In a head full of fractured fog, a venomously savage clarity of the memory of the hatred he had for the man, whom in his eyes, had ruined his whole life.

"Stop. No," Ruevnalynn yelled as he grabbed Feroshi's arms, pinning him back to the ground.

"What are you doing? This is all his fault," Feroshi frothed.

Even in his weakened state, Feroshi put up quite the fight. Needing him to calm down quickly, Ruevanlynn mounted Feroshi, restraining him with all his weight and strength.

"Mumma Rue is your brother. Do you trust Mumma Rue?" Ruevanlynn prompted for a request.

"What are you doing, Rue? Yes. Yes, I trust you. Now get off me."

"Boo, you're not gonna like this, but Theron's one of us. He risked his life saving you and your grandmother, baby boy."

The fight left Feroshi the moment he heard the words.

"One of us? Grandmother? How long was I away?"

Ruevanlynn dismounted Feroshi, helping him to his feet in the process. The two men hugged each other. Finally safe and together again. Separating from their embrace, Feroshi wobbled on his legs, still not back to full strength.

"Probably gonna take a few days till you're back to your beautiful self again," Ruevanlynn reassured as he helped Feroshi get his balance.

"Firstly, Theron, let's get one thing clear. I trust Rue, not you. Secondly, I don't know about any explosion. The last thing I remember is them injecting me here." Rubbing on the back of his neck. "I think there's something in there."

"They've put a tracker in him. We need to get that–" Theron exclaimed.

Woo! Woo! Pit breach! Pit breach! Woo! Woo! Pit breach! Pit breach!

"They've found us," Lemra yelled. "Everyone listen. Get all the transporters fired up and ready to go. Arm the men. Evacuate the women and children. You know the drill."

"Argh. What the...". Feroshi yelped in pain.

Theron had used his sword to quickly slice Feroshi's neck and rip out the tracker. Throwing it to the ground and stamping on it to discontinue the signal it was transmitting.

"Look, all done. Now, I'm going back for Yvanny," Theron stated.

"Oi, soldier boy, be safe." Ruevanlynn smiled at Theron.

"Rue, I need you and Feroshi on the first transporter out of here," Lemra ordered.

"Yeah well, that's not going to happen now, is it?" Feroshi jeered.

"I didn't think so. Please stay alive, boys. We're counting on you." He nodded before turning to Theron. "Come on then, Yvanny's in the family quarters."

Using the tracking signal and scans of the Outer System, the Hav Guard had sourced the entrance to the Pit. Drathon, Keeper Thon and the Higher Powers watched on through a viewing glass. From the safety of the stage in the Great Hall, Drathon could not help laughing maniacally as the Hav Guard blew open the entrance to the Pit, taking out the homes above and in the close vicinity of Ranoa and Shajo's. Every occupant killed by the blast without prejudice. Hav Guard flooded into the tunnel like vermin. A blade to each mask. A cloak to each soldier with a sole mission: Eradicate the enemy. Anybody drawing breath beneath the ground of the Outer System, not representing the Shadow Empire, was an enemy.

"Never doubt me. I knew he would try and escape, just didn't think it would lead us right to a nest," Drathon boasted.

"This still does not excuse what you did to the archive," Keeper Thon barked in reply.

"Silence. You have done well, Captain. You have found the key to the Emperor's return," Marra El's demonic echo sounded.

The Hav Guard swarmed from the exit of the tunnel into the training hall. The first lines of defence were the unarmed men wrestling and training. Their arms severed as they tried to block. Chests, faces and throats slashed as they attempted to duck and dodge. The front line of attack took a knee. BOOM! BOOM! BOOM! The second line of attack sent all the warriors crashing back into each other with the wall of energy bursting from the batons. Then the charge began. Blades extended like a spear ready to impale. The training army all scattered and piled on top of each other. Clambering and rolling to get to their feet defenceless. In the cloud of chaos, they blindly felt for an instrument, a weapon. Grabbing mainly broken bodies, decapitated limbs or thin air. The scramble for a weapon was ended by the rumbling floor, caused by the armed stampede rushing towards them.

An exploding barrage of belief burst through the stairwell partition. Leading the brigade, Theron with his O'Bohare blade high, he headed straight for the middle of the charging Hav Guard while the armed warriors fanned out behind. Creating a barrier between themselves and the injured. Clashing steel. Screams of pain. Blood splattering. Crashing of bodies against the armour.

"Hold the line!" Theron yelled. "Push!"

Parrying blades. Rolling off charging Hav Guard. Stabbing. Slicing. Blood and sweat soaked Theron raged through the enemy line. Cutting his way to the entrance of the stairwell to the family quarters. Dragging the defensive wall of thrashing warriors with him.

"Theron, we're clear, get those women and children out of here," Lemra ordered Theron. "Any younglings willing to fight, send them this way."

Theron peeled off behind the wave of warriors and into the stairwell. Women and children cowed at the horrific sounds of war. Not knowing if the Hav Guard would break through. Fearing for the lives of their family and friends.

"Come on, it's ok. Head straight for the armoury. Do not look back and do not stop, no matter what," Theron shouted loud and clear to make sure the instructions were heard.

The trail of evacuees steadily made their way up and out of the stairwell.

"Where's Yvanny?" Theron enquired over and over, hoping for an answer on his descent.

Chapter 15

"She's lying on the bed in her room. Left at the bottom of the stairs." Finally he was given a reply.

Trying to not slow down the evacuation, Theron bounded down the stairs as carefully as possible. He crashed through the door at the bottom of the stairs.

"Yvanny," he gasped in relief. "Come on, it's time to go."

"I knew you would come for me. Don't forget the scroll, it's under the bed," Yvanny croaked.

Scooping Yvanny up and onto his back, she interlocked her arms and legs around his body. She was so weak that Theron used one of his hands to aid her in keeping a lock with her hands.

"Rue, they're here. We've got to get them onto the transporters," Feroshi yelled to Ruevanlynn.

Women and children had started to file into the armoury. Some soaked in streaks of blood and flesh from the battle above.

"This way, everyone. Everyone's just gonna get onto the transporters as quickly as possible." Ruevanlynn ushered the way, assisted by workers and anybody willing to help.

In his current condition, all Feroshi could do was help everybody board the transporters. Larger and larger groups poured into the armoury for refuge and escape. Sprinting for the first transporter with space as soon as they entered.

"Lemra, fall back to the armoury," Theron yelled out, as he ran through the training hall with Yvanny hugging onto his back like a shell.

Theron headed straight towards Ruevanlynn. "Get ready, the Hav Guard are coming."

"Feroshi, they're coming," Ruevanlynn shouted.

"Theron, put me down. They need you," Yvanny said to Theron.

"I'm not leaving you until you're on a transporter," he replied.

"I am afraid that is not an option. I will be fine, now go and show them what you can do."

Theron unsheathed his sword and walked over to Ruevanlynn. Preparing to fight alongside him once again. Suddenly, Lemra came bursting through the entrance and flew down the steps.

"Get those transporters out of here. There's too many. Everyone left, get ready to fight," Lemra ordered.

Engines fired up as the rolling doors began to open. Lines of the remaining warriors assembled behind Ruevanlynn, Lemra and Theron, while Feroshi and Joldack bundled as many people onto the transporters as possible, while there was still time.

"There's just too many of them. We have to hold them off long enough to give the transporters time to get out of here," Lemra reinforced to Ruevanlynn and Theron.

BOOM! The blast from a baton blew the entrance doors, flying through the air. One crashing into a wall, the other crushing two warriors. Like a bursting dam, the white masks of the Hav Guard flooded into the armoury. Feroshi agonisingly watched from afar as Ruevanlynn clashed blades with oncoming Hav Guard.

Wave after wave of Hav Guard came surging into the armoury. Piles of body started to make an obstacle course of corpses for them to wade through. One by one the warriors started to become overwhelmed by the sheer number of Hav Guard filling the armoury.

"Get those transporters out of here. NOW!" Lemra screamed at the top of his voice. "Theron, help Rue."

Ruevanlynn was getting backed up between two high sets of racking. Blocking and parrying with everything he had. Stabbing and slashing whenever he saw an opening. He was tiring though, and tiring fast. Theron hacked his way towards Ruevanlynn. Ducking under a wild swinging blade, Theron flipped the Hav Guard over his back, cutting off the head of the one behind. No matter how much he fought, the distance between Ruevanlynn and himself didn't seem to be getting shorter. The area was just becoming far too condensed with Hav Guard.

"I'm coming, Rue!" Theron yelled.

There was just too many. He wouldn't get there in time.

Ruevanlynn had begun to swipe wildly from side to side. Keeping a safe barrier between himself and the swarm of Hav Guard.

"Still a few more of you to die before I go. Come get me, boys," Ruevanlynn taunted.

He was soaked from head to toe in every bodily fluid. His body ached and his reserves were running low. It was over for him, but he was determined to take at least a couple more down with him.

Quietly, Feroshi dragged his body up the side of the weaponry. Straining and whining with every exertion of energy. CRASH! SMASH! He threw his body off the racking and onto the taunting Hav Guard.

Feroshi's fearless act of throwing himself into the middle of the action, even though injured, fuelled the fire of everyone struggling to hold off the Hav Guard. Slash. Slit. Cut. Stab. Ruevanlynn hacked through any Hav Guard around Feroshi. Clang. Theron and Ruevanlynn's swords collided with each other as they both dissected their way through the sea of black armour and white masks.

"Having fun yet?" Theron jested.

"You ain't seen nothing yet," Ruevanlynn joked.

Finally the first transporter was taking off. The two went back-to-back. Slowly circling and battling in every direction. BANG! BOOM! Randtyph's defences blew the transporter full of the innocent out of the sky. There was an outcry of sadness and rage. Once again, spurring on another flurry from the quickly decreasing number of warriors.

"Feroshi, I need you to do something for me," Lemra said, rushing over to the hobbling Feroshi. "Grab whoever is left and get them out through the other tunnel. Rue will show you the way."

"What about you?" Feroshi asked.

"Your dad gave his life for all of us. Least I can do is give mine to give you a chance of getting out of here. My part in this war is over. Yours is just beginning...you'll see. Tell

Ranoa I love him. Now go."

Feroshi relayed the instructions to Theron and Ruevanlynn. Warriors and younglings stood with Lemra; women, men, boys and girls, fighting back the constant stream of guards. Some taking four or five stabs from the enemy before they would go down. Even with their dying breath, they swung, hoping to take one more foe with them into death.

Refusing to leave Yvanny, Theron fought his way over to where he had hidden her and carried her towards the exit tunnel; Ruevanlynn helping Feroshi and Joldack. The last remaining few, that hadn't managed to get a space on the transporters, were already headed for the tunnel. Rather taking their chances among the Faded and Grandors, than remaining below. The transporters were all sat waiting to take off. Waiting for a sign that the weapons were offline before they were stopped. Feroshi held the door to the tunnel open as the rest made their way in.

"Lemra, come on," Feroshi screamed across the armoury.

Lemra fought free of his skirmish to turn and smile at Feroshi as a blade plunged through his back and out his front. Dark liquid began to trickle from his mouth as he looked down to see the white of the Hav Guard blade, still gleaming while it dripped his blood. He unclipped a small black controller from his belt. The blade was removed and then plunged through Lemra again.

"Go..." Lemra struggled, pressing a button on the black controller.

BOOM! BOOM! BOOM! BOOM!

"RUN!" Feroshi screamed to everyone in the tunnel, slamming the door tight behind him.

The entirety of the Pit was self-destructing. Every orb of light, carefully placed fuel sources and the entire furnace laced with explosives as a contingency. A plan in place in case the worst happened and they were overrun by Hav Guard. Fire raged from the training hall, soaring down all the attaching stairwells and tunnels. Anybody not killed in the explosion would burn in the flames or be buried alive. A large area of the Outer System, stretching from the cratered entrance to beyond the wall, began to collapse. Knocking out massive parts of the city's weapons systems.

Taking off as quickly as possible, the transporters climbed into the air. Then in the blink of a blue light, they were gone.

Ruevanlynn hurried and rushed as many people out of the tunnel as possible. Cradling the smallest under his arms and over his shoulders. Refusing to lose anybody else, Feroshi tried to drag Joldack and his lame leg the distance. His body still broken, battered and bruised, but he would not stop. Step after forceful step he made it closer to the exit. The starlit sky, their light to guide the way.

"Just leave me. You'll never get both of us out of here," Joldack yelled, attempting to struggle free of Feroshi.

"You've obviously never seen me in the farm. Now shut up and hold on," Feroshi replied through the gritted teeth of determination.

The roar of the flames caused Feroshi and Joldack to snap their heads back. A shockwave of heat slapped them both in the face, before the purging wall of fire raced towards them.

"Come on," Feroshi yelled in alarm filled motivation.

Like a mythical serpent devouring everything in its path, it scorched the earth.

"Faster, Feroshi. Faster, Joldack," the others screamed from the exit, watching on as the fireball raged behind them.

As if erupting from a volcano, Feroshi and Joldack fired out the end of the tunnel, trailed by streams of flames. Skimming, bouncing and crashing across the broken and upturned ground when they landed.

"You still with me, Feroshi?" Joldack yelled out, hoping for a response.

"I think so. In too much pain to be dead," Feroshi replied.

Both men lay there, flat on their backs. Staring at the sky, catching their breath and in sheer disbelief that they had both survived.

Thick plumes of smoke bellowed up into the air from the cone shaped crater. Where there was no wall, there was no curtain. Funnelling the smog up and out, polluting the clear starlit sky. A raging sea of fire was all that remained of the underground army's stronghold. Ruevanlynn and Theron stood watching on from the edge. Each dancing flame casting an arc of light across each man. Feeling the heat and tasting the ash in the air. Screams of Hav Guard and Outer System residents, caught in the blazing inferno, were drowned out by crumbling homes. The ground giving way below or the materials of the homes catching flames.

There was no grey shade in this sector of the Outer System.

"What do we do now?" Theron asked.

"I have no idea," Ruevanlynn replied.

"We need to get clear of here, it's our only chance. They won't listen to me though."

Theron headed for the main group, huddled and crying in fear. Gripping onto the handle of his sword tightly as he scrambled down the hill of rubble.

"Yo, everyone listen up," Ruevanlynn yelled. "Theron's going to show us how to get out of this."

"Why should we trust him?" the crowd yelled.

Theron gave Ruevanlynn a smile of thanks. Grateful for his attempt to integrate him and a chance to lead. In such a short time, a great level of respect had grown between these men. Not everyone had the same view of Theron though, and he was not sure if they ever would.

"Because I trust him," Feroshi exclaimed.

Joldack was hanging off Feroshi as the two struggled from the distance.

"Look the truth is, I don't really know what's been happening. All I know is Theron risked his life to save me and then again to save Yvanny. I can't tell you what to do. If we stay here we will die though. We need to put as much distance between ourselves and the city as possible. So, Theron, if you have a way, please show us," Feroshi pleaded.

"You heard him, lead the way, my boy," Yvanny said in encouragement whilst smiling at Theron.

Chapter 15

Walking into the dark of the unknown, away from the Faded, far from the feeding Grandors. Eventually the flames of the city became a flicker in the distance. But the escape from the light of the city was only replaced by the incoming beacons of something large in the sky. Closing in from over the sea. The silhouette of an enormous fork-shaped aircraft, very quickly became visible against the black canvas of the night.

Gasps of shock morphed into screams of fear as more of the group heard the humming and took notice of the aircraft.

"Everyone, stay calm. It's probably heading for the city, just stay down," Theron ordered.

Everyone dropped to the floor. People muffling their cries and screams with their own hands.

"That's a PTPPT," Theron muttered to himself.

"What did you say?" Yvanny asked in his ear, still clenched onto his back.

"That's a planet-to-planet prison transporter. They shouldn't have one because prisoners are only ever brought here. They never leave."

"That's not heading for the city, that's heading for us," Feroshi said, jumping to his feet. "Everyone stay behind me."

The incoming PTPPT flew lower and lower the closer it got. Sending dust clouds soaring like a parting sea.

"We got you," Ruevanlynn said, as Theron and he drew their blades. Standing side by side with the unarmed Feroshi.

Rapidly descending right in front of the terrified group, the lights and dust from the PTPPT were blinding but the three men stood tall. Even as its legs pressed against the ground, the men did not move. The entire crowd fell silent. Petrified of what may exit the transporter.

"Here we go, baby," Ruevanlynn said excitedly, as a ramp began to lower from the transporter's undercarriage.

Joldack hobbled up behind the three, dragging his leg until he reached Ruevanlynn, throwing his weight into him.

"Joldey, get back there, baby. You're in no fit state," Ruevanlynn insisted.

"Look," Joldack replied, pointing to the figure slowly being revealed at the top of the ramp. "He's a friend."

"Niloc," Theron gasped.

Troop Commander Niloc Ecurb was stood there, smiling.

"You lot want to get off this rock or are you starting to like it here?" he yelled.

The first of the crowd helped Joldack up the ramp, while Feroshi, Ruevanlynn and Theron ushered everybody onboard.

"Your mother and father would be so proud," Yvanny proclaimed, grabbing onto Feroshi's hand as she passed. "Argh."

She dropped to her knees, gripping her chest.

"Yvanny." Theron rushed to her aid. "What's wrong?"

"He is coming. You need to get everyone out of here," Yvanny ordered, getting to her feet. "Run!"

A cold gust blew through the air. It carried a chill of fear and sadness with it, causing the hairs on the back of a neck to stand up. From the shroud of darkness, an even darker shadowed figure approached. Purple flames burned along the blades of evil, gripped in each of the spiked gauntlets.

Chapter 15

Snorts of exhaled air streamed from the faceless hood, clouding in the cold brought by this figure of death.

"Hurry, now," Yvanny ordered.

"We're not leaving you," Theron exclaimed.

Yvanny threw off her top layer of covers and in the same movement unsheathed an O'Bohare blade. The blade radiated light. She kissed her locket to her lips before lifting the sword to her face.

"Give me the key and I shall let you leave," Karantha El's voice echoed. "Deny me what I want and I shall make you watch, as the last of your blood line dies. Before you die, you shall feel the power of the Shadow one last time, Yvanny Angel of the Light."

"In darkness the light shall burn through."

Yvanny was no longer weak and frail. She flew through the air. Crack. Crash. Snap. Clash. She danced through the air, defending and attacking. Rolling and spinning as she clashed swords with Karantha's. Like waves of light and dark crashing in an ocean of colour, the two moved beyond that of mortal beings. Moving like ethereal phantoms dancing a tango of death.

"We've got to go," Niloc yelled, firing up the PTPPT.

"Not yet. We wait for Yvanny," Theron screamed.

"You're not the Captain now."

"Bitch, if Theron says we ain't leaving then you best believe we ain't leaving," Ruevanlynn barked.

All Feroshi, Theron and Ruevanlynn could do was watch as this battle of the elements tore through the fabrics of reality. Blending and swirling through the air.

CRACK! The sound of thunder threw out shockwaves as Karantha crashed his blades together, causing an eruption of shadow energy to fire out in a vortex. Yvanny managed to swallow the darkness into the O'Bohare blade. But it depleted all of her newfound energy. She crumpled to the floor. Her whole body limp. The sword flopped to the floor. The blade did not have the same radiance it previously had. Like Yvanny's life force was tied to the blade and both were fading.

"Yvanny!" Theron screamed as the three men ran to her aid.

One of the swords retracted, as though becoming another shadow floating in the dark figure of Karantha. The flames flowing from the blade and up into him. The dark edge all the way into his gauntlet. Throwing up his arm caught all three men. Lifting them as they floated paralysed, trying to move and even breathe. He held them there powerless, struggling and suffering. Unable to do anything but watch as he stalked Yvanny.

She struggled to hold consciousness on the ground. Feeling around at the cold ground beneath her hands, she could feel Karantha closing in. His darkness shrouding her. Her vision. Her mind. Her life force. Even her locket was repelled. The Light Stone inside attempting to escape the darkness of the Higher Power.

Feroshi gargled and frothed as he tried to escape the choking grip of Karantha. He could feel the tingling in his hands moving and then exploding like fireworks throughout his entire body, breaking his legs and arms free from the paralysis. Swinging his limbs wildly and attempting to reach out to grab Karantha. Feroshi ripped at his throat, choking. He looked to the sky and thought about Simeskey. Staring at the black of night, he noticed the moon was glowing the most brilliant, bright shade of blue.

"You were supposed to be a queen," Karantha cracked at Yvanny. "Now you will all die and I will take–"

The ground began to rumble causing Karantha to lose focus, dropping the men to the ground. Theron crawled over to Yvanny as quickly as his body would carry him while the other two struggled to catch their breath on the ground. Feroshi watched as Theron rushed to her. He had to take a double look at the flower growing from the ground next to Yvanny. The yellow and peach petals as clear as day.

"Mum?" Feroshi questioned aloud, thinking of the Grandors, Blue Moon and Flower.

The rumbling ground turned into bouncing ricochets. Thumping and crashing had everyone looking into the dark.

Theron looked down to see Yvanny's finger pointing to his locket. Karantha El produced his second flamed sword once more, ignoring the raging stampede of noise coming towards them.

Theron grasped at the locket as Karathna soared towards him. Fumbling it. Finally unclipping the lock and releasing a beam of light. Karantha screeched, rolling out the way. Only to see a pack of Grandors charging at him. They snarled and roared, launching their attack, but Karantha dissipated on impact.

"Come on," Feroshi yelled, picking up Yvanny and Theron.

All four rushed for the PTPPT. The moment they set foot on the ramp they screamed for the transporter to take off. Soaring off over the water. The Grandors howling up at them as though to wish them goodbye.

"Does anybody have any idea where we are supposed to be heading? There's only so long we can travel across water before we hit the opposite side of Randtyph. Shadow tech engine so a nice smooth ride ahead either way," Niloc shouted.

"Anywhere that isn't here. It's all over anyway. The army's dead. Lemra's dead. You really think the Outer System is going to survive this?" Joldack started to moan hysterically.

"Enough!" Feroshi shouted, jumping to his feet, trying to stabilise himself as the aircraft soared into the air. "There must be about thirty people on here, you think they need that? No, they don't. Yvanny, something tells me you know where we should go."

"Nlackavoir," Yvanny uttered as she rolled her head to the side to look at Feroshi from the ground. "Ruevanlynn, it is time for you to meet your grandmother."

"Hell yeah, baby. Nlackavoir it is," Ruevanlynn hollered.

"Feroshi, can you come and sit next to me please? I think it is time. There are a few things I need to tell you," Yvanny disclosed. "Oh, and this belongs to you, my boy."

Yvanny handed her O'Bohare blade to Feroshi as she rolled the leather case, protecting the Keeper's Scroll, under her head like a pillow. Plugging a destination into his controls, Niloc pointed the ship skyward, fired up the Space Jump drive and set them off into the Cosmic Web wormhole in the blink of a blue light. Like a twinkling star that was there one second and gone the next.

***

Drathon awoke to being naked and strapped to a gurney, in an ominous reverberating room. A glass like shine to the shadow. He felt the swoosh of air as Karantha El appeared beside him.

"It is time, Captain." Karantha moved over to the Captain, holding a glowing purple rocking his gauntlet fingers. "It is time to shed you of this useless form. You are the one with the darkness within. You are the one to serve at my side. You shall wield power great enough to lead the armada.Kill Feroshi and the angel. Kill all of them."

"No, please, nooo..." Drathon begged as the stone was slammed into his chest.

His pleading turned into squeals of pain and the terrified noise, of somebody in so much agony they wished for death. The Shadow Stone was consuming and unleashing its malevolent energy. His cries cracked under the strain of blood vessels bursting. Screams that released snaps of purple energy ripping across the room. Arcing like jagged bolts of chaos-infused bolts of lightning.

www.ingramcontent.com/pod-product-compliance
Lightning Source LLC
LaVergne TN
LVHW041113080826
845145LV00007B/1790
* 9 7 8 1 9 1 6 5 7 2 7 4 4 *